Mother

Book Two

by Angelina Maffeo
First published September 2018
Second Edition 2020

Cover design by
Angelina Maffeo

Copyright 2020

ISBN 978-1-7327517-4-3

Before you start...

Thank you to all the writers and artists whose music often inspired the writing. I believe you created and performed with the intention of sharing your message, emotions, and talent with the world. If the readers don't know who the music came from, it's damn time they learned. They should stop posting photos of their lunch and acquaint themselves with real music and the warnings and messages you gave us through your music. Mother does work in mysterious ways.

Thank you to the real Shepherdess, Lizzy, who tended to all the beasties so I had the time to write and her endless insight, inspiration and dedication to reading every chapter.

Thank you to the real Violet, for her knowledge on series and fiction. Who told me a coupla times, as only a Virgo can, "Mother I'd tell you if you should stop, trust me. Keep writing!"

*Mother was penned to express
my enduring gratitude to
the Mother Goddess
for always catching me before
my ass hit the pavement.*

For Laurel
Thank you for all the insight from the other side of the veil and your Purple Kamikaze recipe. I miss you every day.

Chapter 19
She's a Killer

*"What on earth gave you the idea
that I lie awake at night
thinking of you
at all?"*

7:30 am EDT, October 4,
Dancing Goats Farm
Moon Mountain, North Carolina

Nick banged into the kitchen fuming, as Reno came upstairs with the latest zombie report, "What has you so pissed?"

"I thought I could stall her from going out on patrol because she wasn't good enough with a rifle. Gave her an Mk3 and she passed with flying colors!"

Reno frowned. "I could have told you that."

"Why the fuck didn't you, when I brought it up yesterday?"

Reno shrugged. "Because you said a *big gun*. I thought you were talking about training her on an AK-47. That's what *we* call the big gun. She prefers a hand gun

7

over a *big gun, which is what she calls
an Mk3 rifle*. That's why she took the
Glock when we went out yesterday. She
calls the AK47 the *giant gun."*

"Well aren't you a fucking wealth of
information! Which I wish you had shared
with me yesterday! I would have brought
an AK out this morning. Now she's
insisting she's going to town with me
today." There's a look of confusion on
Reno's face. "I know - I know I said we'd
make the run tomorrow but this zombie
shit has changed things. Have Dark Lady
and an SUV ready in an hour. You and four
of your choice in the SUV. Carmichael can
ride in the truck with the Killer Queen
and me."

Reno was openly laughing now. "Will
do, Boss. Wait till Charlie hears how she
tricked you."

Nick ripped the report out of Reno's
hands. "Get the fuck out of here."

At 8:32 they headed out for town.
Moon Mountain is a quiet rural small town
with a population of 986. They don't know
their population data is short the 152,
who live at Dancing Goats Farm. The Law
in town is enforced by four deputies from
the Surry County Sheriffs department.
It's economy is based on agriculture,
small shops, two wineries, and a small
amount of tourism.

On the ride to town Gianna read the zombie reports, passing the pages back to Carmichael as she finishes them. When he's done Carmichael asks if this is *real* zombies. Gianna shook her head no. Nick is still irritated at being tricked, but he's interested to hear her analyses. He does love the way her mind works. "Carmichael, there are two types of zombies. The Voodoo zombies who aren't actually dead. They're rendered semi-comatose by their belief in dark magic and drinking a concoction of powerful plants. The other is a creation of comic book science and Hollywood horror. If there was a virus that screwed up the brain making humans act like zombies, it would still need the body's circulatory system to function. Half bodies clawing around is not physically possible. They might have festering wounds and maybe a flesh rotting virus like leprosy but they wouldn't be rotting dead people walking around. Further more if the saliva carried the virus then so would the blood. Zombie killers who get splattered in the face or cover themselves with blood and body parts would contract the virus and turn without being bitten.

That said, a few years ago there were cases of people behaving in a *zombie like* manner. I think there was a case in Florida of a guy eating another guy's face. The cops shot him five or six times before he would die. And a woman who ate her child. That wasn't a virus, it was chemically induced brain trama. *If* we have zombies in North Carolina, it's from some fucked up drug. You can stop worrying. You won't catch it. Just don't eat anything while we're there." Nick was smiling. He loved the way she could analyze and deduce any situation.

There were cars cluttering both sides of the road as they approached the town. There was a burnt out pickup sideways in a ditch. Nick drove at a 20 mph crawl down Main Street. Down a side street they could see a few buildings had burned but nothing like the damage caused by the plane crash in Holly Springs. There were a few teenagers hanging out at the gazebo on the green. They were loud and acting pretty high. The ground floor windows were boarded up on the remaining buildings. Carmichael spotted a man with a rifle in the window above the Hardware store, watching them as they passed. Nick pulled up in front of the Sheriff's station. It was a store front satellite office. The Emergency Clinic next door looked closed. The windows of both were boarded as well. Nick left the truck running. Nick turned to Gianna, "You stay here. *I mean it* stay in the truck. Carmichael stay with her." Nick headed for the door. The team got out of the SUV and surrounded their vehicle. Gianna watched Nick disappear inside annoyed to be left in the truck like a child.

Reno has taken the spot outside

Gianna's window. She turned the key and
rolled the windows down. An eerie feeling
hanging about the town. The smoke from
the burned buildings still flavors the
air. "Reno I know most of the people live
outside town but this is wrong. They
should be here working together."
Reno, not taking his eyes off the street,
says, "Ma'am do not attribute the values
we have at the farm to the people here.
If they were like us this town wouldn't
look like this."

Suddenly the stillness is broken by
shouting, punctuated with blood curdling
screams. The group of teens they had seen
are making their way up the street. The
sounds grow more manic with each step.
The next second Gianna hears the staccato
of safeties being released. She takes her
Glock from her shoulder holster. Nick and
two deputies are approaching from her
left. Nick stops on Reno's left. The
deputies walk into the center cf the
street and begin telling the crowd to
disperse. The teens keep coming as the
deputies back away. Gianna turned and
sees two come from behind to the right.
She yelled to the men. They turn in time
to shoot one. The other launches herself
at the guard sinking her teeth into his
shoulder. Another guard splits her head
with the butt of his rifle. The mob is
three feet from the deputies when Nick
says, "Take them down." Carmichael tries
to open his door. Nick growls. "Do Not,
leave her side." He turns to deal with

11

another group approaching from the clinic behind them.

With Nick's attention elsewhere Gianna opened her door and got out. "I didn't come to be babysat." Carmichael was next to her in an instant; between them they take out four zombie-teens emerging from behind parked cars. Reno turned his gun on several running towards them from the side street. Reno hits three, Carmichael gets the one off to the right. Two of the ones Reno hit are getting back up. Both men fire again and the zombie brains splatter on the street. "Hey, you two could have left one for me."

Despite the current state they find themselves in, Reno laughs at her comment. Bodies litter the street and sidewalks, thirty four in all. One deputy has been bitten badly on the shin. The guard is in better shape. Gianna retrieves her first-aid kit. She works on the deputy first. Reno and Carmichael flank her 6. The deputy tended to, she calls the guard over. His is more of a bruise he says he'll get looked at when they get home.

Gianna returned the kit to its place under the front seat and turns to find Nick standing *right* behind her. He takes a step closer. He has his '*not happy with her* face' on again. "Don't you know how to follow a direct order?" he hisses through clenched teeth. "I ordered you to stay in the truck."

Not intimidated in the least, she smiles at him and says, "And I chose not to. I'm not some bubble head here for a ride-along. I killed two and would have shot a third if Reno and Carmichael weren't so greedy."

The men are snorting trying very hard not to laugh cause they know the Boss is ripping mad. None of them would dare disobey an order let alone talk back to him. Nick is not amused. "I told Carmichael to stay in the truck too. Now you have my men disobeying orders."

"*No you didn't.* You told him not to leave my side. Which he didn't. Would you rather he'd stayed in the truck? If he had, I would have had a better kill number."

Still fuming Nick grabbed her by the arms and pulled her to him. "I'd like to turn you over my knee and whale your ass. Now get in the truck." She thinks of a retort but understands he has to have the last word; she did disobey a direct order. She shakes off his hands and gets in. Nick slammed the door and said "*Stay there!*" He shoots Carmichael a look that says *you* I'll deal with later. Then he went to have words with the deputies.

Carmichael got in the back seat and

Reno was once again at her window. Gianna, unfazed by Nick's bad temper, continued to lament her lack of kills. "Well Reno it was rather piggish of you two to kill so many." Reno, Carmichael, and two off the guard standing within earshot bust out laughing. Nick looked over at them, still wearing his pissy face. When he finished his conversation with the deputies, Nick walked past the laughing men and says. "*Don't - encourage her.* Get in the vehicles you assholes."

Nick's bad mood permeates the air in the truck. It's dead silent until they clear the edge of town. Then Carmichael starts laughing and can't stop. Nick snaps at him, "Carmichael what the fuck is wrong with you? Is this some sort of battle fatigue?"

Still caught in a fit of laughter he tries to explain. "I never heard anyone" laughing "call taking out the enemy" laughing "piggish before." laughing "She said Reno and I were piggish" more laughing "because we didn't leave her a few more to kill." still rolling on the seat laughing.

Nick's face softens. He glances in the side mirror. In the SUV behind him he sees Reno is laughing too. Nick imagines her saying it, a smile creeps across his lips. He looks over at her ignoring him watching out the window. "Do you lie awake at night and think of ways to drive me insane?"

Without turning her head she says "What on earth gave you the idea that I lie awake at night thinking of you, at all?" A mile later she asks, "Well Gusgus, are you going to share what the deputies told you?"

Still intent on teaching her protocol Nick says, "You'll have to wait like the rest of the team until we get back. What is a Gusgus?"

"It's a dimwitted mouse." Carmichael dissolves into another laughing fit.

10:32
am EDT, October 4,
Dancing Goats Farm
Moon Mountain, North Carolina

Charlie heard them approaching the gate and called Theo, "They're coming through the gate now. Hold on a sec." He waits for the vehicles to stop. "Well most of them are laughing so I guess it went fine. Well hold on, Nicks not laughing so maybe not. Delay that, he has her by the arm and is marching her this way. I'll get back to you."

"Hey Charlie, we found zombies and I got to kill two." Charlie follows them in the house he wants to hear about the zombies. He also wants to find out what she did that has Nick so pissed.

15

Nick let go of her arm and pointed to a chair. The second her ass hit the seat, "There have to be some rules and *you're* going to follow them. In case you didn't notice I was not pleased with my men giggling like a bunch of damn school girls. When we're out there everyone has to stay focused."

Gianna is not in the mood for this bullshit. She stood put her hands on the table and leaned over mimicking his stance. "Shut the fuck up and stop being such a tight ass. In case *you* didn't notice your men just had to shoot a pack of rabid teenagers. KIDS for Christ sake. I made one comment that gave them a moment of joy. In what had to be a really fucking hard moment for a solder. What have you got *your* French knickers in a twist about? Her mention of the knickers undid Nick's bravado and he started laughing." She did have a point.

Charlie asked what the hell had happened. Nick began to explain then Reno came in halfway through the telling, he filled in the piggish part and Gianna finished with the account of Carmichael's laughing fit. Charlie turned to Nick, "*Well Gusgus*, are you going to tell us what the deputies said before Reno and Carmichael went all *piggish*?"

Nick was shaking his head trying not to laugh, "Charlie I'm telling you the same thing I told them, don't fucking encourage her." Then because he knew he'd lost that round, he leaned to Gianna, raised an eyebrow and quietly said, "In fact I do believe... *you do.*"

Then he shared what he'd learned. The deputies were told last night, about the zombie calls in Flat Rock but hadn't seen any of that behavior in town. There were only three of them left. One had been killed two days ago when he tried to stop a gang of looters. They were all sleeping in the station on cots. The Sergeant had gone home to check on his wife and kid at 4:00 am but hadn't returned. The town had pretty much shut down after the EMP. They told Nick the buildings were burned when the looting began. Before he left Nick told the deputies how they could contact him on the farm. He asked them to let him know if they gave up and went home. They were both single and didn't have anyone waiting like the Sergeant. They both said they would stay and protect the town as long as they could. Nick told them to send up a flair if they got cornered and he'd try to send help.

They were all silent except Gianna "*No - you - won't.* No more risking our people on your bleeding heart rescue missions." The three men stared at her. "You keep this up and *you're* going to be off gate duty. I am absolutely serious. No more risking our people. You can contact the deputies and see if they have any skills that will be useful to us. If *I* like what I hear, you can tell them to come here tomorrow. We went today because we had to know. Now we do. Our gas isn't going to last forever. How much did you burn through on those two trips to Holly Springs? Then I stupidly wasted more on the snot-zis. This is not *Thunder Dome*, You're not Mad Max, and we don't have a midget making gas out of pig shit in the basement. No more. Now, if you gentlemen will excuse me, I have to go clean my gun."

Nick watched her limp out. She probably was going to get a drink for the pain. He hated to see how hard this was making her. As shocked as they all were by her outburst, they agreed she wasn't totally wrong. He'd better check in on her when he was done here. The thought of her cleaning her gun drunk didn't sit well.

11:30 pm EDT, October 4,
Dancing Goats Farm
Moon Mountain, North Carolina

Nick and Reno were at the farm to check on the regulars. Reno was going to do a spot check on the posts. Nick wanted to see the barracks and talk to the Sergeant. He stopped in the infirmary first to get the dressing on his shoulder changed. Becky was on her way out as he was going in. "Should you be up already?"

18

"I heard the Lady went on a raid this morning with her leg so I thought I should get my candy ass up out of bed."

Nick helped Becky to the waiting cart. "First, she doesn't have two broken ribs. And second, you do know she's a little crazy right? Third, you take the front bedroom in the house until those ribs heal." Reno pulled up as Becky was driven away. Reno wanted to know how he should deal with men who were screwing up while on duty. Nick said to replace them and send the offender to him at the barracks. On the far side of the green Nick watched Gianna limping out of the Shack. Reno was waiting for the replacement to come down. He was watching Nick watch Gianna. Mendez met her on the path and they walked to the Hall.

Reno said, "Boss see anything you like?"

"Yeah, Those two talking. That will make things run smoother around here."

The replacement arrived and Reno left no wiser. Reno thought he had Nick there but no, not this time.

12:30 pm EDT, October 4,
Dancing Goats Farm
Moon Mountain, North Carolina

Mendez left the meeting feeling good

19

about everything. Gianna had told him she literally trusted her vanguard with her life. He would have to prove to her, she could trust him in that way before she could recommend him to Nick for the Van Guard. Everyone here was skilled at more than one thing. Redundancy was imperative in such a small village. Every person was valued but she had to be able to replace them if something happened. Mendez needed to learn how this place worked. He needed to help with the day to day tasks. She read his file and knew he had grown up on his parents' fruit farm. She asked if he'd seen the greenhouses yet.

Gianna warned him, just when you think you know everything about this place you'll find something new. She explained the roles some of the people filled. Theo is the external hard drive of her brain. He knows as much about this place as her and Nick, some days more. Her niece Alexandra was the Huntress who lived in the 100 Acre Wood. She was the Keeper of the herd of wild deer that lived there. She was also the herbalist healer who worked hand in hand with the people in the infirmary and the animals. On the far side of the wood lived the Jack of the Green. He was many things but most often they refereed to him as their Wise Man. Not far from him lived the Water Wizard, the keeper of our waters. Simon was the culinary artist who kept the Tribe fed. Violet oversaw the baking to feed their bodies and their Priestess

who cared for their spiritual well being.
Sadie was her mini-me. She kicked ass
when Gianna wasn't around. She saw that
things got done properly, that the farm
kept its rhythm. Amber, her niece was
very much like her and Sadie, she and
Dawn were the Green Goddesses who kept
the pantries stocked. Lizzy was the
Shepherdess, the keeper of the flocks.
He'd get to know them and the rhythm of
life on the farm. Yes, it was a Feudal
system and it worked because people got
what they needed and were happy. Most
important was, Nick, if she had not
returned today the Tribe and the farm
would go on. Now that the world had gone
to hell, Nick was far more vital to the
farm than she was. Without him at the
gates, the castle would fall.

Mendez ran into Nick as he was
leaving the barracks. "I just had the
most amazing meeting with your Lady. I
think I just may find my place here. I
don't know how you've kept this place
under wraps for all these years. She told
me you have a subterranean greenhouse
with tropical fruit trees. My father and
mother would have loved it here. Watching
her talk about this place, she kinda
enchants you with her words. I can't
believe the woman I spent the last hour
with is also the Ice Queen."

Nick frowned. "She has a new title
today. Now, she's the "Killer Queen". She
told me she likes shooting bad guys.

Insisted I take her out with me on a run. She killed two. That's four in the last three days. Lost count on how many she ordered to be killed."

"Did you consider maybe, she wants to go with you to watch your back? She told me this place could go on without her but not without you. Think about it. I have a date with a hot redhead, I'll see you later."

Nick was heading back to the Q now that the dressing was off, he wanted a hot shower. He saw Gianna limping to her place. She really needed to rest that leg. He pulled a U turn. "Get in. You look like you're in pain. She got in without a word. She sat there biting her lip. "That bad? Let's get you in the house. You have to get you leg elevated." He pulled around to the back door. He came around to help her out, she was struggling to get her left leg out because she couldn't put the weight on her right one. There was blood seeping through her pant leg. Nick couldn't watch her struggle. "Let's give them something to talk about." He picked Gianna up and carried her inside. Sadie was there. "I think she may have torn a stitch. I'm leaving her in your capable hands. Sadie get her cleaned up, medicated and off the leg." Nick left before Gianna could say thank you.

4:45 pm EDT, October 4,

22

Dancing Goats Farm
Moon Mountain, North Carolina

The reports of zombies were coming in from towns as far away as Roxboro. Whoever was selling the the drugs had cut a path across the top of the state; Pelham, Danbury, Eden, Mayodan, Flat Rock, and now Moon Mountain. The information was slow to be reported because people thought it was a joke. One woman was adamant her sister would not buy or take drugs. Yet she'd ripped out her husband's throat and ate him while he slept. Most attackers were shot. Some were found dead covered in blood not their own.

Antonio told Nick, "This is some real sick shit. It has Tiny spooked. He asked Becky to work on the HAM with headphones on so Tiny didn't have to hear it. She's good with it."

After reading the latest report Nick gave a 'shoot at will' order. He did not want them in here nor did he want them to continue their gruesome murders. They would burn the bodies in the road every morning. He spoke with Tyler about adding some floodlights along the wall. Tyler said he could rig some up with solar panels and batteries if they were too far from the areas powered by their grid. Nick wanted them for the men to light up an area if they heard movement. This war was turning out to be worse than any

action he'd seen in his whole career as a
Marine.

6:00 pm EDT,October 4,
Dancing Goats Farm
Moon Mountain, North Carolina

Amber had asked Nick to have dinner
with the family again tonight. He was on
his way, when the Sergeant flagged him
down. He wanted to know how long the man,
who had been napping when Reno checked on
him, had to scrub the floors. Nick said
he could break for tonight and start
again in the morning at 07:00 hours. When
he was done in the barracks he was to
start on the floor in the Hall. At dinner
Alexandra joined them and admonished Nick
for not coming to her for his shoulder.
She left and returned with a salve.
Violet's baking elves, as she referred to
them, made apple pie with fruit from the
farm's trees for dessert.

7:30 pm EDT,October 4,
Dancing Goats Farm
Moon Mountain, North Carolina

Sitting on the veranda Nick couldn't
remember when or why he had stopped
eating in the Hall. During dinner someone
had come up to the table and asked if
Nick might join them at their table one
night. Her request was met with: *No -*
Violet, *Don't you have someone else to*
annoy? - Alexandra, *Fuck No -* Amber,
Mother said he has to eat with us -

24

Sadie, and He's *my* Uncle - Angelena.
Tyler looked at Nick after the woman had
left and said "Guess you won't be eating
with her, the Amazons have spoken."

Charlie and Freddy were on tonight.
Nick and Reno off. If crazy shit was
going to keep up at this rate Nick had
decided to have shifts for the four of
them, so they didn't burn out. Reno
joined him with the bottle of Jack. Nick
told him about the dinner which set Reno
laughing. Reno said he might have to
start eating in the Hall if it was that
much fun. They were kicked back enjoying
the effect of the Jack when Nick says
"What the fuck is she doing back up...
and out? What the hell is she carrying?"
They watched Gianna walk all the way to
the barn. "She's limping less but she's
weaving a bit." Nick watched her walk all
the way back until she vanished beyond
the edge of the house.

Reno watched Nick watch her as he
called the barn to asked what the Lady
had wanted. Nick told Reno Charlie said.
She brought Carmichael his own pie for
saving her from the asshole who tried to
shoot her in the back. He's being very
piggish about it he won't share.

Reno was laughing so hard Nick gave
him a 'what the hell look, "I really
don't know why it's so funny but every
one of the guys who hears it starts
laughing. She said it in that upper class

Connecticut accent of hers, it's just funny. It's like the day we grabbed the asshole we have in the brig and you told DJ 'Tell the Lady I'll be home in time for tea.' He's still laughing about it. The two of you are a never ending source of amusement for us."

"I'm happy to know I keep you assholes so entertained."

"Truth Boss, she's funnier than you. I thought Jackson was going to have a stroke today trying not to laugh when she said 'And I chose not to. I'm not some bubble head here for a ride-along.'" Nick laughed remembering how pissed he was and how casual she was about it. "Speaking of the asshole in the brig, why don't we set him free? Maybe the zombies will eat him." Nick poured them each another drink and thought about it a while. An hour went by Nick was feeling content. Everything was quiet. He had mellowed considerably with the third drink. Reno filled their glasses again and said, "Hey Boss I've noticed something."

"That's good Reno, since we are members of the Special Ops Command, by definition, *noticing things* is our job."

"Not what I mean, ever since the snot-zi take-down, I noticed you watch her."

"Reno, *watching her* is my job and

yours too."

Reno took another swallow... "No not like a job, you *watch* her watch her."

"Reno, what the fuck are you beating around the bush about?"

He tried again, "You watch her like a man watches a beautiful woman."

Nick took another swallow, turnd to Reno, he had to squint to bring Reno's face into focus. "As it happens, she is a beautiful woman, we're men, so it's kind of a perk that the woman, it's our job to watch, happens to be beautiful."

Reno brought his glass down on the glass table top a bit too hard. Nick looked over to see if the glass table was cracked. "I'm not talking about the job! I'm saying when she is *anywhere in sight, you study her every move.*"

Nick frowned. "Reno, is all this bullshit because you want to know if I love her?"

"At last we're getting somewhere. YES!"

Nick leaned over to fill their glasses. "*YOU'RE A FUCKING MORON*. We've been friends for a decade, we designed and built this place together, of course I love her. What you really want to know

27

is am I *in love* with her..."

"Well, are you?"

"At this moment, no. *Not* that it's
any of your damn business, but if it will
stop all of your bullshit speculating...
She and I agreed a long time ago, what we
were building here would be so important,
to so many people, we wouldn't take the
chance of a romantic relationship failing
and damaging the thing we built."

"Wow, I'm really sorry for the both
of you."

"Idiot, have you considered, the
very fact that we have both deemed each
other as forbidden fruit, might make the
experience more exciting? You know that
first rush, the prelude to coming
together? It last a few hours, a day, a
month, then it dissipates. We've had that
for 10 years. So *yes*, I watch her. She
knows when I'm watching her. And she
watches me. We watch each other. It's the
dance we've chosen for ourselves." They
both take another long drink.

"The night we went to get Mendez,
you think her standing there was an
accident? She knew I could have died that
night. She gave me that image to take
with me."

Reno ran his hand through his hair
and thought about what Nick said. "That's

fucking deep... heavy and deep..."

"Reno, we know who we are. We both have a shitload of baggage and we're damaged, but in different ways. Which, is why we make such a powerful team. We complete each others broken parts. That damage, has made us each in-fucking-sanely jealous people. If we were together and it broke, neither one of us would be able to control our jealousy. Why do you think neither of us is ever in a relationship? One of us would have to leave here. I'm not willing to give up seeing her every day. I'm not willing to give up the life I've built with her."

When I came home the last time, I was sure I would never find a place where I could be who I had become. I'm the product of my government and my own choices. Here, I don't have to *fit in*. I can be who I am. Here I'm respected and even loved for who I am.

When Gianna gets too far out there, she know she can count on me to reel her in. When I'm at the edge, I know she'll pull me back. When she dragged me out by my shirt, she knew I had crossed a line. Yes, I needed to make it clear we all had let our guard down and it could have cost us everything. But the rage, that was something else. She heard the change in my tone, my words, she just knew it had suddenly become about my fear of losing her. She could have been killed and it would have been my fault because I wasn't here.

You want to know what happened when we got to the house? She pushed me in a chair, gave me a $60 bottle of French brandy. She leaned over the table and quietly whispered 'Nicholas, pull yourself together, I'm fine.' On her way out the door she delivered my punishment, 'I'll see you in the morning.' I couldn't see her for the rest of the day.

I sat there for an hour thinking about how many times she's had to let me go into a situation I might not come back from. Never once has she taken it out on her people. She's a fuck of lot stronger than I am. One time she's in real danger and I lose my fucking mind.

I didn't think I'd see her before I left to rescue Mendez that night. Yet, I looked up there she was. She didn't let me risk my life without the image of the woman I love to take with me. So yeah, I love her. I'm just not goofy *in-love* with her.

And you should know, I was even worse when you brought her back to me wounded. After I left her with Andy I sat there with her blood on my hands and I thought about shooting you for a minute."

Reno looked hard at Nick. "I didn't think you had that many words in you that didn't have to do with being a Marine."

"Reno, there's a lot you don't know about me. *And* if you ever repeat a word of this, I'll cut your balls off and feed them to her cat."

9:30 pm EDT,October 4,
Dancing Goats Farm
Moon Mountain, North Carolina

They sat there in silence and finished their Jack. After a while Reno stood, yawned and said, "I'm going to get some sleep Boss. I'll see you when I see you."

chapter 20
this kiss

"Yes, you've been waiting
Not as long as they have!"

9:55 pm EDT, October 4,
Dancing Goats Farm
Moon Mountain, North Carolina

Nick thought about his confession to Reno. 'Was it really the truth?... Was it a lie?... he didn't think it was when he said it... but now thinking about it maybe it was... he *was in love* with her. *That's* what was in the box and now that it was open, what would he do with the truth he found there? What could he do with it? Should he do anything with it? Was it that he didn't *want* to break the agreement, or did he think he *couldn't* because it had been his idea?' He poured another drink and rolled the realization around in his head. 'What if he told her? What if she wasn't in love with him? Fucking Reno and his questions! *This* is why he didn't want to open the box." He threw back the second half of his drink. He didn't want to think about this! This was why he was pushing her lately. Was he

waiting for her to show him it was okay?
He didn't know and he was too drunk to
think about it any more tonight. He
really should go to bed... maybe...

Nick found himself on the other side
of the portal... Gianna's light was on...
she was still awake... walking through
the house... the sound of a love song
drifted down the stairs... at the bedroom
door he stopped... "Gianna"... she
smiled, "Nicholas"... her hand brushed
the side of his face... "You're wet is it
misting out?"

He pulled her to him. Her sent was
more intoxicating then the whiskey. Her
hair was down the way he loves it. He
lifted her chin to meet her eyes. "Gia I
lied to Reno tonight... I told him I
wasn't in love with you. Gianna, I can't
do this anymore. It worked before, but
now I need more... I need you. I don't
want to die never having made love to
you." Then he kissed her.... her arms
circled his neck... in one fluid movement
he pulled her closer, higher, she wrapped
her legs around him and he carried her to
the bed.

5:00 am EDT, October 5,
Dancing Goats Farm
Moon Mountain, North Carolina

The alarm was ringing she's trying
to reach for it but Nick won't release
his hold on her. "Nick let me turn the

damn thing off." He gave her just enough
room to reach it, then pulled her back to
face him. She presses closer. "Nicholas,
I don't want them to know. I don't want
to share this. I want you all to
myself... for a while longer."

Nick buried his fingers in her hair.
His other hand traced the curve of her
spine. It glides over her bodacious ass
slips between her thighs and lifts her
leg over his hip. "Woman don't move an
inch or we will never get out of this bed
before dinner. Do you think I want them
in this? We've waited too long not to be
greedy with us. The only problem I can
see will be, keeping my hands off you
when they're around."

She smiles then frowns, "*Oh no*, the
cameras have you coming in here and not
going out! Amber is coming at 6:30, we
have a breakfast meeting. Take a pillow
and that quilt and put them on the couch
and *put your pants on.* If you're asleep
on the couch when she gets here, we might
get away with it."

She tries to rolls over to get up but
Nick has a very firm grip on the tender
flesh of her inner thigh. "Gia, where do
you think you're going? We still have at
least forty five minutes."

6:30 am EDT,October 5,
Dancing Goats Farm
Moon Mountain, North Carolina

"Angelena slow down. Auntie, the tiny tornado is here."

Angelena spies Nick on the couch. She races over and starts shaking his arm. "Uncle Nicky, wake up we're going for pancakes!"

"Oh not so loud. Uncle Nicky has a very big hangover. How about you go find Auntie Gianna? Amber, morning."

Gianna walked into the kitchen. "Where's my tiny tornado? Morning baby girl. How is my house guest this morning? We have to be kind to Uncle Nicky, he was a wicked boy last night and got very very drunk and now his head hurts a lot. Nicholas would you like to join us for pancakes?"

"Thank you ladies but I think I need a shower and a gallon of coffee."

"Would you like me to make you some before we leave?"

"Yes I would." They'd already had coffee but Nick wasn't ready to let her go yet. He'd rather she didn't go at all. Why did they have to have this damn farm anyway?

Gianna filled the pot way too quickly for his liking. "Nick I'll be over after breakfast. I want to see the zombie reports. I might take a turn in the tower after that."

"You are an evil woman. Don't start an argument with me before I'm even vertical."

Over breakfast Amber asked, "Auntie are you sure you don't want to hit that? He's hot, hung over, bed head and all."

"I'll take it under advisement darling. Now talk to me about the winter crops, before I forget we need to think about a rice paddy in the spring. Wheat we can grow more of if we plow another pasture. I'm worried about rice. We need to start now before our four year supply runs low. Okay, what are you planning for the Octoberfest?"

While they planned menus and crops Angelena danced around the Hall, telling pretty much *everyone* who came for breakfast, she got to wake Uncle Nicky up on Auntie's couch because he'd been a wicked boy the night before. By 8:00 am the *whole village* knew their protector had gotten so drunk he couldn't walk home. Gianna made the excuse, he was drinking because his shoulder hurt from killing zombies.

After breakfast in the Hall, Dawn and Freddy, DJ brought the news about where the Boss had slept, to the Q. Nick was in the shower contemplating their

night together, wondering why they had
ever made that ridicules agreement. While
downstairs the speculating had begun.
Finally Reno said, "I can't tell you how
I know but I know they're not sleeping
together. And I can tell you he was very
drunk when I crawled to bed. I don't know
how he was able to walk there." Tiny
checked the cameras, yes, Nick was
weaving badly. That settled, they all
went to work, before he came down and
heads rolled. No one wanted to be around
Nick when he had a hangover. They would
try to stay clear of Nick for the rest of
the day.

Gianna rode out to Studio City to
find out how much ale and mead Jerry had
for the Octoberfest. Sadie was already
there. She had copied her mother's list
the evening before. She was home now and
taking charge as second in command. She
sent her mother off to tend to other
things. Gianna picked up some salve from
Alexandra for her leg and left for the Q.
Gianna remembered to call housekeeping to
cancel. *That* would have blown their
secret. When she got to the Q, the
kitchen was full. Nick was coming in the
front door, Antonio, Charlie, and Reno
were already in the kitchen. Becky came
from downstairs, the same time Gianna was
coming from the back, both women were
limping. Reno pulled out a chair for
Becky, Nick for Gianna. Nick looked at
the two of them and deliberately baiting
Gianna, said, "Is the hopping difficult?"

Gianna spun around, "I warned you Lorenzini, if I heard either of those two words out of your mouth." she tapped her earring. Through her teeth she hissed in his ear, "Your balls will be in my hand before the clock strikes midnight." Then she tried to punch him in his stitches.

Smiling wickedly Nick caught her fist and held it. "That's something for me to look forward to."

She willed her heart to stop pounding and pulled her hand away. Sitting she said "Nicholas, fuck you. Remember this is a kitchen, there's a large assortment of things I can find to stab you with in here. Now sit down and try not to irritate me too much. You're such a cad, making fun of two women wounded in battle."

Charlie said, "Oh shit it's going to be one of *those* days. It was a quiet night and I'm going to bed." Antonio said he was too. Reno followed them out.

Gianna raised an eyebrow at Nick. She yelled, "Charlie would you bring me a bag of rocks before you go?"

Nick goaded Gianna. "They weren't battles. They were skirmishes."

Looking to head off another round Becky said, "Speaking of skirmishes,

there have been an increased number of
zombie attacks. New towns have been added
to the list. Winston-Salem had a mass
outbreak at a community soup kitchen, set
up on the campus of the University. One
of the volunteers went zombie and soon
after, people who were eating there and
hanging around outside went zombie too.
There was at least one mass suicide when
five people jumped off the roof. Several
on the ground were killed when the
jumpers landed on them. The people are
saying it's viral because of this
incident."

Gianna shook her head. "No, I don't
think it is. I think the food was dosed.
Not everyone, just some turned. If one
dish, drink, whatever, had been dosed,
then only the ones who ate it would go
zombie."

Nick ran his fingers through his
hair at the thought of this thing
spreading. "We have no reports of them
coming back to life, just hard to kill?
There were sick fucks out there before,
kept in check by the law, now there is
none. Becky, pass Gianna's theory along.
It may help them be more careful at the
group gatherings."

"Yes, Boss, but there may not be
another one at that location. No one in
the crowd was armed. The zombies killed
and then ran off in a herd."

"Check to see if there are reports of more of the zombies just dead not from being shot. It's got to be a meth based drug but who knows what combination of shit they mixed together. Most likely something psychotropic. It could cause stroke or an aneurysm which would kill them in the end."

Gianna said, "*That's* good news. At least they have a life span. At some point this could run its course. Nick, what happened with the deputies from town?"

Nick braced himself and tried to head off the tirade. "They should be here shortly. D*on't go off*. You're going to have to start trusting me on this. I know you were pissed about Mendez but I know what I'm doing, Gianna." Outside there was a rush of activity. Frantic blasts of a car horn coming closer. Nick was up and out the door before either woman could get out of their chair.

At the front door Gianna said, "Stay here Becky." She had a good idea what was happening outside the gate. At the base of the tower Gianna yelled to Nick how many he said twenty. Gianna looked around at her men armed with semi-automatic weapons and told him to open the gate. The gates were opening and she was lifted off her feet. Nick grabbed her from behind and set her halfway up the tower stairs. She was almost pissed then she remembered *she* didn't have a gun. Ten zombies had gotten in with the car, another got crushed when they closed the gate. Carmichael finished off the rest in the street. Nick was supervising the removal of the bodies to the street. Gianna made her way around the dead zombies and opened the car door. The deputies were sitting there in shock at how close they'd come to being eaten alive. Gianna said, "Come with me boys you look like you could use coffee and some breakfast." On the way to the kitchen she said to Becky, "I always wanted my own cop car."

Nick returned to find Becky making the deputies coffee and Gianna at the stove making bacon and eggs for them. He smiled. "Isn't this the picture of domesticity? The little women feeding the men."

"*Nick*, I do have a pan of hot bacon grease here, so watch it, smart ass."

He came up behind her under the pretense of reaching for a piece of bacon, he whispered "I do love a woman who knows how to handle meat properly."

"*This* is never going to work, if you keep this up!"

Freddy and Dawn came through the back door. Dawn set a basket of warm muffins and a few apples on the table.

41

"Morning everyone. The muffins are from the kitchen and the apples I picked this morning." Gianna glanced over at her. Dawn had that glow going. She thought 'That's not all you were up to this morning Missy!' Dawn asked, "What was all that shooting we heard coming over? Nick you're looking well and recovered."

Nick said, "Thanks Dawn, for the muffins and the assessment. We just killed a herd of zombies that had these deputies cornered at the gate. Freddy you want to get out there and make sure they don't get out of hand with the flame thrower before you turn in. I told them to burn the bodies in the street. If it's not too late, hold one back. Andy may be able to analyze the blood so we know what we're dealing with. Becky call Andy and ask her to send someone over to draw the blood. I want to get the body in the pile ASAP." He looked at Gianna filling the plates for the deputies. "Thank you."

"Thank you for the stairs. I totally forgot *I* didn't have a gun." Gianna put a plate of bacon and eggs in front of the men as Dawn put a crock of hand churned butter and a pitcher of fresh cream on the table. She waved as she slipped out the door.

The deputy whose leg Gianna had bandaged, looked around the table. "Are we sure we didn't die out there and this

is heaven?" It had been far too long
since they'd eaten a meal that didn't
come out of a can.

Gianna winced as she sat. Nick
caught it. He got up and refilled her
coffee with a smile. "Lady, this is
Derick and Scott. Boys, this is the Lady
you have to thank for this. Where did you
pick up the mob?" In between mouthfuls
they explained they had made it to within
a mile of the farm when the zombies came
up out of the woods and surrounded the
car. They had to drive over a few to
break away. They were just praying there
would be someone at the gate. Nick walked
over and yelled down to Becky, "Tell Reno
I want him to warn the Sergeant there are
mobs of zombies wandering the woods a
mile out. Shoot at will keep them off the
Zone fencing at all costs."

On the way back to the table he bent
over and spoke into Gianna's ear.
"Becky's in the front bedroom because of
her ribs. Can we put these two in the
back bedroom for now? These poor bastards
look like they could use a shower and
sleep." She said yes and asked why he was
whispering? "I needed an excuse to smell
you." Reno banged through the front door
as Nick sat. Nick looked at the the
deputies. "Boys, when you're done there's
a shower upstairs and you can catch some
sleep in the room on the right."

Reno turned to the man behind him

holding the deputies bags and pointed up
the stairs. The deputies stood and picked
up their plates. Gianna said, "Just leave
those we'll take care of them. Go before
you both fall over." They said their
thank you ma'ams and left.

Reno put the plates on the counter
and sat. Nick said, "They were attacked
about a mile out. Reno these are words I
never though I'd be saying,... *we have
zombies circling the farm.* Are they
finished with their Bar-B-Que out there?"

"Yes, the mess is still smoking but
we're in and locked down. We'll aim to
shoot them as far away from the walls and
Zone as we can. That may help with the
stench when they start to rot. The kid
came and took four vials of blood for
Andy. I think we should hold off on
anyone leaving until we deal with this.
Do we have any idea what this is?" Reno
looked over at Gianna clearing up the
breakfast mess. "Lady, you look tired,
how is your leg?"

With her back to him she answered
"I'm okay Reno, just didn't get too much
sleep last night. Kept trying new
positions all night... ya know with the
leg."

Nick nearly choked on his coffee. He
coughed and said, "The Lady has a theory
and I think she's right. There's a crazy
serial killer out there who knows there's

no one to stop him. He's taking advantage of the chaos. From what Becky has gathered people, who wouldn't do drugs are being affected. We think he's passing out the drug and dosing batches of food. Normally we'd go out and find the fucker but no. We have no idea where he is and we're not risking our men to hunt for him. Becky is warning people on the radio. That's all we can do for them. We need to focus on keeping zombies out of the Zone."

Gianna said, "I'll have Sadie make sure the Tribe knows to alert the Sergeant if they hear anything. Need to let Alexandra, Jack and the Water Wizard know too. Nick, are there enough cameras on the back wall?"

Nick was smiling because he knew where she was going with this. "I'll go over that with Tyler when we finish here. We can pull as least two off, just inside the wall. Do you really need four cameras pointing at your house?"

"I don't needed *any* pointing at my house. If they're that far inside the wall, we're already fucked. Can we get those moved today so I don't have to worry?" The sound of two shots echoed across the yard. Reno said he take care of it.

Nick said, "You slipped that right in there. Very nicely done." He stood and came up behind her again. "I'm going to go take care of that now, so you can stop *worrying*. Go take a nap. I have a feeling you're not going to get much sleep again tonight." He kiss her neck and left.

**10:00 am EDT, October 5,
Smokey Mountains, Tennessee**

The mountain compound had suffered no more intruders. They assumed the one who got away had told others about the sharp shooting women who lived there. Once a day, two or three of them would go through the woods and check on Harvey and Barbra. Their days took on a monotonous routine of replacing water, fire wood, cleaning out the ashes, and washing laundry by hand in buckets in the tub. Dan put some seeds in pots for tomatoes and spinach. They fought their cabin fever by reading and reorganizing their supplies. The only news of the outside came from their time on the HAM radio. They had reduced their air time to two half hour segments to conserve on gas. At 1:00 pm so they could check in with Rory and the women, then again at 7:00 pm. The lack of a central government worried them. It began to dawn on them this might go on longer than first expected. This caused them to rethink their food consumption. The news of the zombie attacks frightened them all.

**12:00 pm EDT, October 5,
Damascus, Virginia**

Rory and the women at the Inn were not frightened of the zombie reports in the same way that those at the mountain compound were. Cindy had treated overdose cases at the hospital. This sounded like a more powerful form of a drug whose street names were Bliss and Bath Salts. She didn't believe there was a virus causing this behavior. She did warn her group that the people on these drugs could be very violent and should be shot. They had created a brush barrier wall all along the picket fencing. Fir trees and brambles piled 5' high interspersed with 4' pikes jammed in the ground. They had filled the woodshed and now had four cords stacked on the front porch. The porch stack hid the generator from view and absorbed some of the sound. Ann had rigged the front steps to collapse under more than two pounds of weight. Cabin fever was not an issue for them. They spent hours working on their new garden room. Rory and Ann were working on plans to add two skylights. They were not pleased to learn there was no central government but they had figured out very quickly this was going to be a long haul.

1:30 pm EDT, October 5,
Dancing Goats Farm
Moon Mountain, North Carolina

Andy had thought Gianna had gone a bit over the top when she bought a $100,000 mass spectrometer for the lab.

Alexandra had wanted one to analyze the plants she used in her herbal compounds, so her Aunt bought it for her.

Now Andy was very glad they had it. Some of the Tribe were worried the zombie virus would get into the farm. This morning one of the 'ungrateful twats' Gianna had sent her asked, "Miss Andy, are the zombies part of Mother's revenge?"

Andy had replied, "No, this is humans fucking up as usual." She wanted the science to show the girl and the people the farm would be fine.

Gianna had come down to check on the laundry and found Nick standing in her kitchen. He walked over to her and opened the door behind her. "Just step in here for a minute."

"Nick there's two problems with that suggestion... the first is, this Pagan came out of the broom closet back in high school, the second is, how would we explain *why* we'd been in there to begin with? Which makes the point of going in there *moot*."

"Good point." He closed the door and kissed her... and Amber walked in.

"*I knew it*! The act was perfect this morning. You fucks made me doubt myself. But when you said you'd take it under

advisement I wondered again. Cause you
always say straight up No. Did you two
Scorpios think you could fool this
Scorpio? Sex is my middle name. Don't
worry, I won't say anything."

Gianna looked at her niece. "Amber,
you have *never* been able to keep a secret
in your entire life."

"Ahhh but Auntie, this is a
conspiracy! That's a whole other game. I
excel at conspiracies, *as you well know*."

"Amber we simply don't want to share
this. It changes nothing for them. We
deserve the privacy. We have devoted
years of our lives to them. This is not
their business."

"Fuck them, I got your back guys.
Oh... *that's why*... Tyler told me Nick
had him removing the cameras that covered
your house, to put them on the walls for
zombies. Nice one Nick. I'll see you two
at dinner. Your absence and Nick's
presence is causing talk. A nice family
dinner will shut them the fuck up." And
she was gone as quickly as she had
appeared.

Nick looked at Gianna questioningly.
"Could be a blessing, could be a curse,
we just won't know for awhile. You heard
her, I'll see you at dinner. Oh, you
better drop some clothes off today, or
you'll be doing the walk of shame in the

49

morning."

Amber pulled up to her cousin's Vardo. Violet is working with the belly dance troop on their choreography for their performance at the Octoberfest. No one can shimmy like Violet. She tells them to continue practicing. "Hey Ambie, what's up?"

"Auntie and I went over the menu during breakfast and we want to know if you want to add anything else before I hand it to Simon."

Violet scaned the paper. "No, this is everything I would have picked. Do you have a large white pumpkin to serve the pumpkin ale in?"

"Yes, it should hold close to a gallon. Dawn has been babying it for the last month making sure it's perfectly formed. She found a squash bug on it yesterday and went bat shit. She put DE all over it. We'll cut it in the next few days so the stem has time to cure."

How's mom's leg today? Is she walking better?"

Amber answered as she was pulling away. "Yes, she's doing great today. I think the salve is working wonders." She thinks 'Yeah, a salve called *Nick*!'

50

2:00 pm EDT,
Moon Mountain, North Carolina

The *Zombie Maker* parked his Spyder
in front of the recently abandoned
Sheriff's station. He peered through the
glass door, then picked the lock. "This
will do nicely. Love love love the irony
of it. What's needed is some light." He
rummaged in a closet until he found a
hammer. Outside he removed the boards on
the windows. That done, he tossed the
hammer through the glass door of the
Emergency Clinic then went back inside
the station. Back in the closet, he found
a roll of duct tape which he used to tape
over the word **'Sheriff'** stenciled on the
door. In the desk he found a marker and
wrote FUN in big red letters on the duct
tape. He stood back to admire his *handy*
work. The door now read **'FUN STATION'**.
"Simply lovely and just what this town
needs about now." Tossing the marker into
the street he went back inside. With the
sweep of his arm he cleared the desk,
then opened the drawers and emptied them
onto the floor. He retrieved his bags
from his bike and placed their contents
neatly in the drawers – he has a
system... Then he sat with a grand
flourish as if he were lifting coattails
and said, "Folks the Fun Station is now
open for business!" He smoothed back the
tendrils of his greasy red hair , put his
boots on the desk, laced his fingers
behind his head and waited... eagerly

51

anticipating the arrival of his first
customer.

4:34 pm EDT,
Dancing Goats Farm
Moon Mountain, North Carolina

Andy read the analysis of the blood
taken from the zombie. It's blowing her
mind. She called Nick she wants to
discuss the results in person. She's
still trying to make sense of them when
he got there. "Nick, This drug is very
bad." She handed him the printout. "This
is what's in this shit:
Methylenedioxypyrovalerone, Mephedrone,
Pyrovalerone , Cocaine, Methamphetamine,
Methylone, Arsenic and Peyote. This drug
was designed to drive people mad and
eventually kill them. The qualifier
"psychoactive" means that the drug
crosses the blood-brain barrier and
causes changes in neurochemical
functions." Nick looked a little lost.
"The result is, it has an amplifying
effect on mood, thought, perception and
behavior." She let that sink in. "Which
is why we have zombies running around
eating people! It seems to remove all of
their learned civilized impulse controls.
The *best* thing you can do for these
people is put them down."

Nick thanked her and left to find
Reno. He liked being right but there was
no feeling good about being right about
this shit storm. What was this sick

52

bastard's goal, just to kill off the rest of the country's population? Nick had gotten spoiled over the last ten years. With the exception of a few isolated incidents, his life had been damn peaceful. Not that life with Gianna could be considered peaceful, but his job wasn't to kill all the time. It wasn't that he didn't believed her when she said this time would come, he just hoped she'd gotten it wrong.

Nick found Reno and told him what he'd gotten from Andy. Nick wanted all the men on both shifts to be made aware of the facts. He'd let Charlie know tonight. Nick suspected Reno had a fascination with Lizzy and asked him if he wanted to join them for dinner tonight. Reno said yes and he'd meet him there at 6.

Nick went to inform the Sergeant about the drugs. The Sergeant told Nick they shot four zombies approaching the Zone fence shortly after lunch. He asked if Nick thought the bodies would bring in scavengers like coyotes or even bears? And if it did, would the animals be affected by the drug? Nick told him to shoot the coyotes and he'd check with Andy about the bears. Neither of them wanted bears high on Bliss roaming the forest. Normally when a bear was spotted in the area they put the low voltage on the fence. After being shocked a few times it didn't come back. Before going to dinner Nick checked back with Andy. He didn't like the answer. She said it would depend how long it had been in the person's system. How much they took and a host of other variables but it was a real possibility. Fuck, now they'd need to remove the bodies or have to shoot the bears. No one wanted to shoot the bears.

6:00 pm EDT,

Dinner was a boisterous affair. The Amazons were in rare form. Angelena insisted her place was between Auntie and Uncle Nick. Nick watched Reno and Lizzy and wondered if it had become more than fascination. Violet pointed out no one dared asked Nick to eat with them after they'd put Blondie in her place last night. Simon came out and had a beer with them. Angelena kept Uncle Nick to two beers so he didn't end up having to sleep at Auntie's again. He saw Becky having an animated conversation with one of the regulars. And Ferret was holding hands with one of Amber's greenhouse girls. They ran into Freddy and Dawn on the way out. Nick offered to drop Gia at her place. Sadie thanked him for saving her a trip since she had a hot date to get ready for. Nick wondered why he hadn't seen all the romance going on around him before now. Gianna said it was because he didn't want to see what he couldn't have.

8:30 pm EDT,

Charlie was waiting for Nick when he got back from dinner. "This zombie shit is becoming more widespread. I think we should light up the fence and keep it hot. I know the Lady doesn't want to keep it on because of the animals in the woods but you need to talk her into this."

Nick exhaled. "You're right. If a big enough mob hits the fence they could damage it. Warn the Sargent to tell the regulars it's hot. No one should be out there but make sure they know anyway. I'll go over and let Tyler know so he can adjust for the extra draw on the grid. I'll have Gianna let the Tribe know in the morning. Go ahead and put the fence on now."

"Are you sure we want to do that before you talk to her? I don't want to see you two at it in the morning cause Bambi got fried over night."

Nick chuckled at the image that popped up in his head. "Don't worry she'll be fine with it."

Charlie's not convinced. "You've said that before and it didn't end well. You should just marry her. You fight like you're married, you should get the perks that go with the fighting." Three shots echoed across the yard. Charlie and Nick walk out to the gate.

Freddy yelled down, "There's a gang

of nine, *not zombies*, demanding all our
food or they will attack and kill us."

Nick asks sarcastically, "Do they
have a convoy of 18 wheelers to carry it
away in?" From the tower Nick can hear
the asshole at the gate is still running
his mouth. Nick is sure the guy is one of
those men who never got over having been
a football star in high school. Now he's
in his fifties, bloated and evidently
stupid. Nick tells Charlie, "Light the
fence up and ignore him."

Nick was turning to leave when the
asshole yells "For making me wait I'm
going to fuck the bitch with the long
silver hair and then shoot her when I'm
done."

Nick turned back and shot him in the
forehead. "Freddy kill the rest of them.
No one threatens Gianna and lives. We'll
clean it up in the morning." Then he went
to find Tyler. Amber answered their door.
wanting to know what the racket was.

Nick likes how she always gets right
to the point. "Just some asshole who
wanted all our food and to first fuck and
then shoot your Aunt."

"Nick, tell me you shot the pig."

"*Yes*, of course I did. I just
stopped by to tell Tyler we need to turn
the fence on now." He glanced over at

Tyler sitting on the couch. "Are we good?"

"Yes, it should be fine Nick."

"Then I'll say goodnight." On his way to the house he calls Charlie and tells him it's a go on the fence. It's quiet in the house. Nick thinks she might be asleep. He took a detour to the basement. He opened the safe and removed the box he kept there. He found the smaller box he'd come for and put the larger one back. He left his boots at the bottom of the staircase in the hall. He didn't want to wake her if she was sleeping. He placed the box on the bed table and started to undress.

Gianna rolled over. "I heard you come in babe, what took you so long?"

Nick climbed in bed and spooned her to him. "Had to get something from the safe." He put the box on the bed in front of her. "I had these made eight years ago before we made our agreement." Gianna open the tooled leather box, her breath caught in her throat. Inside were a pair of platinum bands etched with vines. Nick slid the small one on her finger. "I think it's time we started wearing them." Gianna put the other on him. He rolled her around to face him. There were tears on her eyelashes. "Gianna I've always loved you." Then he showed her just how deeply...

Amber was dreaming of a time before everything changed.In the dream, Angelena had been playing on the bed with Amber's phone. Now it was ringing and couldn't find it. She was searching through the blankets... Tyler nudged her and passed her the phone from the bed table. Still half asleep she answered it. "Amber it's Becky wake up this is an emergency. Answer me! Wake up your husband now."

The urgency in Becky's voice brought her around. "What time is it? What the hell is going on? Tyler wake up."

"Listen to me...There's a camera that covers your Aunt's back door. Someone just turned it on. I need Tyler to run and unplug it NOW right this fucking second! Then get your ass over here and help me fix this."

"Okay we'll unplug the camera and be right there."

"NO, not Tyler just you. Don't bring him with you. This is really bad get over here."

Becky rang Ferret next. "Ferret wake up it's Becky I need you for a serious computer problem in the command room

58

now."

Ferret had only just gotten in bed. She'd been on a late shift in the Shack. "Okay should I bring Adrian?"

"NO, no men just get here."

Tyler and Amber are fumbling into their clothes. "*Fuck*, Nick and I were talking about where to put that camera and then he got called away and I just left it unplugged and we both forgot about it. Someone must have plugged it back in."

That got her *full* attention. "Oh fuck, I know what she's talking about. Just rip it out and get back here to Angelena. I'll be back... I don't know when just don't tell anybody... don't tell anyone about this." Ferret and Amber reached the portal at the same time. Downstairs the door to the com room was locked. "Becky it's Amber, Ferret's with me."

Becky opened the door, pulled them in and locked it. The normally calm, cool, nerves of steel soldier, Becky, is at this moment frantic. Even her hair is a mess. "I was sitting here when the monitor for that camera suddenly came on. I don't know why but it's taking stills. I turned the monitor off, but *Fucking Tiny* did something, so only he can edit the recordings. I can't figure out how to fucking erase them."

Ferret pushed Becky aside. "Show me what you're talking about." Becky opened the file.

Amber says "Holy Shit! No wonder you freaked out. It's not often you get to see *both* of your bosses naked! Well they do make a hot couple. Oh that one is very nice. At least she looks great. It'd be bad if she looked unattractive in the pictures. Too bad the porn industry is gone, they would have been instant stars."

Becky is not as amused as Amber. "Ferret can you get them off the hard drive?"

Ferret is laughing. "Keep your panties on Becky this is a piece of cake. Give me a new disc."

"What? NO! Are you making a copy? Why? No!"

Ferret snatched the disc. "*Yes Becky*, I am. These are really beautiful photographs. If they were me and my lover I'd want to keep them."

Amber says, "Oh wait, zoom in on their faces on that one."

Becky is horrified. "Amber!"

"Shut it Becky. Look at their hands. Those look like wedding bands to me... they *didn't* have them on at dinner last night."

Becky's voice softens. "You're right, look at their expressions. They're *really* in love."

"All right you voyeurs back it up and let me do my magic."

"Shit, Beck someone is coming down the stairs." Amber checks to make sure the door is locked.

Freddy rattled the doorknob. "Hey Becky open the door."

Leaning on the door Amber answers him. "Freddy it's Amber, what do you want? We're having a girl thing in here you can't come in."

Annoyed Freddy says "I don't know what you're up to but you better open this door right now. Becky are you in there?" Pounding on the door.

"And we're done." Ferret slips the CD case down her pants. "He wouldn't dare look there."

Amber opened the door and Freddy fell into the room. He starts bitching them out. Amber pushes Becky and Ferret up the stairs and gives Freddy her death look. "Freddy shut the fuck up or I'll tell Dawn what an asshole you're being. This was important Amazon business. If you don't like it, you can take it up with my Aunt!"

Outside Amber asks Becky if she's off shift. Yes, she was just giving Tiny a break, "Thank the Goddess you were on and not him. Well I think we can use a drink. I don't think any of us can go back to sleep after *that*. Let's go to my place. Tyler's probably back in bed by now."

Tyler yelled from their bedroom. "Hey babe what happened? Was your Aunt naked or something?"

Amber rolls her eyes, "Tyler, I want that camera off that fucking pole before breakfast. Yes, she was, and she wasn't alone. And if you repeat any of this I'm very sure she'll have Nick kill you. Now go to sleep. Baileys and coffee ladies?"

Ferret looked at her sister conspirator and says, "Amber you weren't surprised were you?"

"No I wasn't. I walked in on them kissing, in her kitchen this afternoon. I promised them both I'd help them keep the 'change' in their relationship a secret.

Thanks, both of you. They just want some privacy. We all owe it to them. It's

no one's business but their own. How long
have they waited for this? I couldn't
wait ten fucking years. Ferret quick
thinking on the CD. Once they get over
the shock, I think they'll enjoy having
them.

    Beck they owe you a big one for
catching this. Becky under fire... keeps
her head and makes all the right calls...
too bad we can't give you a medal for
this." Amber thought it best not to
mention the state of Becky's. " Until
this little fuck up, I was the only one
who knew." As she hands them their mugs
she says, "We're keeping it between us
three. Becky if there's a problem for you
over locking Freddy out, call me and *I'll
handle it." Not only is it good to be the
Queen but it's also good to be the Queens
niece.*

chapter 21
PLEASED TO MEET YOU

*"In which we meet the man who brought
Bliss to the Apocalypse"*

**3:45 am EDT, October 6,
Moon Mountain, North Carolina**

In the sleepy little town of Moon
Mountain, in the abandoned Sheriff's
station, in the chair once reserved for
the Deputy Sergeant, sat the Zombie
Maker. His dusty boots were propped up on
the desk. He'd just finished gnawing on a
chicken drumstick. He tosses the bones
over his shoulder on to the evicted
contents of the desk drawers and wipes
his greasy hands on the leg of his
quilted satin pants. "Southern women,
they do make the best fried chicken, even
in the middle of the apocalypse." He
squints his eyes at a pair of shadows
moving against the building across the
street. "What have we here, Customers or
Distributors?" The shadows move on. "Ahh
the shy type." He picks bits of chicken
flesh from between his snaggeld teeth
with his yellowed, three inch long, pinky
nail, as he waits.

Nine minutes float by before the shadows appear in the doorway. He spreads his arms wide. "Come in, the Fun Station is here to fill your needs." A slimy grin belies the truth behind his black shark eyes. The man and woman cautiously move toward the voice. They're soiled and disheveled. 'Hmmm... she's a junkie, badly in need. Oxy I think. Yes, yes, that nasty scarring on her arms is fresh. Tsk-tsk No Doc, no Druggist here in the apocalypse... he's looking for 'medicine' for the little woman. Clearly a Distributor.'

Sounding like a barker at a carnival, "No need to speak sir. I can see your dilemma by the expression on her pain racked face. I have what you need to ease her pain. You're wondering how you're going to pay..." The man shakes his head yes. "I'm just a man who wants to help in this time of chaos and need. I have what you seek. All I ask is a small favor... help me ease the pain of others in this sad little town." He slide his feet to the floor and took a small plastic bag from the drawer. Standing he stretched out his hand, "Just call me Ziggy." As he shakes the man's hand he palms him the packet. "This one is for her. Here, use this mirror. Pour her a lovely healing line of bliss. Let's get her fixed up toot-sweet." Ziggy slides a piece of broken mirror and a straw across the desk. 'If the Deputy Sergeant could only see what his station's lavatory mirror was reflecting now. Tsk Tsk he can't, because his wife and son ate him.' The Zombie Maker watches the woman's face as the dust dissolves and the chemical cocktail hits her brain. "There, isn't that so much better?" She starts to giggle. Ziggy turns to the man. "I can see how relieved you are now that she is out of that intolerable agony." He reaches in the drawer for three more packets and hands them to the man. "These are for you to share with the good people of this town. Some don't know how desperately they need the healing. You'll have to be brave and kind and help them. Just sprinkle a pinch of this pixie dust in their food or drink. These are for you to give away. When she needs more just come on back. My door is open twenty four seven." Ziggy sits and puts his feet back up on the desk. The man understands the transaction is over and leads the giggling woman out into the gray predawn light.

Had there been anyone on the sidewalk they would have heard the sound of Ziggy's singing echoing off the walls of the dead Deputy Sergeant's station; "*Ah, what blissful day in the neighborhood, won't you try my Bliss.*"

5:32 am EDT,
Dancing Goats Farm
Moon Mountain, North Carolina

Charlie and the guard were dealing

with a fresh wave of zombies at the gate. It was the third time since he started his shift at 6:00 pm . The thing that worried him was the type of people these zombies were, before they went zombie. They were grandparents, shopkeepers, farmers, not druggies. Many of them he knew by sight from living in this town for the last eight years. These were not people who would take recreational drugs. They went to church, tended their gardens, had family dinner on Sundays. Nick was right, some very sick bastard was behind this. But how was he getting them to eat it?

The good news tonight was the fence was working. The Sergeant reported two zombies had fried outside the Hundred Acre Wood around 1:00 am. Nick would have to figure out how to remove the bodies when he got up. Alexandra would have a shit fit if they had to kill the bears. Charlie made it a rule to not piss off a woman who was that good with a bow.

Gianna held her hand up in the morning light to admire her wedding ring. "Nicholas, you know my love we have really shitty timing. Last month we could have run away to an elegant hotel or a Bed and Breakfast in the mountains. Now, we can't even go out for a frigging cup of coffee!"

Nick took her hand and kissed it. "So now you want to abandon our life's work? He teased.

"No. *Maybe*... I don't know. I do know I want time for us without prying eyes and stupid smiles aimed at us. I don't want you to leave me and go to work now."

"We still have twenty-eight minutes."

She rolled over to face him. "It's not enough!"

Her pouting amused him and made him want to give her whatever she asked for. "Fine. We'll stay here until you're ready to face *the prying eyes and stupid smiles*. I think we've earned our honeymoon. There's nothing I'd rather do than spend two weeks locked in here with you." Nick reached for his Catsear. "Charlie, I'm taking a vacation."

She could hear Charlie asking when. "Now?" Charlie asked, "What the fuck are you talking about?"

"Charlie, you told me I should marry her. *I did*." Nick turned the earpiece off and threw it in the drawer.

Charlie stood there, in the middle of the kitchen, with an incredulous look on his face. Reno asked, "What the fuck did he just say to you? You look like you don't know whether to shit or wind your watch."

Charlie sat down. He was at a loss for words. 'Did Nick really just say he married her? Nick sounded serious, but what if he was joking?'

Freddy says "Does this have to do with whatever Amber, Becky and Ferret were up to early this morning? Tiny was bitching after they left that a file from one of the cameras had been removed from the hard drive. He wants the three of them strung up. Ferret was the only one of the three who has the skills to do that and she doesn't have the clearance to access that system."

Reno asked, "Freddy what the hell are you talking about? Shut up, we'll get to that next. Charlie, what did the Boss say?"

Charlie said, "Nick said he's taking a vacation... *now*. The fucking apocalypse is at the gate, zombies and all and *NOW*, after ten years he wants a frigging vacation!"

Freddy and Reno sat down too. "Did he say why? *Does* it have to do with what Freddy's talking about? Charlie, snap out of it, did he give you a reason?"

Yeah he did, but I couldn't tell if he was joking so I don't want to repeat it."

"For Christ sake, stop with all the cryptic bullshit. Just tell us what he said."

"He said... *he married her.*" Freddy and Reno's mouths dropped in unison. Charlie got up, at the doorway he said, "Reno you're up. I'm going to bed. If this insanity is still going on when I get up, we'll rework the schedule." and he left.

Reno found his voice before Freddy did. *"Holy - Fucking - Shit."*

6:30 am EDT,

Gianna went down to make them coffee. She found a silver tray with matching bowls of fresh strawberries and fresh sour cream. A dome covering warm scones and a bud vase with a single rose. There was a CD case with a note on the counter next to the tray:

Auntie,
There was an issue with one of the cameras early this morning. Becky called me. I had Tyler disable the camera. Becky and I had Ferret take these off the hard drive. This is the only record.
Love
Amber

While the water was boiling Gianna put the disc in her laptop on the counter. *"Oh - Fucking - No. NICHOLAS get down here NOW!"*

Nick ran into the kitchen naked, "Gia, what's the matter?" Gianna pointed to the computer and handed him the note. Nick read the note then scrolled through the pictures... *twice*. A wicked smile spread across his face as he pulled her into his arms. "I have a very sexy and photogenic wife, but two weeks may not be long enough for *this* to blow over."

While she finished making the coffee, Gianna called her niece. Amber explained the early morning antics required to secure the pictures. Laughing Gianna thanked her. She said to tell anyone who had a problem with their behavior, that they were acting on her orders. And please, do not tell anyone what they erased. Gianna said to tell Ferret, Nick said thank you very much. He's threatening to print them and frame them for the bedroom. Amber said Congratulations, she'd seen the rings. Gianna told her Nick had just told Charlie, so it wasn't a secret anymore. She finished with; "We are taking our honeymoon. You all know your jobs, do them. Tell Sadie to step up to first chair. No one, but Reno, Charlie or the four sisters can contact us. And no one comes within fifty feet of this house. Oh wait, Nick says security around the house is to be solely under Becky's control. Nick says to tell her, she's now a

71

Lieutenant, and the front bedroom is permanently hers. He also says he'll shoot anyone who comes to the door, unless it's Becky or one of you sisters leaving food. Oh, I guess Becky can call too. We'll come out, when we're ready to." Then she hung up and had breakfast with her new husband.

Amber found her two cousins, her sister and Becky, then she filled them in on the phone call but not the early morning antics. Violet bitched that of all times for Amber to learn how to keep a secret *this* wasn't it. Amber ignored her and let Violet know she would have her hands full getting everyone to mind their own business, since Vy was in charge of the Tribe's state of mind. Sadie said anyone she caught talking about them would be put out, with nothing but the clothes on their back. Alexandra said no, if she heard them fist, she would put an arrow through their heart.

They called a Tribe meeting for after lunch. They explained to the Tribe and the security teams: The news of the nuptials of their founders; The shift in power to the four sisters; Reno's charge of the vanguard and regulars; Becky's promotion and responsibility for the manor house; The rules of behavior to be followed by everyone within the walls, in regard to Nick and Gianna's relationship; And the punishment if they broke them even once.

Then, *with the apocalypse at the gate, zombies and all*... the sisters four took over the running of Dancing Goats Farm...

1:00 pm EDT,

Becky ran into Reno in the Q kitchen. It had been an eventful 12 hours. She had posted four of the regulars around the manor house. Now she needed a shower and three or four hours sleep. "Hey Reno, any zombie shit today?"

"Yeah, but it's under control. Had a group of beggars an hour ago. They moved on after ten minutes. So what were you doing in the command room with Amber and Ferret? What the fuck were you thinking giving Ferret access to that system? You've got a lot to answer for."

Becky turned to face him and crossed her arms. "Let's start with, how about you watch your fucking tone of voice with me. You no longer out rank me. I'm now a Lieutenant.

It was an *extraordinary situation*. I dealt with it in a manner I saw fit. Evidently the Boss agrees with how I handled it, cause he made me a Lieutenant for *my handling of the situation*. It had to do with the security of the manor house, which is now, solely under my control.

73

Were you not at the meeting just now? The only people I answer to are the Boss and the Lady. Now I'm going to my room to get some sleep." At the stairs she turned and said, "Oh, one more thing, If Ferret *wanted* in that system, she wouldn't have to be in the command room to do it."

Antonio and Lee came through the front door. Lee said "What the hell's wrong with you? You look like somebody shot your dog."

Reno shook his head "Where do I begin? Shit's changing by the fucking minute around here. Becky is now a Lieutenant in charge of the security at the big house. The Boss is taking a leave of absence, we have women and children begging at the gate, fried zombie bodies we have to get up and burn before the bears eat them and go zombie, I've got 'Andy and Barney Mayberry' out there that should go in with the regulars but the Lady hasn't vetted them, have no idea when she'll be available to do it... that about answer your question?"

"You're just riled up because they got married."

"Lee, if you like breathing, you better not mention that subject again. If Alexandra hears you she will put an arrow through your heart. I think the Amazons

made that *very clear* at the meeting. She
has trained them very well. Don't think
for a minute, they aren't as strong as
her. Now, go make me a few of those
grappling hooks you use to catch gators
with *bayou boy*. We're going to use them
to reel in the zombie bodies.

2:00 pm EDT,

Life on the farm that day ran as if
Nick and Gianna were at the helm. Sadie
vetted the deputies, passed them, and
told Reno to get them to the Sergeant for
training. She reviewed the zombie reports
with Reno. After the patrol missed the
two that fried on the fence during the
night, they agreed to switch to six hour
shifts so the men would be less likely to
miss anything out of boredom. Reno told
her he and Charlie would stick to twelve
hour shifts, they were used to it.
Charlie had Freddy as his second and he'd
take DJ for his. She agreed DJ would have
been her choice too. Reno said he'd cover
all of it with Charlie and Freddy when
they came on at 6:00 pm.

Sadie was in the tower with Reno
when twelve assholes tried to breach the
front gate in an old pickup with a plow
on the front. Once the driver was dead
she told Reno, "Take them all out they'll
only annoy us by trying again. Keep the
truck. It might be useful for parts or on
the farm." She suggested they install a
heavy gauge chain across the drive to

slow them down before they got close enough to damaged the gate next time. Reno had the chain in place by 4:00 pm.

Violet kept the Tribe from gossiping by first telling them she'd rip their hearts out and then by putting them to work assembling the infrastructure for the Octoberfest, which was only two weeks away. She ordered it to be a costumed affair with prizes in several categories. People were too excited and busy thinking about their costume to be pondering her mother's sex life. Theo was elated at the higher level of power Gianna's absence afforded him.

5:12 pm EDT,

Things got more than a little dicey, when Reno sounded the general alarm. A herd of 90 zombies attacked the farm. They swarmed the front gate first. The chain did help to slow them down. When the bat phone went of in the bedroom, Nick and Gianna climbed up to the roof with binoculars. Gianna spotted Alexandra standing on the roof of the infirmary with her bow. She was picking them off as the herd started to move through the woods along the Zone fence. One zombie had managed to climb the fence and got caught in the razor wire. He hung there now with an arrow through his eye. Nick said the children all seem to be performing very well.

Gianna asked Nick if he noticed the zombies didn't have guns or knives. They were throwing rocks with an abnormal amount of strength and speed. Nick pointed out that from up here on the roof she probably could not accurately gauge the rate of speed of the rocks. She pointed out on the roof was not an optimal location to irritate her. Nick agreed. She counted at least six injured from the rocks. She said *however fast* they were throwing them the zombies didn't have very good aim. They threw far more rocks than people they hit. Which Nick pointed out was a good thing for our side.

By 5:55 pm the last zombie was dead. Dancing Goats Farm had lost no lives but 10 went to the infirmary with rock injuries. Nick said they'd used a fair amount of rounds. It might be wiser to save the bullets for people who attacked them with guns. Nick said they needed to talk to Alexandra about training a squad of archers. They watched as Renc had the bodies piled on the road and the flame throwers used. Gianna said the stench was disgusting. Nick told her it would have been worse if they had been left to rot, and then there was the issue of possible zombie bears. Gianna started to laugh because it reminded her of a really bad movie she'd come across about zombie beavers.

Out in the tower Sadie said they

needed the wind to change. She looked up
at the roof where her mother stood
watching. Gianna raised her arms...
whispered a prayer to the mighty Thor...
the breeze shifted direction... carrying
the smoke and stench away from the farm.
No matter how often Nick had seen her do
it, she always amazed him anew. *His wife
could raise the wind.*

**6:45 pm EDT,
Moon Mountain, North Carolina**

It had been an equally busy day at
the Fun Station. His latest happy
customers, the twenty-ninth of the day,
had just left. A trio of youths traveling
to Asheville to join their families. They
had paid for their five packets of Bliss
with; a ham and American cheese on
homemade sourdough, a liter of orange
soda and a chocolate bar. Chocolate was
getting so very hard to find. Because
they were such nice young people Ziggy
had an instant two for one sale, to
insure they'd have some of the pixie dust
to share with the whole family.

Ziggy had just taken his first bite
of the ham and cheese sandwich when the
faint scent of burning flesh drifted
through the door. "Ooooh that smells
promising. A family B-B-Q perhaps? I do
so love when verification floats in. Too
often I don't have the satisfaction of
seeing the results of my *handy* work." By
the fourth bite the air in the room was

becoming quite pungent. "Dare I hope for a mass suicide? That would be the perfect end to my rather successful day. By my calculations, there should be at least 100 new zombies running around the town of Moon Mountain tonight. The little devils will take out the rest of the town's population with their insatiable appetites.

It *was* tricky getting my chemical concoction to trip *that* trigger in the brain, but I must say I've done a smashing job of it. It feels like my work here is done. As soon as I finish this delicious chocolate bar, I'll be on my way to the next town on my list. Let me see what is it called? Oh my memory is simply not what it used to be. Oh yes yes Levelcross. I simply can't wait to visit the Anchored in Jesus Baptist Church!"

Ziggy wiped the melted chocolate from his fingers on the front of his quilted shirt. He looked down and thought the chocolate smears went well with the electric pattern. He took the bags from the drawers, tucked the liter of orange soda under his arm and walked to his Spyder. With his goods safely packed in the side compartments, he turned the key. Backing out he glanced up at the black pillar of smoke rising in the evening dusk. "Oh maybe just a quick peek. After all how often does this happen when I'm still around to enjoy it?" He pulled an elaborate U turn in the center of the deserted street and slowly drove through town. "Oh that looks like results of my *handy* work. One for me. Oh there's two, three for me." He counted the chewed on corpses that were scattered along the street and sidewalks. He'd counted twenty by the time he'd passed the edge of town.

7:05 pm EDT,
Dancing Goats Farm
Moon Mountain, North Carolina

He drove leisurely, savoring the stench with every breath, as it grew closer and stronger. Thirteen miles out of town he rounded a bend and screeched to a halt. In the center of the road up ahead there was a burning mound. The beautiful smell was coming from the mound. "No no no no no this can't be." His hands slid up the sides of his face, his fingers wrapped around his greasy hair and he began to pull. "No no no all my work gone up in flames!" He got off the bike and began to jump up and down. "You fools what have you done? This is my work, my sacred task. You have no idea who you're screwing with." He stopped jumping and listened... there were voices. He crept closer. There was a high fence and a tower. "Just a few feet closer and maybe I can learn who has dared to commit this sacrilege." A woman's voice asks how many?... a man answers 90 maybe 95. A high pitched squeal escapes him as he clutches his chest. "I must leave this sinful place."

80

He rose up and in an act of defiance and contempt he thrusts his fist over his head and shook it at the people in the tower.

As he lowered his fist something whizzed by his head and his hand began to feel as if it's on fire. He ran for his Spyder another whiz went through the wide cuff of his coat. He started the bike and flew down the dark winding road leaving his beloved pinky with it's three inch yellowed nail, behind.

Reno looked up at the hay door. "Carmichael what the hell are you shooting at?"

"There was someone in the shadows. I think I hit him but he ran."

Reno and four men went out the gate and search the area with flashlights. One of them says, "Reno, I got something here." The guard picked it up by the yellow curved nail. "It's fucking creepy."

Reno told him to get it to Andy. Reno followed the blood trail another ten feet and then it's gone. Back inside Sadie asks him what he found. Carmichael is running towards them. The guard holds up the finger. "Hey Carmichael you killed a gnarly pinky."

"Cool. Can I keep it Reno?"

Reno snaps, "*No*, it's going to Andy. Maybe when she's finished with it. Get to dinner. Simon held back serving dinner until the fighting was done." Carmichael heads off to eat, Reno watches him go. "Just when I think he's gotten normal he says shit like that! Sadie, it was black out there. I had trouble seeing with the flashlight. His eyes are like a frigging cat's. I don't know how he saw anyone out there, let alone shot their pinky off. He's four sandwiches short of a picnic but he's a frigging ace sniper."

"Hey, don't pick on my Carmichael. He probably took out more than both of us put together tonight. Mom's right he has wicked mad skills, and Reno, you're not bad yourself."

"I'm not picking on him. He's a good soldier. You just can't take the boy out of the sniper nest. He doesn't quit until *he knows* the job is done. The night the escort team got hit everyone else had stood down, but not him. Those fucking cat eyes of his saw that guy when no one else did. He saved your mothers life.

Sadie, you're going to have to pick up the slack with him. She treats him like she's his drill sergeant. He lives for her. After he took the guy out she didn't gush like a girl. When he said 'I got your 6 ma'am'. She just said 'I know you do babe.' Then later she brought him

82

his own pie and he was an ass and wouldn't share even a bite. Keeping Carmichael in check is another of you new duties."

Amber spots the deputies casting about for a place to sit. "Hey Andy and Barney, come sit with us." The deputies walk over glad to be included at the table of one of the Amazons. "This is my husband Tyler, our daughter Angelena, and I think you know Becky."

"Thanks for inviting us, ma'am, but our names are Derick and Scott."

"I know what your names are dipshit sit down. We have to torture the newbies. It's a rule. You're local law, down the hill from the real Mayberry so yep, we'll call you Andy and Barney till you prove yourselves."

Scott aka Barney says, "If you keep feeding me like this you can call me anything you like. Can I ask a question?" Amber nods. "How do you have phones that work?"

"We have a brilliant tech team. See Brian over there next to Theo, you met Theo right, well Brian has created our own WiFi system for the farm. Only some of us have the phones the rest use radios. Managers, many of our security force and my daughter has one because Angelena wanted one and her Grand Auntie

adores and spoils her." Angelena shows
him her pink flip phone.

"You have no idea how lucky you
were when Nick let you come here. We had
an idyllic life before the Earth Changes.
Now, even though we may have to deal with
shit like today, we'll continue our
enchanted way of life because Nick and
Gianna had a vision and busted their
asses *and* ours to build it. So while the
rest of the world is drowning, being
roasted by fire, or turning into zombies,
we're here. Some day you'll understand
just how fucking lucky you are."

7:30 pm EDT,

Becky called Gianna, "I'm dropping
off your dinner so please keep naked
people out of the kitchen for a few
minutes. And tell the Boss not to shoot
me."

Becky's call had woken them. Gianna
hung up and asked Nick if he was hungry.
Nick grined as he ran his hand up her
thigh, "*Always*. They say life is short,
maybe we should have dessert first."

Smiling she answers him, "*We
could*... but if I know Simon, there are
rare lollipop lamb chops sitting in our
kitchen..."

"You are a wicked woman to make me
choose. His lamb chops are *almost* as

84

tasty as you are."

"True darling, but I'll still be
warm in an hour, *the lamb chops won't
be.*"

chapter 22
WHO ARE YOU?

*"I knew who I was
when I woke up this morning
I fear I changed
several times since then"*

10:45 pm EDT, October 6,
Moon Mountain, North Carolina

Ziggy was lying on the floor of the abandoned Emergency Clinic, his hand wrapped in a dirty strip of gauze he'd found on the floor of the ransacked exam room. The physical pain from his missing pinky was excruciating. It burned a trail from the tip of his missing finger up to his fetid arm pit. His despondency was compounded by the loss of his magnificent pinky nail. 'They would pay for the assault on his person and taking of his limb.' *Yes*, he thought of the finger as a special limb. 'Their evil wretchedness would be punished by the Mother herself!'

11:00 pm EDT,
Dancing Goats Farm
Moon Mountain, North Carolina

Sadie, Amber, Lizzy and Carl sat in

front of the fireplace in the Hall. Reno
was due to join them. Carl was reading
through the zombie reports. He looked at
the women. "This is like reading Sci-Fi
shit. Do you have today's report on
what's going on in the rest of the
country? I've been getting them every day
from Adrian, but the zombie herd
distracted me today."

Sadie started the meeting. "Yes,
Reno should be bring them. Carl we need
to find out who is turning the people
into druggie zombies. While the guys were
tightening up after the attack,
Carmichael shot at a guy who'd been
hiding in the bushes. Carmichael swears
the guy stepped out and shook his fist at
the wall. Carmichael hit him as he turned
and ran. Reno found a blood trail in the
road, that ended abruptly. He figures the
guy left on a bike. One of the guard
found a pinky finger Carmichael had taken
off below the knuckle. The finger has a
bizarre three inch nail. Andy says there
is trace from the drug on the finger but
not in the blood. There wasn't a lot for
her to work with."

Lizzy handed Carl a paper. "This is
the chemical breakdown of what Andy found
in the blood of the first zombie and what
was on the finger. This drug is designed
to drive people mad. The zombies probably
die within twelve hours of taking it.
From what I saw today, they don't seem to
understand when they're in danger.

87

Several looked right at me tonight and didn't appear to understand the situation. If they could have gotten through the fence they would have kept coming even though I was about to shoot them in the face. The eyes show rage and nothing else. We're looking for someone with a heavy background in chemistry. The cocktail of drugs is too precise to be just some jerk tossing shit together. This guy is a twisted fuck. We need you to help us find him."

Reno walked through the door. "Sorry I'm late, it's been a fucking busy day. Here are Adrian's reports for today and this evening. I need a beer. Carl you want one? Ladies?" Carl says yes, as he scans the reports. He passes the pages to Lizzy as he finishes each one. Reno returns to find them all engrossed in the reports. "I haven't read them yet. I don't know how you're keeping up Sadie but I found out today how hard it is to be Nick. Watching him and being him are very different. And I lost Becky today. She has taken care of the brunt of these reports since she broke her ribs. I didn't know how much shit she was sifting through, to give Nick just the meat."

Without looking up from the page Sadie says, "Fuck yeah. Why do you think Lizzy's here? I had to pull her in to be 'me' to help me carry mom's load. I really 'owned' their redundancy rule today. Bonny had to step up as

Shepherdess. Alexandra got a call from Nick telling her to put together a squad of archers. She's going through personnel files with Theo right now. She'll have a list for you in the morning so you can schedule them to work with her. She called woodworking to get them started on producing arrows in the morning. It's a fuck of a lot to be them."

Amber says "And they've been doing it non-stop for ten years. They probably got married just to have an excuse for a vacation! During the attack Tyler was in the Q reloading, but I was inside the infirmary with Angelena. Those two watched the whole zombie battle from the roof. I would have loved to hear their assessment of how we handled ourselves." They all stopped and looked at her.

"What? You know they were grading us. They really have eyes on everything all the time. *Stop looking at me like that.* I'm not discussing their *sex life*, just how they're everywhere all at once. I think we did very well for our first day, considering it just got dropped on us before breakfast."

Reno asks, "You think they'll stop arguing now?"

"Fuck no. That's who they are with each other. That's not going to change. Its a big part of why they're such an amazing team. I have it with Tyler. We

Scorpio women, are cunts. Come on Lizzy, back me up here."

That's who we are. Few men can deal with it. The ones that can like the give and take of the game. Beside, if they stopped, we'd lose half of our entertainment around here. Vy'd have to come up with roving combative comedians to pick up the slack. Knowing mom... and Nick, he said something up there today and she offered to toss his ass off the roof."

"Yeah, they were even doing it ove... *never* mind."

Lizzy frowned at Amber. "Come on Amber, you think we haven't figured it out? Tyler racing across the green at 4:30 in the morning while you and Ferret race toward the Q. They got caught on tape having sex in the... guessing kitchen. Becky's promotion..." Lizzy stops. They're all looking at her. Amber's face says *Shut Up!* The other three clearly had not figured it out...shit. "I can't help it if y'all don't pay attention like us Scorpions."

"Lizzy what were *you* doing out there at 4:30?"

"Reno, daahh I'm up with the animals."

Amber still trying to shut Lizzy

doen, "This is just what they don't want people doing Liz!"

"Fuck Amber, you know she doesn't care what we say behind closed doors. She just doesn't want to hear it or see it on our faces."

They all burst out laughing. Sadie says, "So was the tape good?"

Amber gives then all a wicked smile "First consider the cast... dumb question. Second let's just say Ferret copied before she deleted, and Nick wants to have them framed for the bedroom."

Laughing Lizzy says, "So they were good. You go mom. If you're going to get caught on tape having sex in the kitchen, it's important you looked good doing it."

"*That's what I said when I saw them.* Stop asking me these questions besides, you know Nick, he will put at least one of them in the bedroom, if for nothing else just to bust her balls."

Reno says, "How did this happen? Nick and Tyler moved the cameras to the walls yesterday."

"All but one. They were trying to figure out where to put it and Nick got called away and they both forgot about it. The one camera they should have taken down *first*."

Lizzy says, "Enough, back to the Zombie Maker. Carl do you think Mendez would be helpful to you? He not doing much besides screwing one of Amber's girls. What's her name?"

"Molly, at least he's helping in the orchard greenhouse so he can hang with her."

Reno offers, "Carl, he's a Marine from Special Ops Command. He's got some unique skills."

"Good idea Lizzy. And I like the name, Zombie maker. We have to call him something. The only other option is 'sick fuck'. I'll talk to Mendez in the morning. If I want him I'll let Theo know to reassign him to me. I'll need a room to work from to correlate what data we have so I'll need to talk to Theo about that too. Reno, is Mendez really good?"

Reno shrugged. "Nick thinks highly of him. I don't know if the Lady has changed her opinion of him. She did offer to shoot him at least twice."

"I'll look at these tonight and get started in the morning. Reno can I keep these overnight? I'll have them copied in the morning. Becky has an excellent mind for data analysis. Think I'll ask her if she wants to be part of the team."

Amber says, "Carl, if you want my two cents worth, she recognized the problem, shut it down, called in the people she needed to eliminate it in 60 seconds. She's been under used as a foot soldier. Not that she isn't a good one, but she has more to offer."

Sadie agrees. "Amber's right, but Lizzy knows her best."

"Yeah, we hang out and get drunk in the barn sometimes. I mean how much of her time is the manor house going to take up? She's very intelligent."

Sadie says, "Alright, sounds like we have a plan. Let's hope we put enough of those poor people in the ground today to have a quiet night. Oh Reno, I'm going to need my own bat phone."

"Right, see Theo about that. He'll get Brian on it. Goodnight all. I'm beat. I don't know how he does it."

Carl stands to leave too. "Good night ladies."

"I'm too awake to sleep. Either of you want to come to my place for a drink?"

Amber shakes her head no. "I need to get home. I've been up since 4:30 and unlike Super Sleuth over here, that's way too early for me, mother of a tiny tornado."

"Sounds good Sadie, let's work on our plan for tomorrow."

1:45 am EDT, October 7 ,
Moon Mountain, North Carolina

Ziggy had passed out from the emotional devastation he felt at the loss of his finger. He lay there now staring at the ruin of his left hand. 'He'd have to learn to play the guitar without his pinky and it's nail. How would he ever learn how to use a pick. He'd only ever used his pinky nail.' "Wait until I tell Mother about this! She'll smite those evil bastards." He got up and searched for something cleaner to wrap his hand in. He found new gauze in a box under the exam table and took it back to the Fun Station.

The blood had dried and caked on the old gauze. He howled as he ran it under the rust tinged water until the tap ran dry. "*Fantastic*, no more water! Who would have thought in this water logged apocalypse, I'd run out of water when I needed it the most?" He soaked his hand in the puddle of toilet water in the bottom of the bowl. The sight of his deformed hand set him crying again as he wrapped it in the new gauze.

In his agony he had forgotten his bags in the Spyder. He brought them in for safe keeping, along with his liter of orange soda. Now, he was hungry. He sat cradling his arm. "How could this have happened to me? I am a messenger of the Mother. Doesn't this afford me some sort of mystical protection? I failed her this is my punishment!" He ruffled through his leavings on the desk. He found a crust of sourdough and a missed square of chocolate. "Well it's something. They've murdered all my Distributors. How will I get to all the rabbits hiding behind their locked doors? Things had gone so very well yesterday... until the massacre. I shouldn't have gone to look. I should have gone on to Levelcross as planed. It was my ego that drove me to seek the gratification of seeing my *handy* work. Do I stay and seek revenge, or go on about my ordained task? Best leave the revenge to Mother. How would I get inside those walls anyway?"

Ziggy looked down into the bag of Bliss. "I could do with a bit of bliss right now. Bliss, Pixie Dust, Star Dust, Moon Beams, these are lovely names I've chosen." Ziggy had tried the early batches on himself. Then he woke up in a hospital on a 48 hour hold. After that he used street people for the tests. No one missed them when they disappeared. He could only dream of how wonderful it would be to try the finished product once his work for Mother was done. "Well no sense dawdling, best be on the road. I'll have to leave the rabbits to Mother along with the revenge." Ziggy gathered up his bags and soda. As he revved the Snyder's engine he looked back at Main Street and shrugged. "Just have to chalk this one up to a total failure." Then he was gone.

Ziggy's Total Failure had already caused the death of 25% of Moon Mountain's population. That would leave 739... except another 184 have died as a result of the Earth Changes, 206 have left in search of food and safety. Moon Mountain's population is now 349 not including the Tribe at Dancing Goats Farm.

5:45 am EDT, October 7,
Dancing Goats Farm
Moon Mountain, North Carolina

Alarm clocks are sounding throughout Dancing Goats Farm.

Bonny is already in the barn releasing the animals. She has her clipboard with a list of all the Head Shepherdess is responsible for each day. The three barn hands are forking hay into the cart to wheel out to the pasture. The goats in milk, are on their milking stands chomping down their morning ration of sweet feed. She is determined to prove to Lizzy she's ready for the job.

Lizzy is brushing her hair while mentally reviewing the list she and Sadie made the night before. She's going to

deal with the Q interaction today. Sadie
wants her to keep an eye on Reno making
sure he's up to the job, while not
letting him know she's checking on him.
Sadie thinks he is up to it but she'll
feel more confident with Lizzy's eyes on.
Liz also has to deal with the Hall and
Simon. Sadie doesn't get along with Simon
so Lizzy said, rather than have a
confrontation the first week on the job,
she'd take Simon off Sadie's list.
Lizzy'd been going back and forth for
fifteen minutes over; should she or
shouldn't she carry her Ruger P 95 today.
Screw it, she slips her shoulder holster
on and slides her stainless steel beauty
in place. She doesn't want to be in the Q
and have to ask to borrow a gun if shit
happens... which it seem to be doing
every day lately. She heads over to the
Hall to grab a coffee and see to Simon's
needs for the day.

   Becky's in the Q kitchen pouring her
first cup of coffee when Reno came in.
"Good morning would you like a cup I just
made it?"

   Reno smiles. "Yes, thanks. Listen
Becky, I'm sorry I was an asshole
yesterday. I think it had just hit me,
you know what we're not supposed talk
about, and I shouldn't have spoken to you
that way, and Congrats on making
Lieutenant."

   "Thanks Reno for the apology and the

congrats. You can say the Boss and the Lady getting married. They just don't want us gossiping about it. Or acting stupid when we see them."

Reno nodded. "I hope we don't have too much shit happen today so I can get the normal stuff done. The good news is Sadie was real easy to work with yesterday. Oh and I think Carl might want to talk to you. We had a meeting last night about the guy responsible for the zombie drug. Carl was impressed with your reports. Oh yeah, good catch on the camera."

"*How do you know about that?*"

"It came up at the meeting. Amber was being closed mouthed and Lizzy told her to stop the crap. Lizzy spelled it out like we'd all figured it out... only we, Sadie, Carl, and I, hadn't. But Lizzy did cause she was up and saw the three of them running around at 4:30 in the morning. It'll be fine as long as no one brings it up until they do. So we don't mention it to anyone outside the circle."

Becky shook her head as she handed Reno a mug. "*The fucking circle keeps getting bigger.*"

Tyler woke Amber to say goodbye. "Hey babe I see you for lunch. I have to go hang your Aunt's nudie cam in the Q."

Amber grabbed him by the beard. "Tyler don't think because you're married to me Sadie won't toss your ass out or my sister put an arrow through your heart. *Never*, mention that again. I love you go to work."

Sadie got to the office as Theo was pulling up. "Hey Brian, just the man I want to see. Can you come in a minute? Morning Theo, where's your hat today?"

"I didn't feel the need for it since mom and dad aren't fighting. I'm going to assume, even if they do venture forth, Nick has her in a very good mood."

"Theo *that's* just the type of comment Alexandra will shoot you for."

"*Never happen*, she loves me. What do you need my Brian for?

"I need my own bat phone. It doesn't help me if it goes off in her room. How do I know if she'll even respond?"

Oh stop, they were on the roof watching the whole thing last night. I don't think they were up there sunbathing."

"Theo you never leave the building how the hell do you know everything that's going on everywhere?"

"I have Brian, our resident

communication genius. I have listening devices everywhere you can think of and quite a few more where you would never imagine."

"*You're lying.*"

"Alas yes, but it sounded good didn't it? We'll get you hooked up this morning. Where do you want it? The bed table like mom's? Come ,we'll go over the day's list."

"Oh Theo, Carl is going to need a room. He has a project he's working on for us. Long table, chairs, a board to tack or tape things to, he may need more. We need to catch this evil drug dealing mother fucker before he kills any more people. Those were locals last night. Our little town lost a hundred people in twenty minutes. That's crazy and sad."

Freddy walked upstairs with Tiny, as Charlie came in the front door. "Good morning Lieutenant."

"Morning Charlie, hi guys. Quiet night I hope?"

Freddy starts a new pot of coffee. Charlie answers her. "Yes, it was pretty quiet. We had more beggars moving west. Caught Sal trying to give them food. Reno, he's off the wall from now on. Nick never did finish interviewing the men about that. I'll finish the ones on my shifts today. Tiny has a list of the men on your shifts with Nick's recommendations on the ones he interviewed."

Thanks Charlie. I'll get these finished today. We don't need that shit starting. Did you see DJ out there?"

"Yeah, he's in the barn assigning work to the shift. Thought he was you for a minute when he started on the condition of the equipment."

Reno smiles as Becky says, "Tiny you're glowering at me. Spit it out big guy."

Tiny takes a breath. "No one touches that system. I am responsible for the data in there. I want to know what was erased and why you let an unauthorized person into it."

I'm sorry you space was breached. I had no control over the incident that caused me to act as I did. As for the data, I'm sorry it's above your pay grade, along with everyone else in this room. I was functioning under direct orders from the Lady. I really don't think you want to demand she tell you, what she had taken off her system. As for Amber, she was speaking for her Aunt. Ferret was there because you had put software in place I couldn't get around. Tiny you are very good at your job but you are not a world class hacker. It took Ferret less than one minute to get around your lock. I'll tell you what I told Reno, if Ferret wanted in that system she would not need to be in the room to do it. She works in the Shack. *Everything* runs through there. Theo trusts her and the Lady trusts her, a recommendation doesn't get any better than that around here. Know this, she is very grateful for the home she has here. She will never hurt the farm. You might want to get to know her. She may have a few tips for you so you can be even better at your job. Are we good?" Tiny didn't say anything. "Tiny if you don't believe me you can ask Amber. At some point you can ask the Lady herself. Tiny, I didn't get promoted because I fucked up."

No one heard Lizzy come in. "She's absolutely accurate with what she said. You may still ask Amber and mom too, but if you do, mom may not be too pleased you didn't believe Becky, Me or Amber."

Tiny uncrossed his arms in surrender. "Okay, I'm good. It's just the system is my baby. Maybe I will talk to Ferret and see what she can teach me."

"Great, Good morning gentlemen. Reno and Charlie the Q is on my list today. Charlie anything you want to go over before you go about your day?"

"Morning Lizzy, I'll sit in for the

meeting."

"See you later Lizzy. I have to go get *the breakfast*. Reno said Carl might want to talk to me."

"I just saw him go in the office and yes he wants to talk to you."

Freddy asked "Lizzy do you mind if I sit in?"

"I have no problem with it, it's up to Charlie and Reno."

6:30 am EDT,

Charlie nodded for Freddy to sit. They reviewed the morning's report. The zombies were showing up in Asheville. Lizzy said the drug had to have been carried there. The zombies can't drive or walk that far. She checked that the information had been sent to the Shack. Carl would be wanting it. They discussed Nick wanting a squad of archers. Lizzy recommended pikes through the fencing in the Zone because of what she saw defending that side of the wall. Alexandra wanted one of them to get her the number of crossbows there were and she wanted one to be brought to the wood worker to see if they could make some out of wood. Charlie really like the idea of pikes. They wanted to know if there was any flack about the fence being hot. Lizzy said she didn't know if mcm knew

103

but she and Sadie were good with it.

7:00 am EDT,

In bed over their breakfast, of French toast with an apricot butter syrup, Gianna asked, "Nick, I love having you naked but might you like to have some of your clothes brought over? It's not a complicated job. You wear black jeans and black T shits every day... and yes, you look *very sexy* in them. Reno could get them or Becky. Any thoughts on this?"

Nick looked very seriously at her. She was licking the syrup of the tip of her index finger. "If *I* start wearing clothes, then *you'll* start wearing clothes. I'm not sure how I feel about that."

"Well darling, it was kind of tricky on the roof yesterday. You almost lost that towel... *a coupla times*... and, *as previously discussed,* I don't share well... and I'm not interested in sharing you at all... or *all of you* as the case may be."

Nick slid the breakfast tray aside. "Point made. Tell Becky to bring three of each. Now come over here wife, there's something I have in mind for the rest of that syrup."

7:45 am EDT, October 7,
Levelcross, North Carolina

Ziggy parked the Spyder behind the church. The lock on the rectory door was a simple one designed to keep honest people out. It took longer using his right hand to get inside. His left hand throbbed. He thought he could hear it echoing in the room. He curled up in a corner. A little nap was what he needed before the service and so he slept.

Beneath the gauze a frenzy of activity was taking place. There had been a legion of bacteria living in the puddle of water at the bottom of the toilet bowl, in the dead Deputy Sergeant's abandoned sheriff's station. For almost thirteen hours now, they had been feeding on his torn ragged flesh and traveling up the super highways of his veins. They gobbled up the meat and blood and they were now making their way into the bones.

But there's more... The first gauze he'd found on the floor had come from the Bio-Hazard bin. It contained a rich colony of Staphylococcus. If the world hadn't spun out of control, the lab test for the patient would have verified this. But it did spin out of control. The Woman died but not before infecting two family members. All three became part of the statistic of 184 who died in Moon Mountain due to the Earth Changes. The colony of Staphylococcus incubated moist and safe inside the red plastic bio-hazard bag, until a starving dog had ransacked the bin, as Ziggy was driving through town counting corpses. The dog tore open the bag and dragged the gauze around the room and dropped it where Ziggy found it 45 minutes later.

The dog left with no food but he did have a mouthful of Staphylococcus which he would give to the next four people he met. The gauze patiently waited for Ziggy snacking on the dog's saliva.

The Staphylococcus and its toilet buddies had a death grip on Ziggy. His fever spiked and his twisted delusional brain leaped to new heights of madness. He was having ham and American cheese on sourdough sandwiches with Mother while they drank orange soda from beakers in his lab.

Outside the quaint white clapboard church, in the shadow of the steeple, two men were hot wiring Ziggy's Spyder, as Mother and Ziggy drank their orange soda. When the two men reached the intersection of I-77 they pulled over to see what was in the side compartments. They danced a happy snoopy dance at their great fortune. One said he'd take one bag and work his way south to Charlotte. The other took the bike and the other two thousand packets and worked his way northwest up 21. He was headed home to Kentucky by way of Damascus Virginia. Though Ziggy would miss the show, he would have been ever so pleased his work was being carried on.

9:00 am EDT, October 7,
Dancing Goats Farm
Moon Mountain, North Carolina

Carl had drawn a map, now stuck with
push pins, indicating the locations where
zombie activity had been reported. They
clustered around the route, Carl
believed, the drug dealer took. Once the
Zombie Maker arrived at Moon Mountain the
incidences began to spider out from town.
Mendez and Becky were studying the map
with him. Carl was saying, "It's true our
data gathering is primitive at best, but
I think we have a pattern we can work
with. The question is what happened here
that caused him or enabled him to spider
out like this."

Mendez said, "It could be as simple
as right time right place. Maybe the
other towns were not in the state of
devolving as Moon Mountain was when he
got here."

Becky added, "If that was the case,
he may have spent more time here than the
other towns. No other place has reported
a herd the size we dealt with yesterday.
Or we haven't heard about it because the
people were not as well armed and are
dead or, had a place to defend and didn't
have the advance warning or a radio. Fuck
we just don't have enough information and
a shitload of maybes." Both men looked at

her. "Sorry guys, I've been at this for days. You just joined the party."

Mendez asks, "When was the last time anyone was in town? Let's talk to the two deputies. They may have some information for us."

Becky went to the door and asked, "Theo can you find Andy and Barney and get them here?" She turns and finds them both looking at her again, "You Guys need to stop that you're creeping me out. Reno called them Andy and Barney cause they're local law from the real Mayberry. Which is Mount Airy. Amber made it a rule we are to call them that until they prove themselves."

Mendez looked over at Carl. "I say we talk to them and take a trip to town."

Becky shook her head no. "I can't go. I have to be on call for the manor house. In fact I have to do an errand for them. I just got a text. You guys talk to Scott and Derick and I'll check back in later when you return."

10:30 am EDT,

Carl and Mendez interviewed the deputies then went out to talk to Reno about a vehicle. Out in the barn Mikey was just finishing a camouflage paint job on the truck with the plow on the front. Carl saw it and asked how it ran. "The guy must have been a bit of a motor-head. It's souped up."

"Where did we get it from?"

"They tried to ram the gate with it demanding our food. Carmichael took out the driver. Sadie was here and said take out the rest they'd just annoy us by coming back. But keep the truck. So here it is."

Reno showed up and Carl told him the plan. Reno said Nick had grounded everyone. But He and Sadie were in charge and they felt the information was important, so if they wanted to make a run in it they could.

10:45 am EDT,
Moon Mountain, North Carolina

The ride to town was uneventful. Town was another story. In the first block they came across a zombie eating one of the corpses Ziggy had counted. Carl slowed the truck and Mendez put it down. They saw movement in the window above the Hardware store. Carl stopped the truck. Mendez got out and showed the man his badge and mimed for him to open the window. When he did, they asked what had been happening. He told them about the deputies leaving and not coming back. They asked if he'd seen any drug deals going on in the street. He said not in the street but he suspected it was going

on out of the sheriff's station. There
was a weird guy with strange brightly
colored clothes who road a three wheeled
motorcycle, red with black spiders on it.
After the guy had showed up the zombie
stuff started to happen. There'd been a
lot of people going in and coming out
laughing. Carl asked if he had food and
water. He said he wasn't sharing. Carl
said he didn't want to take his food, he
had some to give him. Carl said he'd
leave the box by the door the guy could
get it after they left. They put the box
and two gallons of water at the door and
went to look at the Sheriff's station.
There was noise coming from the clinic so
they went in there first. It was a cat.
They found Ziggy's blood on the floor.
Next door was more informative.

Ziggy had been doodling in between
customers. Carl took photos of the
ramblings of a madman. In the bathroom
they found the bloody gauze. The toilet
and sink were splattered with Ziggy's
blood. Carl was confident the rest of
Carmichael's pinky had been there. There
was a wallet on the floor near the desk,
it belonged to a Ziegfeld Star. The last
photo Carl took was of the two words
scratched into the center of the desk. In
the drawer they found one of Ziggy's
packets. They drove around and figured he
was gone. They passed the Hardware store.
The box was gone. The man waved pointed
to a can and gave them a thumbs up and
went back to eating the canned beans Carl

had left in the box.

12:30 pm EDT,

Lizzy and Reno were standing in the tower. Reno had called to tell her he'd let Carl and Mendez take the truck to town an hour and a half ago. "Did they give you any indication as to how long they'd be gone?"

"No, he's the Fixer we pretty much give him anything he asks for and we don't ask him any questions. Nick told us the guy runs 'errands' for the Lady. I figured he wasn't picking up the dry cleaning." Reno put his hand up and listens. "There's a truck hauling ass and several following." Reno takes the stairs two at a time.

Lizzy grabs the binoculars off the hook. "Fuck! There's a monster truck on Carl's ass and two Harleys flanking him. Open the gates, sound general alarm, there's no way to stop them from coming in with him." Reno radios Antonio to sound the general alarm and races to open the gate. Mikey is already pulling the other side open. The vanguard are flying in from every direction, some with no shoes or shirt having just rolled out of their bunks. Antonio has radioed the Sergeant; the Q is being breached. Ten regulars stand ready to decimate anyone who comes through the east portal. Carl takes a hard right into the Q.

The Harley riding on Carl's
passenger side gets run off the road into
the brush. Lizzy says, "That's the waste
of a nice bike. Hmmm not sure if you're
dead, this will clear that up." Lizzy put
one through his eye. She turns and finds
Carl has stopped nearly on the steps of
the veranda. The Harley from the driver's
side is in the hands of two of the
vanguard in a move right out of the
movies. Carmichael is picking off the
assholes in the back of the monster
truck, which has stopped halfway in the
gate, preventing the guard from closing
it.

Carmichael signals Lizzy to look
behind her. "Mother Fucker. Reno get that
truck moved there's another truck 60
seconds out. Lizzy takes out another bike
that's riding point. It crashes in to the
woods across from the gate. Lizzy hears
Reno say open the gates and then she
smiles cause she knows what's coming.

DJ has lined Audrey up in front of
the monster truck. Audrey's gun barrel is
pointing at the center of its windshield.
The vanguard have the sides of the
monster truck covered. The second monster
truck screeches to a halt behind the
first. A biker on Lizzy's side of the
trucks is taking aim at the hay loft.
Lizzy puts one through his throat
severing his carotid. Blood shoots out of
both side of his neck. "You don't fuck

with our Carmichael ass wipe."

Through the loudspeaker mounted on Audrey, DJ says, "Say hello to Audrey boys." The second truck has bigger wheels than the first. DJ sent Audrey's calling card through its engine block. The bikers flanking the truck are knocked sideways twenty feet, by the explosion. Lizzy just missed getting slammed by a side mirror that sailed through the tower. Carmichael finishes off two, mostly dead, on his side. Lizzy caps a biker crawling out of the woods. Her ears are still ringing from being so close to the gun barrel but she thinks it's over. She sees the Amazons standing on the veranda. In the distance... yes... mom and dad are on the roof!

Violet surveys the damage and death. "This is a Fucking Mess. Carl, did you at least find out who the zombie maker is?"

"Yes... it's *Ziggy Stardust*.

chapter 23
LOCK AND LOAD

*"Screw defense,
we're going on the offensive
Lock and load sisters"*

6:00 pm EDT, October 7,
Dancing Goats Farm
Moon Mountain, North Carolina

It had taken the efforts of the whole farm four hours to clean up the wreckage in the Q. The vanguard had ten injured mostly because they hadn't had time to get to their vests. Three were serious but the Doc said they'd make a full recovery. One had a dislocated shoulder from getting slammed by the mirror that had whizzed by Lizzy's head.

The gates had taken some damage from the blast. The planks of the Q's fencing and gates were not pine but steel. It could have been worse. DJ had apologized for the damage. Violet said it wasn't like he had a choice and not to worry he'd done good. Mikey had declared the rear end of the first monster truck fucked but they hauled it in for parts they could get off the front end. The second was a heap of twisted metal that littered the road for thirty feet up and down. Freddy shoved it off to the side of the road with the bobcat.

They recovered the five Harleys. The two that had taken the blast were badly damaged but might be repairable. The Sportster from the first rider Lizzy shot in the eye, to her delight, had only a few minor scratches and dents. She claimed it. Amber asked if she was going to ride ride it around the farm? Lizzy said *yeah*. The 15" Springer Chopper that went in the brush across the road would be added to the vanguard's growing fleet of vehicles. The Sportster that had come through the gate on Carl's ass, had veered left, dodging four of the vanguard lined up waiting for him. As the rider turned towards the barn, Charlie's Glock, 10" away, sent a bullet through his brain. The guy fell off the bike but the bike kept rolling forward. Two of the vanguard grabbed the handlebars as it passed between them. It now stood, in perfect condition, in the barn. Reno whistled when he saw the teal full-dress low rider, he claimed that one.

Now; the Q having been returned to normal, the injured visited by Reno, Sadie, and Lizzy, they were gathered in Carl's situation room. Theo had more chairs brought in and a table set in the corner with coffee, sandwiches and a handle of Jack and bottle of Viclet's preferred drink, Kracken Rum. Theo handed her a bottle of the farm,s homemade root beer and a glass of ice. She addressed the group. "I have no intention of shooting anyone tonight, therefore I'm going to begin drinking *now*. Carl, what the hell did you and Mendez find? You do know Ziggy Stardust is dead. He died *with* Bowie. Alter egos have a funny way of doing that when the host dies."

Mendez passed out the photos Carl had taken of the walls and desk in the sheriff's station. They showed: bits of chemical formulas, conversations Ziggy thought he was having with Mother. They learned Ziggy believed his sacred mission had been given to him by Mother and the two words found scratched into the top of the wooden desk; *ZIGGY STARDUST* was now beginning to make sense. While they looked at the photos, Theo passed out information on the man Ziegfeld Star.

Mendez was shocked to learn of yet another of the farm's illegal deeds. Adrian had downloaded the FBI's database of files on 'people of interest', before the lights went out. He asked "How frigging big is your server?"

Sadie said, "Mendez that information is still above your pay grade. Carl you want to walk us through this maze of insanity?"

Carl covered the report on Ziegfeld

Star first. He held four degrees; a Ph.D. in Math, a PH.D. in Chemistry, a Ph.D. in Molecular Biology, and was a Doctor of Sacred Theology. He earned his first at the age of 15 from Oxford. Ten years ago, while working for the largest agricultural company in the US, he suffered a catastrophic breakdown. The company carried on with Dr. Star's groundbreaking work without him. Star remained in a semi-catatonic state for eight years, then one day started talking again.

He was released nine months ago in the care of his 70 year old mother, who died two weeks later. Then Dr. Star vanished. The FBI had found journals in the home indicating Dr. Star now felt he was a rock star in contact with earth's alien Mother. This Mother had given him a sacred mission to purge the earth of contaminants. Star was written off as, I quote, 'A FRUIT CAKE' and forgotten. Ziggy's writing was a bit frenzied by then. The tech misread contaminants, it actually said contaminators. Adrian said in the first few days of search for the composer of the Mother email, Star had been a person of interest, but the FBI had eliminated him because of the fruit cake remark in his file.

Carl moved on to the scribblings Star had left on the walls. "He believes he is Ziggy Stardust. The man over the Hardware store in town told us he's

dressed in what sounds like a glam rock
Bowie costume. He's driving a three
wheeled bike, guessing it's a Spyder in
keeping with the Ziggy delusion. Because
he has the knowledge buried under the
delusion, he had the skill to create the
drug that is turning the users into our
zombies. Carmichael did wound him, rather
badly from the amount of blood we found.
He's gone. We don't know where for sure
but we believe he might be dead. Just
before the meeting Antonio picked up a
conversation regarding a brightly dressed
redhead found with a hand wound hiding in
a church. The hand was badly infected.
When they tried to amputate it he went
crazy and they shot him. They did not see
a Spyder or any sign of the drugs. We can
assume the Spyder was stolen along with
the drugs. Antonio is passing the word
through the HAM network to let us know if
they see this red bike with spiders
painted on it. Also that the drugs the
new owner may be selling are dangerous
and most likely what is causing the
zombie behavior. We do not have any idea
of the quantity that's out there. We did
find a sample which Andy has. So yes
Violet, now Ziggy Stardust is dead... *for
a second time.*

Alexandra asked, "The drugs are
still out there but you think they've
left our town?"

Right, unless whoever stole them
comes back here with them. We'll know

when the next zombie reports come in."
Which they were doing as Carl was
speaking. Elkin, Sparta and Hamptonville
were having a rash of zombies.

7:00 pm EDT, October 7,
Sparta, North Carolina

The man parked the Spyder in the
parking lot of the now closed Burger
King. It was boarded up like most of the
businesses he'd passed that day. The King
hadn't served food in seven days. The man
made some cash and bartered for food back
in Elkin. At Stone Mountain Park he had
bartered twenty bags for two gallons of
gas. He stopped here to see if he could
do a little business for a gas can that
would fit in the empty side compartment
so he could barter for more gas. He
planed to hang for an hour then he head
on to Damascus to spend the night. They
made quiet a fuss over his Spyder at the
park. One guy saw his panther tattoo and
said he should call himself Spider Cat.
He'd been trying it out in his head all
the way to Sparta. Two people came over
and asked what he had to sell. He
introduced himself as Spider Cat Man and
told them he had dust for trade. A deal
was agreed upon. The buyers returned
eight minutes later with a red plastic
gas can that fit in the compartment. It
held three gallons so he gave them thirty
bags. Knowing they would sell them around
town he headed out for Damascus.

7:30 pm EDT, October 7,
Statesville, North Carolina

Henry had walked 35 miles to get to
Statesville. He'd wandered around and
found a crowed of twenty and unders
camped out at the Hilton indoor pool. The
kid at the desk, playing hotel clerk,
gave him the keys to a room for one pack
of bliss. In his room he hid the bag in
the air conditioning vent after he had
stuffed his pockets full of Ziggy's pixie
dust. At the pool he bartered for five
warm beers, and a plate of some kind of
rice dish. After the second beer he
started taking jewelry for payment. It
all went very bad after that. He should
have only bought four beers, he never got
to drink the fifth.

7:30 pm EDT, October 7,
Dancing Goats Farm
Moon Mountain, North Carolina

Dinner had been a busy time for the
Tribe. Even those who had eaten at their
place showed up to talk. They had all
been deeply shaken by the breach of the Q
walls. This had never happened with the
exception of the time Samira had let two
men in. But that wasn't the same thing.
Samira had been working in the kitchen
scrubbing pots, pans, floors, whatever
Simon said to. Gianna said it would give
her time to think about what could have
happened if the sisters hadn't run out
when they did. As she cleared dinner

120

dishes she listened to the accounts of what had happened today and she got it. She thought Gianna was being dramatic when she yelled at her after the snot-zi thing. She never really believed anything bad could happen inside the walls. Tonight she saw her neighbors and friends, frightened or worried, some even cried. When things didn't get any calmer the sisters took center stage.

8:30 pm EDT,

Sadie started. "I know today was rough but we're all tightened down again. Our vanguard kicked ass. Let's stand and give them a hand." They did and the mood lightened a little. "While you're standing lets hear it for our regulars who protect us every day and were at the portal in 60 seconds." Most started to feel better but a few still cried. "Nick and Gianna have taught you how to defend this place and I think some of you have gotten a little complacent. That doesn't work for us, any of us. Every member of this Tribe has to give 100 percent to the Tribe. That's the agreement you signed when they gave you the gift of living here."

Lizzy interrupted her, "I'm still hearing fucking crybabies back there. There's no crying... we won, we held our ground, our home is safe, because we're not fucking crybabies. I was literally on the front line today... *do you see me*

121

crying?"

Amber saw Lizzy was a heartbeat from going full Scorpio on them. She stood and took the floor before somebody got slapped. "I have heard some of you question why Nick and Gianna aren't here tonight. My question to you, is, *why are you asking that question?* News Fucking Flash... You are Responsible for You. It shouldn't matter if they're here or in Kat-fucking-mandu. You, sniveling back there, it's time to stand up, put your big girl panties on, and step up to the front line with the Amazons. You'd be crying a lot fucking harder if I put your sorry ass *outside* the gate!"

Alexandra jumped up because her sister was going mega Scorpio. "I want every person to sign up for archery training. See Violet to sign up. I think some of us are just out of practice. I'll get you back in shape." She looked to Violet.

Violet stood. "I want you to look around at the amazing family we are. Go home, think about the things the sisters have said. Then, thank the Mother Goddess, that you are standing here, well fed, with a warm bed to go home to, because Nick and Gianna created this place, where you will wake up tomorrow, and not be killed while you sleep."

Sadie looked at her sister laughing,

122

"And you were doing so well right up to the last four words."

Then a voice through the speakers said, "Mother said you need to dance to some kick ass rock and roll." Katmandu came blasting out of the speakers followed by Old time Rock and Roll... and the Tribe danced their fears away.

9:30 pm EDT,

After the Hall had emptied they sat and drank. Reno said, "Well ladies, that was very motivational, in a threatening sort of way. The music was a nice ending." They said in unison we didn't do that.

Lizzy said, "My money's on Ferret. She's been delivering Mother's messages through the blog so why not the sound system?"

Alexandra said, "I think you're right Liz. I'll get my hands on the two crybabies in the morning and put them in Amazon boot camp. Any word on the traveling drugs Reno?"

"Yes, they are moving toward Virginia. Lizzy, you did a great job out there today. Held up under fire like one of the guard. But... you should have caught that mirror so it didn't hurt my guy."

"*Really?* I'll work on that. It's kinda hard to shoot straight wearing a catchers mitt."

"Nice bike you claimed. I'll have Mikey give it the once over then park it at your vardo. Violet I was worried we'd have a zombie attack during the Octoberfest but it looks like we may be in the clear. We might see a few more if there are any of those bags left. You should tell them no zombie costumes this year."

Amber said, "Liz, you looked very cool up there, you did the Amazons proud today. How many did you tag?"

"Think it was three but might have been four. Carmichael picked me up in one of his bear hugs for capping the one that was aiming at the loft. Reno, I hope you're right but I think as long as there are drugs out there on the streets assholes will take them."

Violet said, "I think I'll add a crystal spell to the Octoberfest. I need to get the Airy-Fairies to put a glamour on the gates."

Sadie looks around at their faces and then blows their minds. "We're taking control of the road. Tomorrow we're blocking the road both ways, 20' out from the gate. We'll leave just enough room for a pickup to pass through with a cattle gate. They'll have to stop to open the gate. We won't have the type of shit storm we had today. If they try to ram the gate it will fuck up their front end. I want 12" spikes welded to the front of the gate.

Alexandra, I want to know how many archers you can have ready in a week. I want a walk added to the inside of the gate for them to shoot from. Reno get your vanguard trained on bows as soon as you can. Lizzy, get those woodworkers busy on those wooden crossbows. We can't reuse bullets but some arrows we can. Check with the metal shop. See what we have we can turn into steel bolts for the crossbows.

After the Octoberfest we're taking back the town. I think we should hunt down any assholes who are making life hard for those just trying to make it through. We might arm them with the guns we took off the Holly Springs mob. I've had enough of this shit. Screw defense, we're going on the offensive. Lock and load sisters, they're about to find out who they're fucking with. On that note I'm going to bed."

They watched her leave, after a minute Reno said, "I think she just turned into her mother."

10:00 pm EDT,

Nick and Gianna listened to what had taken place in the Hall via the intercom. Nick waited for her reaction to Sadie's last. "I was wondering when she was going to find her footing. She's found her fire and not a minute too soon. I like the plan... I like it a lot. I'm quite pleased with all my girls. Amber and Lizzy did rough them up a little but they needed it. It's nice to be nice but sometimes you need to crack the whip across their ass. I find out who was bitching about us not being here I'll slap the shit out of them. How fucking dare they. Darling, some people may have to go. I won't tolerate candy asses or in-grateful fucks." She had been pacing. She stopped. "Nicholas, you know what this means don't you..." She walked across the room, put her palms on his chest, looked up with a *'cat who ate the cream'* smile and purred, "We can stay right here where I can have you all to myself."

11:30 pm EDT, October 7, Damascus, Virginia

Spider Cat Man rolled through Damascus looking for buyers of his pixie dust. The streets were empty, the darkness seemed opaque and deep. He couldn't see more than a few feet even with the headlight. He could smell rain was coming. He pulled around the back of Food City. The lock on the bay door was broken, he rolled it up and rolled the

126

bike inside. The darkness was even thicker and deeper inside. He felt around the floor for something to lay on. He found a pile of rags in the corner and fell asleep, not knowing he wasn't alone.

When his breathing slowed and he was still, the women crept toward him. Their flashlight batteries were all but dead; it emitted a dim pale yellow light. The older one shown the light on his face, the younger one slit his throat with a box cutter. They wanted his food. He had no food left. They rode the bike down to the camp of refugees at the town park. They would use the bike to scavenge when the sun came up. A hundred and fifty ragged, dirty, hungry souls huddled in groups, seeking protection in their numbers. Some slept, while others gathered near the meager fires. When asked, the two women said the bike had been sitting beside the creek. No food but happy powder might help with the hunger. A few said what the hell... when the giggling started more joined the party... by midnight ninety-seven of the retched were dancing wildly, their hunger, now forgotten, would soon return with a cannibalistic vengeance. Zombies had come... *'Damascus will no longer be a city but will become a heap of ruins.'* Looks like Isaiah was right.

1:30 am EDT, October 8,
Dancing Goats Farm
Moon Mountain, North Carolina

127

Tiny missed Becky. Without her he had to listen to the zombie reports. Freddy came in to find the mountain of a man shaking as he documented the information. "Tiny what's wrong?

"This stuff makes me cringe."

Freddy knew Tiny had a box of medals from combat. He couldn't believe the big guy was shaking over this. "I'll be back."

Freddy found Charlie in the tower and told him Tiny was having trouble, he wanted to send Gabe down to deal with the HAM. Charlie agreed. Charlie watched the road. He couldn't see anything but he had a feeling something wasn't right. After years in combat you develop a heightened sense of the night. It was making the hair on the back of Charlie's neck stand up. He called Sadie. She'd made it clear when she'd called him at 11:30 that she wanted to be called if anything was out of place. They'd done serious damage to the attacking force today. She had a feeling... like her Aunt Laurel used to say; 'somethin' somethin' ain't fucken right.' Charlie was getting that feeling too. Sadie answered on the second ring. Charlie told her he was getting the feeling. She was out the door before she hung up, she dialed Lizzy as she ran. Lizzy hadn't been able to sleep either, something was coming. She dialed

Alexandra as she ran. Sadie called
Amber and told her she was up too.

When Sadie stepped out on the
veranda, she could feel it. She told
Freddy to put the Sergeant on standby.
And get the guard out. And wake
Carmichael. Freddy said Johnson was in
the nest. "He's very good but nobody's
better than Carmichael at seeing in this
soup." A fine mist had begun to fall and
a fog was rising from the forest floor
across the road. She told Freddy to get
Audrey out, send a pair of night visions
up to the nest. Lizzy came up behind her
and told her Alexandra was on the way.
"Lizzy go up to the tower, tell me which
way they're coming from."

Once Audrey was out, Sadie ordered
the lights in the Q killed. She called.
Carmichael "Nothing yet but I can feel
something."

"Carmichael, Do I have time to get
Audrey in the street?"

"I believe you do."

As Audrey rolled through the gates Sadie
asked, "Lizzy which way?"

"Not the way they came earlier
today, is what I'm 'hearing'."

"Carmichael get up in the cupola and
tell me when you see them."

Gianna sat up... something was wrong. She went to the window. Amber was running toward the Shack. She took a wrap off the chair. Nick looked so peaceful she didn't wake him. She slipped her phone in her pocket, the binoculars over her shoulder and climbed to the roof. Gianna saw Audrey in the street as the gates closed. Lights out good girl. She scanned the tree line. The tiniest glimmer of light flashed. She reached for her phone as Nick's arms closed around her, so intent in her task she hadn't heard him. "Sadie tell Carmichael maybe three klicks out." To Nick, "I didn't want to wake you, it's just a feeling."

"I always know when you leave the room, you take the light with you. Let me see those." He *was* six inches taller than Gianna. "Two rolling slow. Sadie is she ready to fire?" Nick had his Catsear in so Gianna put her phone in her pocket.

"Who are these assholes?"

"I don't know yet babe."

"Nick, I was talking to myself. Trying to get a read on them."

"They just went dark... Carmichael sees one on foot... It's your call Sadie... Good call."

"Hey how about sharing..."

130

"She's holding for another twenty feet closer... Yes, we're both on the roof again... You got the roof of the truck yet Carmichael?" Gianna whispered who's in Audrey? "Freddy and Sal... Sadie, if there are only two trucks, then they should both be in range... Carmichael's taken out the scout... Audrey's taken out the two monster trucks... Shit, there was a third truck... looks like it's damaged from the blast... the fuckers are running... Sadie...and Lizzy are running them down."

Gianna sees the gates opening all the way and the guard rushing through after her girls, the general alarm is ringing in her bedroom below, regulars are rushing through the portal filling the positions vacated by the guard. Alexandra is now standing on Audrey shouting orders. Charlie is doing the same at the barn. Three Harleys peel out the barn door with four dirt bikes on their 6. Twenty seconds later an explosion splits the darkness, a column of flames rises above the treetops. Gianna runs for the trap door. In the bedroom she retrieves her phone, tosses the robe, slips on her T-shirt and turns for the door. Nick grabs her up short by her arm. "Nick, I have to..."

"Not bare assed." He hands her a pair of fatigues.

"Oh yeah, thanks babe."

Outside they're getting in the cart; Nick is talking to Charlie, Gianna calls Amber in the Shack. "Get the water trucks to the Q. Put the Tribe on full alert. Lock down the Hall with the little ones. We're under attack." Nick tells Charlie to open the barn to let the water trucks through and get the Humvee out in the yard. He and Gianna are on their way. Have Freddy reload and stand by.

In the office Theo and Brian arrive as, Amber hits the Full Alert alarm... then '*This is it*' blares out of the Farm's sound system. Theo says "*That'll* wake them up.

Nick and Gianna arrive at the Q's gates as Reno returns with Lizzy. "She's taken shrapnel to her left side." Nick helps her off the Harley. A regular helps Nick get Lizzy into a cart, headed to the infirmary with two other wounded. Gianna's anger rises at the sight of her daughter's injuries.

Nick turns back to see Gianna getting on Reno's bike. He grabs her around the waist and sets her back on the ground, nodding to Reno to leave. "You are not going out there on the back of a bike, when I don't know how many are still out there. Now get your ass in the Humvee."

"Sadie's still out there. She could be hurt like Lizzy. They were running together."

"*I know!* Stop talking and get in." Nick gets in behind the wheel, he adds, "Gia, don't you know how to obey your husband?"

Gianna gives him a death look, "Oh, You didn't just go there! Fuck you and drive."

Violet is on the green watching as the members of the Tribe run, stumble, and wander out of their homes. Those running are armed. She addresses the rest of them. "This is not a fucking pajama party. Where are your weapons? Wake up you assholes it's time to defend your homes. You two, get the children in the Hall and lock it down. The rest of you report to the Sergeant. NOW." Then she heads over to relieve Amber, so Amber can go to the command room. Across the green Violet sees Lizzy being put on a gurney. 'You fuckers hurt my sister?'... the Kracken awakens.

Theo takes one look at Violet's face when she walks in and says, "I've got this, you go with Amber to the Q." Theo does not want to be trapped in the office with the Kracken, Violet's alter ego would not be happy stuck inside with all that's happening out there. She needs to be out there where she can kill

133

something... other than him.

Amber catches the look on Vy's face. She starts the cart, "Come on sista-cousin, I'll find you someone to torture." Like her Aunt, Amber slides into Ice Queen in the blink of an eye. Like her Aunt she misses nothing, and analyzes the data with the same frosty detachment. Inside the com room Amber scans the monitors, her sister is still standing on Audrey, shouting orders, looking like the Goddess Diana with her bow across her back and quiver hanging from her shoulder. One of the guard is pushing a prisoner into the yard. "There Vy, you can have him, do your worst babe." Violet leaves to obtain intel from the attacker. Tiny looks over at Amber questioningly. "He's in for a very bad night. Tiny, just be happy I found a target for her rage and she's not in here with us." She puts a headset on.

Nick and Gianna's Humvee is traveling slowly through the hunks of metal littering the blast area. Nick says, "The third truck was rigged to explode. That's why they bailed. They were going to use it to blow the gate. None of their men survived this morning's attack to report back what's inside the Q. I'd say they've been watching us for awhile. Most likely a fertilizer based bomb." The water trucks have the fire out. Steven has sent the other truck back to refill from one of the ponds. He's soaking the roadside underbrush from the other. The last thing they need is some smoldering cinders catching the woods on fire. Nick pulls off the pavement and stops alongside one of their army jeeps. When the truck exploded he'd left the nest, Carmichael is now standing with his rifle resting on the roll bar of the jeep watching the woods. Night goggles are pushed up on his forehead.

Gianna lets out a feral screech/growl, sounding something like a pissed off big cat. Nick looks. Reno is coming towards them with Sadie in his arms. "She's not dead ma'am. She's got a lump on the back of her head. Believe that's what knocked her out." Gianna examines her daughter. Nick and Reno put Sadie on the seat of the jeep. Carmichael leaps in to the back of the Humvee to make room for her.

Gianna starts to get in the jeep. Nick puts a hand on her shoulder, "Are you sure you wouldn't rather stay with me and hunt these fuckers down?" He knows her so well. Sitting by her unconscious daughter she'd begin to rant about killing the people who hurt her child, then she'd come right back out here. Gianna nods for Reno to go. DJ comes up to tell them he's sent seven to the infirmary including Lizzy and Sadie and we have two dead so far. The news of the dead sends Gianna back to the Humvee. Carmichael has the top canvas rolled back and is set up on the roll bar. Nick spends another minute talking to DJ about who they lost and how bad the wounded are, then he gets behind the wheel. Nick sees her sitting ridged with her shoulders back and her chin tilted up. He knows her silence and posture are the result of her now lethal state of mind. The gears are turning, she's plotting the annihilation of their enemy. Her face is tight, and her hazel green eyes have gone black, never a good sign. He doubts even God can save the people at the receiving end of her wrath tonight. They've never lost anyone before. He moves the Humvee forward.

1:55 am EDT,

From the command room Amber sees Violet has the prisoner's head submerged in a bucket of water, she's using his ponytail as a handle. Alexandra has come down off Audrey to keep an eye on Vy, to make sure she doesn't drown him before they have the intel. A message from the nest comes through Amber's headset. There's activity at the east end of the road. She calls Freddy. "Turn the girl around they're coming up on your 6." Freddy aims Audrey's gun barrel at the darkness and wait's for Amber's command.

The Humvee has just cleared the last of the wreckage from the truck bomb, when Nick hears Amber's orders. He stops and relays the information to Gianna. She

136

hears him and sits a little tall and breaks her stoic silence. She picks up her phone. "Amber tell Tyler to increase the voltage on the fence to instant crisp. Tell the Sergeant to add some of the Tribe to the walls. They are to shoot anything that moves. We're not going to distracted by this and leave the Farm open to a rear attack. I want the drones in the Q in fifteen minutes. Send them to me once they're there. Ambie, I want to arm them with vials of Nitro, so send them along with Bill. Get the front-loader out front clearing a path for Audrey to follow us once Freddy has taken care of the issue at the east end and make sure they restock Audrey's ammo before they come." The recon had returned while Gianna was speaking to Amber. They knew the location of the camp. "Oh and Amber, tell Violet we no longer have a use for that piece of shit."

2:05 am EDT,

Nick pulls forward ten feet and turns the engine off. "We'll wait here for the rest of the convoy." Nick puts one leg out of the Humvee and stops. "Carmichael."

"I know Boss. I've got her covered."

Nick studies Gianna's profile, sitting there motionless with her 'Dirty Harry' across her lap. He leans over and whispers in her ear, "You're very sexy when you're in an evil state of mind." He kisses her neck and leaves to talk to the men. Gianna didn't move a muscle at his statement or his kiss, but her eyes went, what Nick called, smokey.

Amber heard from the hay loft, the vehicles approaching from the east were within range. She said "Freddy introduce them to Audrey." Audrey's voice echoed through the darkness for the second time tonight. When it was done, Amber told Stephen to get the water trucks to the east of the gate. Two of the guard brought Freddy and Sal more shells for Audrey as Bill left the yard with the drones and nitro packed in cotton fluff.

In the yard Violet got her mother's message. She pulled his head out of the bucket and kicked him over on his back. Alexandra stepped up and put her boot on his throat. Violet stood over him. "You hurt my sisters and attacked my home, and you're a weak excuse for a soldier for giving up the information." Then she shot him twice in the balls and once in the femoral for good measure. To the guard standing next to her she said, "Drag this somewhere and let it bleed to death." She and her cousin went to the tower to check in with Charlie and to view Audrey's latest conquest.

2:18 am EDT,

Amber called Andy for an update then

138

passed the information on to Nick. "Gia, Sadie's awake, with a concussion. Andy is watching her very closely she believes she'll be fine in time. There's no new swelling around the bump. The ex-ray shows no intracranial swelling. Amber said Lizzy is doing just fine too. Amber could hear Lizzy in the background, loudly bitching at the Doc, to work faster so she could get back out here. The men are fine to stable. We lost Bruce and Sam. Audrey is on her way. She left two more vehicles totaled and eight or nine dead. Charlie wasn't sure there were a lot of parts."

Another of their jeeps pulls up behind the Humvee. One of the men brings Nick two vests. He put one in Gianna's lap. "Put this on."

She pushed it on the floor. "I hate those things they squish my boobs."

Nick whips around, takes her by the chin, growling through his clenched teeth, "Put-the-fucking-vest-on-NOW!" He picked it up and handed it to her. She put it on but didn't do the Velcro straps. Nick finished with his and yanked her vest closed. "Keep it on or I'll do more than squish your boobs. I promise, *you won't sit for a week.*" Carmichael knew he wanted to be far away if that happened.

chapter 24
I FEEL THE EARTH MOVE UNDER MY FEET

"Freddy, level it.
Bill, give Freddy sixty seconds
then send in the drones"

2:45 am EDT, October 8,
Moon Mountain, North Carolina

The group that had attacked the Q was run by the Thacker brothers. Their camp centered around an old brick farm house, set back from the road maybe fifty feet. The Thackers had encircled their house with a continuous line of vehicles. Welded wire fencing surrounded the vehicles, their half assed attempt at a first line of defense.

The only sound emanating from the camp was the put-put-put coming from a gas generator providing power for the Halogen light bar rigged to a pole, illuminating the driveway. Twenty to thirty armed men stood on the rooves and hoods of the barrier vehicles.

Nick stopped the Humvee at the outer edge of the light. Audrey rolled up and stopped alongside Gianna. The rest of the assault team rolled up behind them. Reno's jeep pulled up on Nick's left.

2:58 am EDT,

For thirteen minutes Gianna could discern no movement within the camp. She studied the demeanor of the men on the vehicles. "Pretty fucking cocky and obviously incredibly stupid. They can't possibly believe their hunting rifles and shot guns are a match for the tank pointed at them. I love dealing with arrogant men... their own egos defeat them before a single word is spoken. Angelena could outwit these idiots." Then a stick with a white cloth attached began to wave over the plywood gate. The gate began to open slowly, Gianna pulled her long hairpin out and shook her hair free, she pulled Nick to her and whispered in his ear, "I love you Nicholas." Then she stepped up on the seat to commence the annihilation of their enemy. Nick let her take the lead. The fools might mistake this woman as weak. He grabbed a handful of fabric behind her knee, ready to yank her down 'if he felt she was in danger.' He realized how incredulous the thought was... fuck it, was all relative to the game.

Two men came through the plywood gate. They walked ten steps and stopped. The one not holding the flag yelled. "Hey pretty lady, we want to talk. I think we may have a misunderstanding here."

Gianna stared at him. Nick thought
'Of all the things that could have come
out of his mouth, pretty lady was the
fucking worst.' Nick knew her so well, he
tightened his grip on her pants and said
"Carmichael?"

"On it Boss, on her right."

"You attacked my men on the road and
breach my gate, wounding ten of my men.
You tried to attack my farm again tonight
and blow it up. Your truck bomb; killed
two of my men, injured two of my
daughters, and injured five more of my
men. *Now you wanna parlay?*... Here's my
answer." They started to run and she took
the top of their heads off with Dirty
Harry.

Nick pulled her down into the Humvee
and took control. "Freddy, level it.
Bill, give Freddy sixty seconds then send
in the drones. Drop their load around the
perimeter." The vanguard moved in front
of the Humvee and started picking off the
men on the cars, who hadn't run, when
Gianna shot their leader and his brother.
From his perch standing in the back of
the Humvee, Carmichael killed the ones
who tried to run with his 'wicked mad'
accuracy. Freddy and Sal pumped six
rounds from Audrey into the camp, then
halted. They couldn't see where to fire
through the smoke. Nick said "Stand by
Freddy." The nitro vials exploded on

impact, sending cars and trucks tumbling
into the yard like matchbook cars. When
they stopped tumbling Nick said, "Reno,
sweep it... for Sam and Bruce." The
vanguard moved forward in full riot gear.

Nick watched through narrowed eyes.
If they hadn't killed two and wounded
fifteen of his men *and* Sadie and Lizzy,
and if Nick was a forgiving sort of man,
which he wasn't, he might have felt pity
for the hell they had rained down on the
residents of the camp. Nick was sure
these bastards had bullied, robbed and
most likely killed some of the town's
people, who were scattered throughout the
countryside, people struggling to survive
events they didn't understand.
Satisfaction is what Nick felt, *not pity*.

Gianna, reached over and patted
Audrey's side "Good job girl. Very good
job."

Nick looked sideways at her, "Gia,
Audrey isn't a pet. She's not alive."

"How would you know? Have you ever
had a conversation with her? *No*, I have."
Nick thinks 'I didn't know it was a Mad
Hatter raid'.

After ten minutes, they no longer
hear gunfire. The guard start emerging
from the cloud of dense smoke still
hanging over the rubble. Reno stops by
the Humvee and tells Nick the place is

leveled. He didn't shoot the dog they found chained outside the circle of trucks, he set it free. Other than that, between Audrey and the nitro, and their mop up, there's nothing left alive. There was one upper arm wound and we'd lost two of the six drones.

Nick nodded and Reno gave the signal. The men load into the vehicles, then the deadly convoy headed home. Gianna starts to remove her vest. Nick grabs her hand. "Gia! Leave it on until we're back in the Q. I don't know if any of their people were outside the camp and escaped the attack. One could be hiding in the woods along the road." The words no sooner out of his mouth, when a bullet pings the side of the jeep behind them. The guard in the jeep deal with the shooter. Nick gives Gianna a 'don't fucking move' look and picks up his speed. He needs to get her behind the safety of their walls. A vest can't protect her from a head shot. Nearing the Q Nick looks at the piles of twisted, burned metal on either side of the road. "Sadie has her barrier almost completed."

**4:00 am EDT,
Dancing Goats Farm
Moon Mountain, North Carolina**

When they reach the Q house Gianna's out of the Humvee before it stops. She runs up the steps, ripping off the vest as she goes. She hands it to Amber who's

144

coming out the door. She kisses her niece
and tells her job well done, then runs
for the infirmary, Nick's right behind
her.

Sadie is awake and joking with
everyone. Lizzy is siting on the end of
the bed, bitching to Sadie and anyone
else in earshot, that she is ripping mad
they got left out of the big assault. A
relieved Gianna kisses both of them then
leaves to check on the other wounded with
Nick.

After the rounds are made, outside
the infirmary Gianna starts for the Q.
Nick pulls her back by her waistband.
"Where do you think you're going?" She
opens her mouth to answer and he puts a
finger on her lips. "Home, is where
you're going. You've killed you quota for
the night." She tries to talk again.
"Evidently you don't understand... when
you husband speaks, you listen." Before
she can swing at him he puts her over his
shoulder. "Woman, the Honeymoon is
nowhere near over." As he's walking to
the house she's telling him the many very
very bad things she's going to do to him
when he sets her free. Ignoring her he
keeps right on talking. "You have no idea
how hot you are when you're killing
people. Be a good wifey and come to bed.
Do we have any of that apricot syrup
left?"

In the kitchen he puts her down and

takes her face in his hands. "You were amazing tonight. Now, let go. We stepped in when we had to. Gianna, we put it in their hands, don't take it back now, they'll feel like they failed. Which they didn't." He looks into her eyes and sees she's capitulated. "Seriously Gianna... *Do we have any apricot butter syrup left?*"

4:15 am EDT, October 8,

Amber tells Reno and Charlie to take care of their men. The rest can wait for the morning meeting. She tells the Sergeant to stand down but be aware some may have escaped their punishment. She tells Theo to get two hours sleep before they have to start again at 6:30.

She finds Alexandra and Violet in the infirmary. Andy comes in and says she has sick people here who need their rest and throws the trio out. They agree to meet in the office at 6:30 for breakfast and a meeting with the staff heads involved in tonight's events. The Green is now quiet once more... Tyler is talking to her about the night's events. Amber doesn't hear him, she was out ten seconds after she hit the pillow. Violet and Alexandra decide to stay up and sleep after the meeting.

Becky made sure the guards are posted around the manor and leaves the farm for her bed. She needs at least twenty minutes under a hot shower first. She didn't take the hit Lizzy and Sadie did but the blast knocked her off her feet, lading her on her ass in the brush. Everything hurts.

Reno passed out, face down on Nick's bed. He didn't have it in him to walk back to the house he shares with Charlie, Freddy and DJ in the barracks yard. His last thought was, 'I'm sure the Boss won't need this tonight.'

Charlie and Freddy have their feet up on the veranda at last. Normally they don't drink On Duty. Tonight they're having one. They don't think Nick will object after the fucking two days they put in. Charlie asks, "Do you think this shit takes a break or does it just roll on nonstop like this?"

Freddy says "Don't really know much about apocalypses, this being my first one. Sure as shit hope there are breaks. This is as bad as doing a tour."

"Freddy, I think the Lady knew it could get this bad, that's why she only took combat Vets. She wanted men she could be sure would be able to perform under shit like this.

How does she know this kinda shit? Guys like Carmichael could never have made it out there. He was an outcast for his behavior. Here he can be a flake and when she needs him to kill he's right in the game. She and Nick chose each one of us very carefully. Did you know about a hundred were rejected? It's been a fucking easy life for me here. I don't think I would have found a life like this on the outside."

Freddy asks, "Maybe she knows if there will be breaks. Think I'll ask her tomorrow."

"No you won't. Not tomorrow anyway. There was a disagreement outside the infirmary. Nick carried her off. He was heard telling her the honeymoon wasn't over."

"She was pretty tight tonight. Kept it together even when her girls got hurt. That's when she called for the nitro and the drones. Took her rage and used it. I would have shit my pants if I was one of those guys. When she stood up out of the Humvee she was cold as ice. The Boss had her by the leg just in case. Blew their heads to shit. That Smith and Wesson 29 of hers has a kick. She barely moved between shots."

"How the fuck do you know this, you were inside Audrey?

We put some peep holes in her, back in May. I had a birds eye view to the whole show. They're still the same you know."

"Nick and the Lady? Yeah, I imagine they are. That's never going to change. Still can't believe he took me seriously. I was just joking. Next morning he calls and tells me he married her."

"Bet you won't make *that* joke again. Carmichael road with them the whole time tonight. He said they got into it over her not wanting to wear a vest. He said the Boss told her she wouldn't sit for a week if she didn't wear it. I think it fucked with Carmichael's loyalties to the both of them. He was real happy that she gave in and wore it. Do you think they had one of those Pagan ceremonies?"

"Freddy I think that's above *both* of our pay grades. I wouldn't ask if I was you. He must have thought about it for a while. Otherwise where did the rings come from? I won't be asking Nick *that* question either."

"Guess you're right. I went to see that Dawn was okay afterwards. She's damn amazing herself. She had two girls and all the kids locked down in the Hall. I got there as the last parent was leaving. I said I'd walk her home. As we're leaving she says wait a sec and goes back for the Glock she had on the mantel, in the event she had to protect the kids. Pops it in her bag like it's her lipstick. Just so frigging casual. Speaking of women... how's the Parson widow?"

"None of your damn business. That's how she is. Keep your mind on you own woman."

"Touchy subject? For not being in the military the Amazons are kicking ass. You put them all working together and they make a super version of the Lady."

Tiny opened the door and stuck his head out. "Guess you two idiots don't know your Catsears are still on. You better hope the Bosses' is off." It wasn't... Gianna and Nick found the whole conversation highly entertaining.

6:00 am EDT,

Nick couldn't sleep. He looked at Gia asleep with her head on his chest. He never believed he would ever be this happy or in love. If he wanted to hold on to it, he needed to keep her and this place safe. That meant, events like the ones in the last few days, had to stop. He had to get his head back into the game. War was a game of chess. He hadn't been paying attention to his opponent and he'd almost lost his queen... several times. He needed to find out how many more camps of assholes were out there. He needed to eliminate or neutralize them before they even thought to come after the farm.

Then there was Gianna. He needed to make her understand what it did to his focus when she took unnecessary risks. That stupid argument over the vest. He didn't want to control her or tame her or take her power. He needed needed her to take the same care she took with others, with herself. Unless she had some bracelets he didn't know about she needed to wear a vest when going up against people with guns. He loved the Amazon warrior side of her. It was really hot heading into a confrontation with her beside him.

"Nicholas, I can hear your brain working, what is keeping you from sleep husband?"

"I was wondering if you had a pair of bracelets that deflected bullets?"

"Alas I do not. I left them in my pocket in my last lifetime. This is about that stupid vest."

"I want you beside me, but you have to stop taking stupid risks 'because, the vest *squishes your boobs*.' It causes me to think with my heart and not my head. I lose my focus and people could die."

"That's why Amazons of old had armor that molded to their breast."

"Well, we'll have to get some Amazon armor made for you."

"Nick... I thought we were discussing armor..."

"We are, I'm just making sure I know what size you need."

6:15 am EDT, October 8,
Dancing Goats Farm
Moon Mountain, North Carolina

Ferret put the report of all the activity going on outside the walls on the table in front of the chair at the head of the table. She wonders who'll sit there, Reno or Sadie? Mother had showed her Gianna wouldn't be here. Ferret really needed to talk to Violet. The dreams hadn't stopped. She thought they would since there was no way to publish the information now. But no, the hits just kept on coming. There must be a reason. She couldn't figure out what Mother wanted her to do with that information. She stopped by the table Theo had filled with an array of tasty breakfast foods. She selected a warm ham and Swiss croissant and a cup of coffee to take with her. Simon had begun to ration coffee yesterday. It would no longer be served. People had to learn to get their caffeine from tea. Ferret thought she might need to find excuses to go to the Q. Rumor was, the vanguard still got coffee. Violet walked in as Ferret was leaving. "Morning Vy. If you have time today I need to talk to you

152

about what to do with the new information in the dreams."

Violet assumed they had stopped since Ferret hadn't brought them up again. "Shit why didn't you say something sooner... okay it's been fucking crazy around here. I'll come find you later today."

"I think I saw what happened last night, the night before."

"That changes things. I'll find you after the meeting. Wait, what did you see last night?" They talked until people started showing up for the meeting. Vy said she'd see her in awhile.

At the door Ferret turned to look back at the room. Sadie and Reno were standing on either side of the chair, as in her dream. She closed the door behind her thinking, 'hey, the data's still good'.

Sadie leaned to Reno and said, "Why don't you take the other end chair?" It wasn't really a request. The sisters had the seats to the right and left of the chair they were standing near, so he walked to the other end of the table. He was trying to remember if Nick outranked the Lady so he could figure out where he stood in the chain of command.

Sadie sat. Before she could speak

Violet did. "I have some interesting news. It seems Ferret is still getting dreams from Mother. She just told me when she dropped off the report, she saw part of last night's battle. She didn't understand it was our battle she saw. I'm meeting with her after this to find out what else she's seen. I will have her report to me every morning from now on, to go over her dream from the night before. Mother is giving them to her for a reason." Every one was looking at Violet. "Don't look at me like that. How was I to know the kid was still dreaming? It's not as if I've had a lot of time to hang out and chat lately."

Amber came to Violet's defense, "Right, you've been busy drowning and shooting people. Oh and tearing the Tribe a new one every time they screw up. See if you can squeeze dream interpretation in that busy schedule." That got the laughs she was going for and the meeting moved on.

Sadie asked Reno if he would like to start the meeting. This time it was a question. He went over the events of the day ending at 4:00 am. Lizzy asked if he had a count of how many they'd put to rest last night and then the number for the last week. Reno said forty to fifty he could count. He had no way of knowing if there had been any in the house. Audrey had imploded it so it fell in on itself. As for the week's total including

154

zombies, he figured it was just north of
300.

The people who didn't have to clear
away all the bodies were taken back.
Alexandra helped him out by adding 'But
They were all bad, right?' Theo said he
was beginning to understand how Noah must
have felt.

The Sergeant said the Tribe had
performed well with a few exceptions.
Which he had a list of. Sadie said good,
because Gianna had texted her asking for
the names of anyone who didn't do well
and as she put it, 'the ungrateful fucks'
bitching that she and Nick weren't at the
Hall. Sadie added, "I think we may have a
few vacancies soon. That part of the text
was .in all caps. Violet maybe you and
Alexandra can take the names and see if
any of them can be saved. If there are
some on the list because they don't shoot
well maybe they can be scheduled to train
with the regulars."

Carl said he'd like to keep the room
and Mendez and Becky as well. He wanted
to track events going on outside and
analyze the data to see which, if any,
would have an effect on them. He felt
they still needed to track the drugs. He
had begun to suspect by the numbers
coming in, Ziggy had left a rather large
legacy of his deadly dust behind. Then
there was the question of whether Dr.
Star had all the drugs with him or was

there a supply at his home. He wanted to see if they could find out where that was. Sadie loved the idea of staying ahead of the curve and the rest agreed.

Lizzy said she had spoken to the metal shop and they were working on the two cattle gates today. Reno said Audrey had done a lot of the work for them as far as material for the barricades. He'd have the men tighten it up with the bobcat today and rig up a way to hang the gates.

Alexandra was pleased with the arrows and bows the wood shop was working on. She found a book with da Vinci's sketches of his crossbow for them to work with.

Stephen said the water trucks work fine. He was going to keep one parked near the wall so it would be closer for next time. No one thought there wouldn't be a next time.

Sadie said she'd promised Andy she would stay off her feet. If anyone needed her she'd be at her place. Limping Lizzy, would try to cover all the footwork today but not to run her ragged. Sadie had seen her fly right off her feet when the the fucking truck blew up. She closed the meeting with, "I believe we all either saw or heard what happened outside of the infirmary last night. I think Nick made it very clear, the honeymoon is back on.

So don't go near the house unless you want Becky's guards or Nick to shoot you. Oh P.S. In case you haven't noticed, they're watching us from the roof."

Theo wondered if he could get a tower built on to the office so he could have that higher a vantage point too. Violet patted his hand and said, "Not this week honey."

11:00 am EDT,
Moon Mountain, North Carolina

The people who had been bullied and robbed by the men at the camp were woken by the explosions and gun fire last night. The people wondered if the men had now gone after the biker farm. By 9:00 am when the men from the camp hadn't come for their daily share of whatever the people had, some began to wonder anew. Could the bikers have killed the Thackers? There didn't seem to be that many at the farm. How did they do it?

At 7:30 am, a 14 year old who had designated himself town crier, Teddy, rode his bike from place to place spreading the news of what had happened last night. After the first explosion he had gone through the woods and come up on the side of the camp. He'd seen the place get blown to hell. Men in swat type clothing had gone through it after the bombing stopped. When they left he'd cut farther down to the road and watched the swat guys going down the road. There was a whole convoy of them. They even had a tank! The lady with the silver hair, who sometimes sold vegetables at the farmers market, was in a hummer. The tall scary guy from the farm was with her driving the hummer. There must have been 35 men in the jeeps and trucks following the hummer. After they'd gone by he went back to the Thacker's camp. Everyone at the camp was dead.

After Teddy left, Mary Thompson looked at the milk and bread she had ready to give to the men from the camp. She thought she should give it to the lady at the farm to thank her. Mary's husband Paul, had been gone for three days. He went hunting for a deer. The camp had hunted so many the rest had run. The Thompsons needed one to make it through the fall. It would be easier now that they didn't have to give the food to the camp anymore. She was very grateful. She locked the house, out of habit. She gave her fourteen year old the shotgun and their last four shells. Then she and her two sons started walking to the biker farm. They had to stop several times to rest. Her eight year old was not doing well from lack of food. She hoped Paul would be there when they got back. If he didn't come back with a deer he said they would have to kill her dairy cow. Mary loved that cow. She'd bottle fed her from two days old. She didn't think she'd be able to eat her pet but Paul and the boys would be fed.

12:00 pm EDT,
Dancing Goats Farm
Moon Mountain, North Carolina

In the command room Antonio saw the woman before Gabe did. Gabe was taking a piss off the back side of the tower when she and the kids came into camera range. Lizzy was up in the kitchen. Antonio yelled up the news. Lizzy limped out and up the tower. When Mary had asked to see the lady with the silver hair, Gabe had told her to wait a minute. Lizzy looked over the fence and said under her breath "Oh crap!" To the woman she said, "Why are you here?"

"I need to speak to the lady of the house." Lizzy said to Gabe. "I don't think she's begging, she has food in her basket." To Mary she said, "Sorry ma'am, my mother is out in the woods right now. What can I do for you?"

"I must speak with her. I'll sit and wait. I'm pretty tired from our walk. I could use the rest."

Antonio had also called Amber because, she told him to let her know EVERYTHING that went on in the Q today. She was now in the room watching the feed on the monitor and listening to the audio. "Shit, *this* is a problem." She thinks about it for a few seconds then

159

calls Gianna. "Hey Auntie I am sorry to bother you but we have a tricky one, I need to know how you want me to deal with it. There's a woman with two kids at the gate. She says she wants to speak to you. Lizzy told her you were off in the woods and she said she would sit and wait for you to come back. Don't think she's begging. She has a basket of food and a bouquet."

Gianna looked at Nick. He said "We could use the fresh air. It sounds like she might be the stubborn type, like my wife."

"Amber, tell her I'll be there shortly." Three minutes later Gianna and Nick are going down the stairs to the command room. Nick sits in one of the chairs. Gianna looks at the woman with the bouquet of wild flowers and the two clearly underfed kids and starts to swear. "Ahhh Fucking no. I don't need this shit." Nick can see the monitor from his seat. The woman and the kids are in pretty sad shape. He watches Gianna's temper tantrum and is deeply relieved. He was worried the ice around her heart might not melt after she'd gone Killer Queen. He watched as the Earth Mother side of her battled for control. "I don't need starving women and children at my gate. THIS is not my job... Nick if I turn around and there is even a hint of a smile on your face... you will be crying." Of course Nick is laughing at her. "I knew it, you're such an ass. Stop laughing at me. You're gonna cry when we get home... no you're gonna be begging." She's trying not to laugh but she's losing the battle. "If we feed them, they come back for more."

"But we have more. We're feeding organic vegetables to the animals because Amber over there, is such a great manager."

"What happens when we don't have more and they keep begging?"

"Why don't we cut this tirade short? You know you're going to feed them. That's who you are. Give it up my little hard ass." Nick stands and takes her hand. "Come on, I'll let you bitch about this when we get back. Let's feed those kids before *I start crying.*"

At the bottom of the stairs she turns to Amber, "Have them send over a basket of greens, potatoes, what ever you've been feeding the animals. Not too ostentatious. We don't want the whole town at the gate tomorrow."

Nick and Gianna open the gate just enough to walk through. Lizzy has the guard standing by in the event it's a trap.

Mary stood and took Gianna's hand. "I'm Mary Thompson, I just wanted to

161

thank you for what you all did last night. Those men have been bleeding us all for our food." Mary stops and shoos her boys back. In a lower tone she says, "They beat one woman cause she had nothing left and they raped a teenage girl yesterday when her daddy had nothing to give."

Gianna turned around and started banging her fist on the gate. She looks up at Nick, through her teeth she says, "Those fuckers. Tell me we can go back so I can kill them again."

Nick takes her hand so she doesn't hit the gate again and break her hand. "Babe you already shot them, you can't kill them twice no matter how much they deserve it. Breath. Besides, I think you're scaring Mrs. Thompson."

Gianna turned around. "I'm sorry Mary. How are the woman and the girl doing?" "They're doing as well as can be expected. That's why I had to come and thank you. When Teddy came by and told me what he saw hiding in the woods last night, I knew we had you to thank for the extra food we'd have for our families now. I brought these from my yard and just a little milk from my cow and bread I was going to have to give the men this morning."

Gianna took the flowers and looked up at Nick with tears in her eyes. "Mary the flowers are lovely and so thoughtful. Thank you. You must keep the food for your children. We have food."

Amber came through the gate and Nick told Reno to get one of the jeeps to drive them home. The basket was full but not ostentatious. On top were a half dozen apple cinnamon muffins. Amber looked at her Aunt and shrugged. "They were just going stale on the kitchen table." She handed the basket to Gianna and takes two muffins over to the boys. While Nick and Gianna are getting Mary to tell them about the other families, they heard the sound of a truck rolling through the barricade ally; Amber pulled the boys back to the gate, Gianna pushes Mary behind her up against the gate and pulled Dirty Harry out of her shoulder holster and held it behind her back, Reno slipped through the gate and stood in front of the women and children, Lizzy has the guy in the back of the truck in her sight, Carmichael has a bead on the driver from the loft. The truck stops. A young man in the passenger window says "Don't mean to bother you folks just looking for a guy by the name of Thacker, who drives a monster truck. They beat my ma yesterday while I was out hunting. The big guy with a tattoo on his hand of a wolf paw."

Gianna takes a breath and relaxes a notch. "I don't believe you have to worry about him any more, dear."

"I'm not worried ma'am I'm going to kill him for what he did."

"Well... I already did that for you last night." Then because he doesn't look like he believes her, She takes her hand out from behind her back. "Really dear, I took off the top of his head with this. And his dirty rotten brother too. Then my husband flattened the camp. Anyone that was in that camp is dead and will no longer be harming our neighbors."

Nick is smiling at the looks on the young men's faces. "My wife has a very bad temper. We tried anger management but nothing seems to work except letting her killing bad men."

Gianna punches Nick in the arm. "Is it wise to make fun of a woman with a 45 magnum in her hand?" To the boys she says, "Mary Thompson just told us about your mom. Is there anything she needs? What's your name?

"Tommy ma'am. She needs ice ma'am, for the swelling but no bodies' got that any more."

Gianna looks up at Carmichael and holds up three fingers. Reno steps away from the women and lines himself up to catch what Carmichael's going to drop. Everybody knows the Lady can't catch for shit. Reno hands the package to Gianna.

She looks inside and smiles up at
Carmichael. She hands her gun to Nick and
walks up to the truck and gives the young
man the contents of the bag. "Here are
three hot and three cold packs. The hot
makes the ache stop but the body needs
cold to reduce the swelling. She should
alternate them. These are ibuprofen for
the pain. Now, go get these to your mama.
Oh and tell her, he ran screaming like a
baby when he saw my gun. Knowing he died
begging should make her feel better."

Nick looks at her, "Was he
screaming?"

From the loft they hear, "He was
screaming and he pissed himself just
before she blew the top of his head off."

Gianna looks up, "Thank You,
Carmichael." To Nick she says, "I think
his father must have been a tiger or some
other big feline. He's got the ears and
eyes of a cat." They turn and leave the
truck sitting there. Reno has the jeep
out, Mary and the boys are already in the
seats. Gabe takes the wheel and Lee hops
in the other side. Gianna and Nick wave
as they pull away. The truck with the
boys follows them.

Nick says "Maybe, I should hold on
to your gun."

She squints her eyes at him and says
"How would you like it I held your gun

hmmm?"

Nick says "Baby you can hold my gun anytime you like."

Amber's voice echos from the speaker. "The 'children' are listening you two... *Get a room.*"

Chapter 25

NEVER

"Plans do change, Gianna"

1:15 pm EDT, October 8,
Damascus, Virginia

The zombies were still running through the small town of Damascus, eating people who were not high on Ziggy dust. They had started on the sleeping members of their camp and moved on to anyone they found out on the streets, which wasn't many at that time of night. A few found Spider Cat Man's body and snacked on him. Several in that group found their way to the roof of the store. Convinced they could fly, eleven of them jumped. Most of them died in the fall. The few that survived with broken limbs were eaten by the next zombie group that came along. Back at the camp, a pair of brothers, who had escaped the bonfire massacre, found the Spyder with the drugs still in the compartment, and took off. They went east simply because, when they got to Third Street, there was a mob of zombies coming at them from the west. They took 91N and picked up I-81 at Glade Spring. They were headed to Lynchburg where they had family. They stopped in

Pulaski and again in Daleville to stretch and take a leak. They managed to barter a handful of dust packets at each stop for food and water. The younger brother wanted to try the dust. His brother told him he'd fall off the back of the bike if he got high. They'd get high when they got to their Uncle's farm in Lynchburg.

The people at the Inn were woken by screams around 2:00 am. Rory flew to the window to see fifteen people throwing themselves on the barricade he and the women had built. He told Cindy to get the other two women, he was on his way to the front porch, oh, and bring your guns. He started shooting as soon as he cleared the door. None of the zombies had gotten over the fir trees and vines yet but two were impaled on the pikes. Their howls split the night. The women lined up along the porch and started killing their first zombies. Ann put the two on the pikes down, just to stop the God awful racket.

Beth said, "They're very obliging. We shoot them and the next one steps up and takes it's place."

Cindy agreed. "It does seem like that doesn't it. Those stories on the radio were right. These bastards are crazy." When the last one was dead, the four of them sat on the porch. Rory and Ann each had a cigarette. They were carefully rationing their limited stash. Everyone agreed that after taking down their first zombie mob, Rory and Ann had earned one. Beth wondered what drew them to the house? Cindy said the rooster had been crowing when she went to wake them up.

Looking out at the zombie bodies littering their barricade Beth said "This shit is never going to end." No one contradicted her because they'd been thinking the same thing. Rory said they'd need to stand guard because there could be more. Ann volunteered to take watch till breakfast. This was a good plan.

As the other three returned to their beds, down at the camp, several others who had escaped the feeding frenzy found a few packets on the camp's makeshift table. Having been asleep during the attacks, they didn't know the dust had precipitated the insanity. They took the dust with them when they went to look for a new camp location - one with no dead bodies. They found a spot on the bank of the Laurel Creek, in the shadow of the big white Inn with a wraparound veranda. After settling in, they thought they needed to get high, cause of all the ugly shit they'd seen. The one carrying the dust, found when he reached for them, all but one packet had fallen out of the hole in his pocket, as they walked through town. Not knowing what it was, they felt more was the way to go. They split the packet and snorted it. At 2:30 am they broke through a downstairs window on the veranda and climbed in. They killed three people, then went running madly down the street. At 2:45 am Ann sitting watch till breakfast popped both of them as they stood in front of her Inn's barricade. She could have saved the bullets. They had stopped because their hearts were bursting in their chests from snorting enough to kill sixteen people. Turns out *more* is not always the way to go.

1:30 pm EDT, October 8, Statesville, North Carolina

Henry had escaped the zombie pool party he'd started. He made it back to his room, locked the door and piled a table, chair and a nightstand in front of it. He waited for hours, ready to defend himself with a butter knife he brought from the pool party. When he didn't hear any more sounds he fell asleep. He woke around noon. It was still quiet in the hall. He raided the mini bar for lunch. When he was done he retrieved his bag from the air vent. He stopped to add what was left in the bar to his bag. Henry chugged two mini tequilas. He removed the stack of furniture from the door and listened. It was quiet in the hall so he made his way to the stairs at the end of the hall. When he got to the bottom the tequila was kicking in. Feeling the buzz, he strolled through the lobby. Thinking as he went 'No zombie ass mother fucker is gonna bite my ass. Henry is way too smart for those dead ass freaks.' He was halfway out the lobby door when he was snatched up by his dreads. The bag went right as Henry went left. Two zombies had Henry's ass for lunch.

3:30 pm EDT, October 8,
Dancing Goats Farm
Moon Mountain, North Carolina

Nick woke to find Gianna sitting at the table in the window. She had papers scattered on the table. Nick could see from the two that had fallen to the floor she's making lists. The woman loved lists even more than Theo. Though his were often neater. Nick lay there watching her in the afternoon sunlight. She had her calculating face on. She was planning something. He hoped it was a way to reach out and help their neighbors. He'd gone along with her 'fuck everybody outside their walls' declaration because she wasn't wrong... it wasn't her... but it wasn't wrong. He'd given her space knowing in time she would relent.

He loved to watch the faces of the lives she touched as Earth Mother. She'd taught him it was okay and even rewarding to connect with people you helped. In war you learn to keep it 'not personal'. The woman and child you help today, you may find dead on the road tomorrow. She'd taught him how to reclaim some of his humanity he'd lost over there. His wife was getting busy; this might mean the end to the honeymoon. He liked the rush he

got when he called her his wife.
Without looking up she said, "Nicholas,
why are you watching me?"

"Because... I love watching you.
What are you planning now?"

"You know what I'm doing. You always
know what I'm up to. Sometimes before I
do. Stop smiling at me like that. I have
to finish this work."

Maybe you should put work clothes
on. That silk thing you're wearing is not
making me think about feeding the
hungry."

"Please come look at this map I
made. I don't remember where all the
places are Mary mentioned. And put pants
on before you do or we'll never get this
finished."

She watched him as he slipped his
jeans on. He said, "Now who's wearing a
wicked smile?"

Nick filled in the farms missing
from her map. Then worked out the route
they would take. Two places were off to
the east. The rest were west. She asked
if they shouldn't take care of them now
and do the others in the morning. He said
no, by the time they got the supplies
together it would be too late. He didn't
want to be on the road after dusk. She
told him the boxes were already in the

truck. "You have been busy calling all around the farm. I thought we weren't talking to people during our honeymoon. Now you've spoiled it."

She got up to change. "Zip it smart ass. You wanted this. I saw your face when you looked at those children. Now don't start with me. We were never going to take care of whole town. I never said I would pick them up after the shit hit the fan. NEVER. That wasn't in our master plan."

"Neither was falling in love and marrying me. Plans do change, Gianna. Let me help you with that silk thing."

She kept walking. "You're insatiable Lorenzini. We have to deliver the food. Now go, before I succumb to your *immeasurable* charms."... Tugging her jeans on she added, "Nick don't you know, I fell in love with you the night we met."

4:00 pm EDT,

Amber saw Nick coming and started yelling orders because the last boxes weren't finished. Nick stopped her and told he only needed boxes for two families. Once they were loaded in the Dark Lady, Nick said, "Good call with the woman and the kids. It was just what Gianna needed to pull her back from the edge. I've been worried about her new

173

attitude toward, how did she put it,
'people who aren't us.' Nice save.

    You're all doing your jobs very
well. We're proud of how you've taken
control. I thank you for the time you've
given us to be alone. Now this relief
effort, doesn't mean the honeymoon is
over. We'll address issues when we feel
we need to but for now, we're going to
leave the running of the farm to you
ladies. Tell the others for me." And he
left.

    Dawn slapped her on the back and
said "I don't think I ever heard Nick put
that many words together, that didn't
have to do with security or safety. Good
for you."

    "Blew me the fuck away."

    picked up Gianna and drove through
the barn. Carmichael got in the truck
with them. Jackson and Lee followed
behind in Pepé. Nick drove to the
farthest farm first. The husband came to
the door with a shotgun. Gianna got out
and said Mary Thompson told her they
might like to have these. She put a box
of produce in the drive then one with
milk, eggs, cheese and butter with a bag
of ice. Mary said they had three
children. A box of store bought can
goods, with loaf of bread and a piece of
meat on top. She finished and said "We
don't have a lot to give but we hope this

helps." Nick and Lee backed the trucks out to the road.

On the way to the next house Nick said, "You do the Lady of the Manor so well."

"That's not how I meant it Nicholas. I was just trying to be kind and not hurt his pride."

Nick smiled at her. "You can't help it babe, that's who you are. We do live in the manor house don't we?"

At the next house their greeting was much the same. Mary had told her they had eaten their last chicken two days ago. Gianna left them a hen, now they could have eggs again. Gianna didn't think there'd be scraps for the bird so she left a bag of scratch. As they reached the Q, the young men from earlier pulled up. Nick got out to talk to them. Gianna told Lee to go get a set of food boxes from Amber. The boys had just come from the Thacker camp. Some of the wire fencing was rolled up in the back of the truck along with other stuff they'd salvaged from the rubble. They wanted to talk guy shit like what did it look like when Nick blew it up and how did he do it. What the dead bodies looked like. And did the lady really shoot the Thackers cause she did a real good job. Gianna let them bend Nick's ear until Lee returned with the boxes. She had him put them in the back of the boys' truck. "How is your mama doing? Did the packs help?"

"Yes ma'am, she's looking a lot better. You were right, when I told her what you said about how they died. She laughed for the first time since all this crazy shit happened, pardon ma'am."

Nick laughed, "She swears like a sailor."

"I put a few things together for you to take home. We don't have a lot but we're hoping this will help. Lee is putting them in the back now. There's a chicken for fresh eggs, don't eat her."

"Thank you folks, this is real kind of you. You shoulda seen those two boys going to town on those muffins. This is the first kindness anybody has seen since it happened."

"You get this home now. We'll stop by the other places Mary told us about, tomorrow. My husband won't let me go out tonight, he's worried some asshole is going to shoot me. Last night we had the big gun so he let me go. Y'all take care."

Nick was still laughing "*I let you go?* If I had tried to stop you, you might have shot me. You could have rescued me sooner."

176

"No, I couldn't. Do we not live in a manor house? Are you not the Lord of the manor? You have to spend time with the serfs dear."

"That is not how I see them. I am not the Lord of the Manor."

"Oh but you are my love, and it's how they will see you now that we've begun your feed the people campaign. Remember you dragged me out and made me feed Mary and her kids. If not the Lord what? The Dark Knight?"

"Be quiet woman or I won't let you come tomorrow."

"*As you wish mi'Lord*"

6:30 am EDT October 9,
Dancing Goats Farm
Moon Mountain, North Carolina

Gianna and Nick left with Pepé and one pickup. The truck beds were lined with boxes of produce, dairy products, cans of beans and spam. Gianna had put back cases of it for just this sort of situation. She said, "It's a prepper staple. It's tasty roasted on a stick. And yes it's high in sodium but a person may not be getting any in a SHTF situation so it works out." She was fond of the black pepper one. It was her idea of junk food. Along with the rest of the boxes there were cages with laying hens.

177

At 4:00 am Alexandra, Becky and
Charlie had gone hunting to cull the two
bucks. They had them dressed and they
were in another pickup as the food convoy
was pulling out. Alexandra said Simon was
in a snit so she thought the people could
use them.

Mary's house was first. Paul had
returned empty handed. When Mary saw the
deer she hugged Alexandra saying. "Now
Daisy can live." Gianna had to explain
Daisy was her pet cow. They added a few
boxes to what they gave her yesterday and
a chicken which the little one said he
would keep safe and feed. Gianna hoped
the people would share the two deer meat
among the families.

Gianna explained to Mary everyone
needed to know she would not be able to
do this again. When they had extra they
would share. People needed to start
putting in hoop houses for winter crops.
She would bring seedlings if they needed
them. If they wanted to learn how to
build a cob oven she would send two
people over to build one with them, then
the families could help each other build
more. They should do it before it turned
cold. Red clay we have, sand, some straw
and a dozen or so bricks were all they
would need. It was labor intensive, but
it went fast with many hands. She would
leave the other deer at the farm that had
five kids. Mary thanked her for

everything and the boys really enjoyed the pulled pork last night. Back at the truck Gianna said "What pork?"

Alexandra said "Freddy was bitching over dinner that he woke up and the pork was gone from the fridge and someone ate all the muffins. Becky had to tell him Amber snuck the pork in under the veggies and put the muffins on top. He wanted to keep bitching but Dawn started going on about how wonderful that was to feed those hungry children. So he shut up."

At each house the men came out to talk to Nick and shake his hand. He was rather uncomfortable with what he thought of as the fuss they were making. His job had been to stand back, look mean, watch and protect her. Now he was in the spotlight, being treated like the Lord of the manor. He didn't think he'd get used to this role anytime soon. He had advised some of the men on security measures they could take. Nick also suggested they set up some form of communication among themselves, other than the kid on the bike. He said he wasn't sure the roads were safe enough yet. He gave them the information on the zombies. They were relieved to find out it wasn't a virus. The women commented to Gianna how handsome Nick was and said they never realize he was her husband. Gianna just smiled and said thank you. And thought *'Neither had I.'*

On the way home, Nick said he wasn't
going through that again. There was no
need for the two of them to visit the
neighbors with supplies. He'd send Lee
and Jackson out next time. They now knew
all the stops. There was no need for him
to be subjected to all that. Gianna
ignored his complaining and said how
wonderful is was to have a day of peace.
She jinxed it.

4:30 pm,

DJ was in the tower when Tommy came
racing up to the gate. He told DJ the US
Army was making the rounds of the farms.
They had taken some of the food Nick and
Gianna had given the families this
morning. The Army was headed this way.

Reno sounded general alarm and gave
the order to 'shut the Q down'!" The
order meant to make the Q look like
nothing more than a farm. The barn opened
and the vehicles and Audrey went through
to the farm. The barn floor was dusted
for tracks and scattered with straw once
the door closed. Barn board panels were
put in place to hide the bunks and
arsenal in the barn loft. The same went
for the command room. A false wall slid
into place.

Gianna and Nick ran to the Q when
the alarm went off in their bedroom. On
the way Gianna called Theo and told him
to have the farm go silent. Freddy had

been Army. He stood in the kitchen and said, "This is bullshit. The US Army would never take food from women and children. I never thought I would have to fight my Army. This fucking sucks." Gianna put Violet and Lizzy sitting on the porch with Sadie, Becky was raking the yard, Carmichael in the nest, Dawn was in the garden weeding. All of the women were surreptitiously armed.

Amber was standing in the doorway to be able to relay what was going on to Nick. Nick tried to go to the tower with Gianna. "No you're not going out there. He wants food for his men he's not going to shoot me."

Frustrated Nick snapped, "When you start with that mouth, sometimes *I want to shoot you.*"

"Nice Nick... guess the honeymoon's over. Nick, I don't have time to debate this with you. Stay. Please." She ran to the tower. Gianna looked over the fence and asked, "Can I help you?"

"We are the United States Army. I demand you open this gate now or we will be forced to shoot." He was tall, broad and dirty. His men were bunched up behind him. One of them had a red wagon stacked with the food they had taken. The sight of the wagon really pissed Gianna off.

"Why, would I open my gate to a man

who just said he'd shoot me?" Nick was in the kitchen. Antonio was feeding the gate audio to his Catsear. When he heard that Nick told the vanguard to move through the east portal then take up positions surrounding the yard and barn.

"If you don't I will shoot this boy. He tells me you have food and a tank. I want both. I have the right to take them." They pushed a skinny kid to the front where she could see him.

"I don't even know that fucking kid. Do I look like I have a tank? If I had one... wouldn't I have used it when you said you'd shoot me?" Gianna pretended to be rubbing her brow. She turned her head and nodded yes to Carmichael. Then one of the men put a gun to the boy's head.

"Alright asshole, don't shoot a child. Since when did the Army start shooting children? I'm coming down." Gianna saw the vanguard moving up to the loft and the arsenal. Nick was suddenly at her side. She put her hand on his chest and whispered, "Let me get them inside. Then he's all yours." He stepped back into the shadows under the tower stairs. Gianna waved Dawn and Becky to the side. She made a big deal pretending the gate latch was stuck. "Keep your pants on it's stuck. Okay here we go." The second the gate was free the asshole pushed through and grabbed her by the throat and backed her up. Fourteen men and the boy followed him. With his hand still around her neck Gianna said, "Just come right in boys, there's plenty of room in here to spread out." They stupidly did.

"I want that tank and all of your food."

"Did you bring an 18 wheeler to carry the food away?"

"Bitch I going to take the tank and anything else I want, then I'm gonna take you."

"Oh, my my that was the wrong thing to say. Light them up boys." Every Army boy suddenly had a red laser dot shining over their heart. He looked at his chest and back at Gianna. She smiled, lifted her chin a little higher and said, "That's not even the bad news. My husband, is a Captain in the United States Marine Corp, Special Ops Command, he's the meanest killing machine they ever produced."

Nick stepped out of the shadows, "Get your hand off my wife." Gianna turned as she heard his voice, knocked the hand away from her neck and dove for the ground. She knew what was coming.

Nick pumped 12 rounds into him before she got him to stop. "He's very dead now Nicholas, you can stop." Nick pulled Gianna to him and just held her.

Amber, Dawn, Lizzy, Sadie, Violet and even Becky were on the veranda clapping and hooting. Whistling and saying things like, "You go Nick! Kill that fucker again!"

Reno had the others, still sporting their red dot, up against the gate. "The first one that talks, lives." One spat at Reno so he shot him. "Anyone else?... No?" He shot another one. "Where did you come from?... No?" and another. "This is getting boring. Last chance."

One says Tennessee. Reno pulls him out of line, then says, "Finish this." The vanguard fires. Reno walks away pushing the talker toward the barn. Charlie dragged the kid to the porch as soon as Nick started firing.

Nick was walking with his arm still around Gianna. "What did I tell you last night about taking foolish risks?"

"Nick, he wasn't going to shoot me, at least not before he fucked me."

Nick stops and Looks at her as if she's gone a little crazy. She says, "Nick, it's very easy to tell when a man wants to fuck me. It's like a frigging ticker-tape across his forehead. He thought he was going to bully me, then he thought I'd give it up, cause I'm a *girl*,

184

then he would have fucked me and maybe shot me. I knew it was never going to play out as he planned. The second he put his hand on my throat I knew his seconds were numbered. Not minutes, seconds. I just wanted to see his face when I told him who my husband was. The fear in his eyes was quiet satisfying. I knew there were going to be a lot of bullets, so I just got right out of your way. And P.S. It would have been more dangerous for you than me. One look at you, and there would have been *gun play in the court yard*." They had reached the steps of the veranda just as Gianna said, 'not before he fucked me' Everyone on the veranda had been listening to her explanation, waiting for Nick's reaction.

All Nick said was "Gianna, we don't have a courtyard."

chapter 26
I WON'+ BACK DOWN

"I'd rather just shoot them because they're assholes... or for touching someone else's wife just not mine."

4:55 pm EDT, October 9,
Dancing Goats Farm
Moon Mountain, North Carolina

"Nick I'm Italian, I'm allowed dramatic license. And don't look at me like that. Your little number out there was pretty fucking dramatic... *Lorenzini.*"

Dawn pouted, "I didn't get to shoot anyone. I was all ready."

Violet patted her on the shoulder. "Look, I think one of them isn't totally dead, go shoot him honey."

Freddy pushed past everyone and went down the steps. Violet asked "Freddy, where are you going?"

"To the barn to find out what that bastard trader has to say."

"Hey, hold up, I'll come with you. You might need my help."

Amber said, "I think we all need a cocktail. Who wants what?" Amber took the orders. Becky went with her to give her a hand.

Charlie still had a hold on the kid. Gianna looked at the kid and said, "You must be the famous Teddy. I hope you learned to stop running your mouth now. You came very close to being dead this afternoon. You put my husband and people in danger. No more talk of what you saw at the Thacker's camp."

Nick said, "Tiny said that Tommy's truck is outside the gate. He's asking if we've seen Teddy, the boys mom is frantic." Charlie took Teddy by the arm and walked him out to the truck.

Amber and Becky returned with the drinks. Becky went to check on the happenings in the barn. Everyone sat around toasting Nick for the manly fashion in which he had put down the pig who had put his hands on mom. They didn't get to tease Nick very often. The girls were making the most of the opportunity. Sadie reenacted the scene for everyone, with a running commentary as she did it. Nick asked if she had the safety on, she said oops, but it really was on.

Becky returned and reported, what was going on in the barn wasn't pretty. Seems the men really were part of the Army troops that had been sent to Tennessee. Freddy went ape shit at the news. Violet had to keep Freddy from killing the guy, by pointing out he still had more to tell them. Which as it turned out, was a lot.

The governor of Tennessee had released all the non-violent offenders from the prisons. Then left the rest to starve in their cells. Family and friends of the ones left to starve stormed the prisons and many prison guards were killed. In the end about three thousand very bad men had been set free on the population of Tennessee. They killed many people for their food. The troops were over run and the survivors scattered.

Some formed groups with citizens while others went rogue like the bunch that had showed up here. Violet and Reno were still getting information when Becky left. Nick said they needed to find out how many of these groups were out there, who could be headed to, or were already in North Carolina.

The families would have to do a better job of fortifying their homes with roving bands of rogue soldiers out there. He hoped that wouldn't mean he had to visit them again. Gianna said it would be easier for him cause he'd be telling them about how best to kill people, a subject he was far more comfortable with.

Nick asked if she really thought he was the meanest. She said, "Hell no but I was trying to frighten the bastard and '*oh my husband is just the best*' didn't strike her as a phrase that would strike fear in the man's heart, so I went with meanest." Again, her use of dramatic license. She did point out Nick could be rather mean at times.

After her second drink, Amber got up and did her rendition of the conversation of how Gianna knew the guy wouldn't shoot her. If you tied Gianna's hands she wouldn't be able to speak. Amber captured her Aunt perfectly with all the right hand gestures. Sadie laughed so hard when Amber delivered Nick's answer about their lack of a courtyard, she almost wet her pants. Dawn was still pissed about not getting to shoot any of them. Becky saw Freddy, Reno and Violet coming from the barn and said "Shit, they need a drink". She went in to get three ales.

6:00 pm EDT,

Reno said he was glad they were all having such a good time while he and Violet were torturing the guy in the barn. Gianna said stop whining and handed him an ale Becky had brought out. Nick asked where the guy was now and what else they'd found out after Becky left. Reno said the guy was in the box and the news was not good. The guy knew of at least forty other groups like the one he was in. After being overrun they had moved to the northern part of the state. There they broke up into groups who wanted to head in different directions. Amber stood up and said this was getting depressing, she was going home to her husband and child. Reno took a seat. The guy said a few groups had gone to Kentucky but most went east toward North Carolina and Virginia. He thought there were at least twenty-five of the groups in North Carolina. They had crossed the state line at Mount Airy with ten other groups. Others were going to cross down at Danville. The size of the groups ranged from ten to twenty. He said not all of the group leaders were like his sergeant. He was one of the nastier leaders.

Lee and Johnson returned. Charlie had sent them to give the people back the food the Army took. Lee said they had bloodied a few of the men who resisted. They were very happy to get the food for the second time. They said to thank Nick for helping them again. Grinning, Lee said one of the younger women wanted to come and thank Nick in person.

Nick smiled at Gianna, she said "*That's not going to happen*. Tell her to send a thank you card." Still smiling Nick asked Lee what else she had to say. Gianna punched him in the thigh. Lee now

laughing said her mother told her he was
married to the woman who had given them
the food and to behave herself. Gianna
said, "Point her out next time we go so I
can slap the shit out of her."

Reno said the last thing the guy had
told them was he figured the other groups
would move into the area now that they
were no longer in charge. Reno asked what
he should do with him. Did he want them
to put him in H&G with the other asshole?

At the mention of the asshole Gianna
said shit she'd forgotten all about him.
She told Nick they should just toss his
ass out. Nick agreed. He said put him out
tonight. With nothing. He told Reno to
keep the other one in the box for a day.
Feed him bread and water; he didn't want
him dead. Nick wanted to release him so
he could find the other groups and tell
them what happens to anyone who goes
after the people in this town.

From his tone Gianna knew Nick was
forming a battle plan that included the
whole town. She thought their lives just
got a fuck of a lot more complicated. She
knew him well, the next thing Nick said
was for Sadie to have signs ready for the
morning. They were to read: "This is the
town of Moon Mountain. Anyone found
harassing the town's residents will be
shot". They would post them at every road
into town and at every home they had
visited. Anyone else in town who wanted a

sign could asks for one. They would leave extras with the families. The townspeople needed to learn to stand their ground if they were going to survive. Sadie said she'd have them ready by 7:00. Nick said 6:30 he wanted to get an early start. On that note Gianna said "We have maps to go over and routes to plan. See you all in the morning."

6:30 pm EDT,

They stopped by the office to pick up maps. Nick took a copy of the day's reports. He wanted to check if there was any sighting of the rogue armies yet. Carl was still there going over the report with Mendez. Nick told Gianna to go on ahead, he wanted to fill Carl in on the information Reno got.

7:45 pm EDT,

Nick found Gianna asleep with her clothes on, face down on the bed. Her boots were off, her toes were hanging off the bed. Nick said, "My tired baby."

"I'm just having a cat nap. I know what we're going to be doing tonight and it has nothing to do with honeymooning. What did Carl have to say?"

Nick sat on the bed to take his boots off. He climbed on the bed and spooned her to him. "Are you upset with my decision? We normally discuss this

192

sort of thing first. It's got to be done babe. If we don't we'll just keep cleaning up messes and some of the messes will find their way to our door like this afternoon. I'll have to keep shooting men for touching my wife. I'd rather just shoot them because they're assholes... or for touching someone else's wife, just not mine."

"Nick, who are you trying to sell... me or you?"

"Probably both."

"I'm not upset that we didn't talk first. Nicholas I trust your decision. I know it has to be done. That girl on the other hand... that twat's gonna be slapped.

Nick told her there had been three reports of abuse by the rogue army bands. One in Greensboro and two in Raleigh. There aren't as many HAM radios around here, we don't know about the rest of the town. They agreed they should expect another band to try to move in so the signs had to go up in the morning. There were zombie reports out of Damascus, Virginia. One group took down a herd that stormed their barricade. More in Statesville. They review the maps and made a roster of teams and the roads they'd cover. Around 8:30 pm Gianna said she was starving. Nick said "I forgot to tell you when I came in there is a tray with your finger foods on the counter."

"Hey, don't make fun of appetizers. Cher did a movie about a woman who felt appetizers are perfectly acceptable as a meal, as do I."

"You're a very strange woman."

"Ten years and you're just figuring that out?"

"NO. You finish that list and I'll retrieve your finger foods for you Mrs. Fleck."

8:30 pm EDT, October 9,
Statesville, North Carolina

Henry's bag of snacks, booze and pixie dust lay forgotten on the ground outside the hotel for twenty-four hours. The following day, while what was left of Henry lay roasting in the unprecedented heat wave, that had all of southwestern North Carolina in it's grip for the last four days, two ten year old boys found it while scouting for food. Kevin and Jamal ate the snacks, tried one bottle of tiny booze and got back on their bikes. The bag was taken to their older brothers who happen to be partners in the street-drug-trade. Jamal and Kevin were rewarded for their find with two cans of soda, two cans of green beans and a can of potted meats. The paper label is gone. On the top of the can, in marker it says, MEATS.

194

It's one of life's mysteries, what kind
or how many different meats are in the
can. The boys feel this was the best part
of their payment and save it for later.
They sat on the curb at Coolidge and
Lakewood, sipping warm soda, and eating
green beans out of the can, as Ziggy's
dust d another day. By 11:00 pm... Ziggy
induced giggles ring out as far south as
Crescent Lane. By midnight the people who
live over on Hope Street, hope the cause
of those blood curdling screams doesn't
reach them. About that time, the street-
drug-trade partners were on Taylorsville
Highway bartering dust for propane, from
the guys who took control of the propane
tanks, when their little brothers were
eaten by four of their corner boys gone
zombie. This is what comes from... *taking
a taste*. Let this be a lesson to you.
Never dip into the product. The potted
MEATS is still one of life's mysteries...
it may never be solved. Zombies don't
know how to work a can opener.

1:30 am EDT, October 10,
Moon Mountain, North Carolina

Dave heard the zombies around 11:45
pm. He crawled to the window on the
second floor of his Hardware store. They
were chasing a cow down the center of the
street. They must have chased it for a
while. The poor beast was starting to
slow down. The zombies were gaining on
it. He wished he could put it down to
save it from being eaten alive. He knew

the shot would bring the zombies to him. He didn't know how many were out there tonight. The numbers had dropped drastically since the weird dude on the spider painted bike had left. He only had four cans of food left. He wondered if they really were FBI agents? He put earplugs in so he didn't have to hear the death bellows of the cow. He fell back asleep dreaming that they had returned with water and another box of food.

At 1:30 the gunshots woke him. One earplug had fallen out. He crawled back to the window. There were people in the street. They shot the three zombies. Dave thought one person had been bitten, by the way he was yelling. They were across the street. One of the men had a flashlight shining on the bite. The bite didn't look too bad. The man started begging, please no. Then the other men shot him. They probably thought it was caused by a virus like TV zombies.

Dave had figured out it was the drugs. Four boys had gone to the Sheriff's station and sat right there on the city bench and snorted the stuff. The giggling started first. Then crazy behavior followed. It took a good hour before they went insane. They began punching their heads. One kid started pulling out his own hair. Another climbed the fire escape and jumped off the building. He landed on a car. The other two ate him.

These guys shot their friend because they thought he was going to turn. Dave backed away from the window. He hoped they would move on. He heard them banging on the boarded up shops. They pounded on his yelling they were the US Army and they had the right to enter. Dave hid in the dark, rifle aimed at the top of the stairs. The leader yelled they were all empty and they moved away. After awhile the banging and yelling stopped. They moved on, and Dave fell back asleep.

6:15 am EDT,October 11
Dancing Goats Farm,
Moon Mountain, North Carolina

The teams were loaded in the vehicles. Sadie had the signs ready as ordered. Each team had ten signs, ten signs on stakes, a ball of wire and a hammer. No way she was going to fail on her first direct order from Nick. Amber had provided a box of food for each truck just in case. Nick gave each team the map for their route and fliers to hand out to any farms they passed. They would take the roads, Nick would go into town. Carl put a box of canned goods and 4 jugs of water in the back of Dark Lady. He was riding with Gianna and Nick. He wanted to check on the guy in the Hardware store. Carmichael showed up assuming he was coming too. Nick started to say no but Gianna stopped him with a hand on his chest. "It's what he does best. We have other snipers for the nest. No one watches my 6 better... I know, I left myself wide open for that smart ass remark on the tip of your tongue. Zip it." She waved Carmichael in.

Just before they pulled out Lee said, "I feel like I should have a ratty sweater and a cap. Hey Sadie say Ride Postman Ride as we're pulling out." She gave him a thumbs up and did as he asked.

Nick got in the truck and said, "You're making the men as crazy as you are."

"There's nothing wrong with crazy, is there Carmichael? We do just fine."

"Yes ma'am we do. We get way with more shit too."

DJ and Sal followed them to town. They had the road to the south of town. Nick stopped in front of the Hardware store. DJ went on. The sound of the trucks woke Dave. He made his way to the window cautiously. When he saw Carl he waved. Carl pointed to the box and the jugs and waved him down. Dave put his rifle against the wall and ran down to unbolt the door. It took a minute they were steep old stairs. The ceilings in the shop below were nearly ten feet high and he had installed several deadbolts. Carl handed him the water jugs and went back for a box.

Carmichael was already out of the truck watching the street next to Gianna's door before Nick could say it. Carmichael said, "On it Boss." The thought crossed Nick's mind that Carmichael might love Gianna almost as much as he did. She treated him like one of her kids. Carl and Nick carried the boxes up the stairs. Dave had a sparse apartment set up in what had been his storage loft. They introduced themselves. Dave said he remembered them all from coming in the store. Gianna had spent many an afternoon in the store. Said she had a passion for old Hardware shops.

They talked about the rogue Army bands and what Nick was planning for the town's protection. Dave told them about the night before and he believed they moved on about 2:30. Carl had stuck a few signs in one of the boxes. They got around to the zombies and the weird guy. Dave was glad they understood about the drugs. He thanked them. They said they'd keep checking in with him, he was their eyes in Town. Nick's foot was on the top step when the first shots rang out.

Nick and Carl raced down, Dave ran to the window. The man that had been by the truck was on the ground. There was blood on his face. He saw the leader hit the woman in the head with the butt of the rifle. Dave ran for his rifle and the stairs to the roof. Nick and Carl burst from the door and stopped. Nick's blood turned to ice.

He couldn't see Carmichael. Gianna was across the street. One of the rogue Army, guessing the leader, had her by her ponytail, there was blood running down one side of her face. Nick counted twelve armed men. Nick controlled his rage and fear and asked "What do you want?"

"We are the United States Army we are authorized to seize all supplies and weapons. We'll be taking the truck too."

"Take it and go."

"Get our gear and get in the back of the truck boys." Gianna could only see out of one eye because of all the blood running down her face, which hurt like she'd been kicked by one of the draft horses. She was looking for an advantage while trying to see if Nick was going to do something insane that would get him dead. If the pain would only stop so she could think. If her blood would stop running so she could see. If this fuckwad would take the gun away from her face, she might have a move. He said. "Move bitch" and started pushing her forward toward the truck. She didn't make it easy for him.

Nick said, "She stays here."

"NO. The bitch comes with me. She

shot two of my men. The dead asshole on the ground shot two more. She's payment. Besides I haven't had a piece of ass in a week." Gianna's mind screamed 'NO DON'T SAY THAT TO HIM.'

Nick's world slowed to crawl, seconds became minutes. He saw Gianna's hand come up to stop him, drops of blood fell from her finger tips, her face turned to her left, blood flew from her cheek, he saw her fingers go round the barrel of the Glock at her temple, Nick didn't realize he was moving toward her, a shot echoed through the morning air, he watched as Gianna slid slowly to the street.

chapter 27
she's like the wind

*"I have to teach you
how to listen to the wind
The wind is Her voice"*

**6:58 am EDT, October 10,
Location Unknown**

The Blogger is now The Flogger: Mother is
still talking to me at night so I'm still
writing.

Those of you who are still here seem
confused. You can't understand how any of
this could happen? Or my fave... Why has
God let this happen? The answer to the
second is two words... Free Will. The
answer to the first is much longer and
complex *or not*, if you boil it down...
Humans are Self-centered Assholes. Let me
break it down for you:

Piss, Shit and **Corruption** – The headlines
taken off my seriously missed buddy –
Google News.

Piss:
Paris encourages tourists to relieve

202

themselves in public with exposed urinals.

ME: Just what you want to see, some guy's dick, while taking a romantic stroll through Paris. Seems like an open invitation to the public Tally-Wacker-Waggers

Shit:
San Francisco starts a 'poop patrol' to deal with human waste.

ME: The Mayor said she had data and was working on getting it up. How about working on the cause moron... apartments are $5,000 a month! If you can't find them housing, how about porta-potties? And shame on you assholes for shitting in the street.

Kenilworth school superintendent Thomas Tramaglini, who stands accused of pooping near the Holmdel High School athletic field in Holmdel Twp., N.J., will collect more than $100,000 until his September resignation, according to nj.com.

ME: They have a video of this and he still gets paid? Don't they have a morals clause in his contract?

Corruption:
Pentagon Spokeswoman, the assistant to the secretary of defense for public affairs; The focus is on allegations of leader misconduct and abuse of power.

ME: I would bust her down to runner. Make her fetch and step for the people she abused.

Cop charged with assault in beat-down caught on video.

ME: And why didn't the other cops help him subdue this guy? And/or stop him? You do know this shit slimes the good cops simply because, they're cops.

Venezuelan Hospitals scrap surgeries, Venezuelans forgo showers as taps run dry. Water cuts are the latest addition to a long list of woes for Venezuelans hurting from a fifth year of an economic crisis that has sparked malnutrition, hyperinflation and emigration.

ME: Wake up people! Five years and you can't get this bastard out of office? Stand up and take back your country. Read our history. A raggedy group of colonists took on the largest empire in the world and we kicked it's ass. Now everyone wants to run here. How about y'all stay home and do your fucking job.

Kenya fraud charges over Chinese-funded $3bn railway Two senior Kenyan government officials have been charged in court with fraud over the building of a $3.2bn (£2.5bn) Chinese-funded railway line.

ME: This is just wrong in so many ways...

This would take six pages to answer.

UK, On Independence Day, Returns Indian Buddha Statue Stolen 57 Years Ago.

ME: How about all the rest of the shit filling the museums of Europe? Why is the Dresden Codex in Dresden? Isn't it Mayan?

The US is $19.9 trillion in debt — here are the countries we owe the most.

ME: Everyone knows the money went to pay for the toilets, hammers and table and chair sets. And giving it to other fucking countries when we had millions of homeless Americans living (and shitting) in the streets.

Mexico violence: Newly elected Congresswoman kidnapped. The kidnapping comes little more than a month after the mayor of the town of Naupan was seized and killed in the same area.

ME: If you'd shoot the drug dealers this shit would stop.

Moral Corruption:
SCHOOL CLOSES AFTER FACEBOOK PARENTS THREATEN TO CASTRATE TRANSGENDER 12-YEAR-OLD GIRL WITH KNIFE

ME: I have only one solution for dealing with rabid motherfuckers who want to mutilate a child. I read about it in your Christian bible.

I just don't care Category:
Woman, 87, tased by police while
attempting to cut flowers.

ME: This is a classic example of the
press whores stirring the shit pot of
social unrest. It should read: Woman 87,
went on to private property, where
children congregate, with a knife,
intending to deface said property and
steal their flowers. The bitch moved here
and can't be bothered to learn ENGLISH,
that's why she got tased. My great-
grandparents spoke Italian at home, but
Nona knew how to speak English to the
customers in their bakery. Get a fucking
dictionary!

Largo mom: Bus driver drops off 6-year-
old miles away from home, police find her
wandering.

ME: The bus driver and the two adults
were supposed to be on the bus Whoever
left that child in the next fucking town,
should be placed in a dark hole, and left
there. Gold star for the Clearwater cops
who found her.

Farmers' Anxiety Grows as Details on
Federal Aid Remain Unclear

ME: Clearly feeding the country wasn't a
top priority in the DC snake pit. Guess
they were too busy ripping each other to

shreds.

SHANGHAI/BEIJING (Reuters) - China's commerce ministry said a U.S. decision to subsidize renewable energy firms and impose tariffs on imported products has seriously distorted the global market and harmed China's interests, firing the latest shot in a broader trade conflict.

ME: The 'Global Market' is a distortion of brobdingnagian proportions and the greatest contributor to the climate changes that brought the planet to it's knees.

Ammunition company operators plead guilty in water contamination case BOZEMAN — Two Montana men who ran a now-defunct ammunition company have pleaded guilty to federal criminal charges over the dumping of lead-contaminated wastewater into the Bozeman sewer system.

ME: Is it any wonder why chunks of the state are falling into sinkholes? My only question is, was it Mother or Raphael the darling who buries demons in the desert? I do believe Archangels are omnipresent.

'Forever chemicals' contamination in eastern Pennsylvania water among worst in U.S.

ME: There's a phrase that should have struck fear in the hearts of the intentionally ignorant. Guess they were too busy sending insipid photos of themselves on their phones.

Cake Shop owner sues after refusing to make a birthday cake for a trans woman. He does birthday cakes, but not "gender-transition cakes."

ME: I have this image in my head; I see this fucking zealot asshole's shop being sucked into the Pacific by TuTū Pele's tsunami. Then the scene from jaws when the shark is skimming along the surface with a body in it's teeth... here's to hoping.

Catholic Church abuse: Pa. priests molested more than 1,000 children

ME: Got to be a special room in their Hell for these dirty bastards. P.S. 'I am heartly sorry for having offended Thee' isn't going to save your pervert ass from toasting.

One of China's highest-ranking monks has quit as the head of the country's Buddhist association after facing accusations of sexual misconduct — including demanding sexual favors from nuns.

ME: Evidently not really a fucking Buddhist! Cause Buddha ain't say that.

6-year-old orders over $300 worth of toys on mom's Amazon account.

ME: This mother needs a fucking slap. There's a photo of the tiny identity thief standing next to the boxes smiling. If she was my kid she'd be working it off at twenty-five cents an hour. She wouldn't see a computer again till high school.

Murder:
VENEZUELAN PIRATES SPREAD FEAR ACROSS THE CARIBBEAN

ME:Rather than fix shit at home, they go out and rob and yes murder people? Are there no Navy destroyers to blow this human garbage to hell?

1. Rockingham County, Man hit in drive-by shooting after vehicle broke.

2. Wave of arson attacks targets scores of cars in Sweden.

3. Fearless Mercedes-Benz Driver Thwarts Scumbag Carjackers.

4.Group on scooters confronts, shoots man in downtown Atlanta.

5. Couple charged with Capital Murder after bloody toddler led police to double homicide.

6. 'We won't survive': Residents speak of ongoing battle in Ghazni.

7. Hundreds of people gathered Monday in Yemen to mourn the 40 children killed in a Saudi-led coalition airstrike last week.

8. Louis Vuitton model convicted of murdering rival Harry Uzoka
Louis Vuitton model George Koh has been found guilty of stabbing his fashion rival Harry Uzoka to death after a heated social media dispute.

9.Kabul suicide bomber kills 48 in tuition center attack.

10. Victim runs to daycare parking lot after shooting nearby.

11. Gunman in deadly Clearwater 'Stand Your Ground' shooting trying to get bond reduced. The shooting happened over an argument over a parking space. Surveillance cameras recorded the shooting. Markeis McGlockton came out of the Clearwater store and shoved Drejka. He pulled out a gun and fired one deadly shot.

12.Arizona Dad 'Killed Man Who Tried to Enter Daughter's Bathroom Stall': Police Report.

13.Eight injured at Walmart in Pennsylvania after shooting in checkout lines

ME: This bakers dozen is a really big

reason why Mother purged her Earth.
Humans can't stop murdering each other.

The US Air Force is ordering more
hypersonic weapons just one week after
China tested one of its own.

ME: Men and their never ending contest of
my dick is bigger than your dick. All I
can say is, thank you Mother for the
cataclysmic EMP. These fuckers would have
blown it up. At least you left us
something to work with. Let's hope the
ones left have learned their lessons.

A word about today's Flog; I don't know
who wrote these news snippets, nor do I
care. If you're still alive, shut the
fuck up and just be happy you made it
into the Flog.

As you all know, *the internet is gone.*
Hence the fliers... flier & blog is flog!
Today's flogging... the double-entendre
is just a bonus. So folks as you're
sitting there with no food, no lights, no
heat, etc, thank Washington, but most of
all, thank yourselves.

**6:58 am EDT, October 10,
Moon Mountain, North Carolina**

David lay on the roof and watched
the exchange between Nick and the Army
guy who had the woman by the hair. He
wished they would stop moving. David
couldn't signal her without giving his

211

position away. When the men went back in the cottage, David knew this was his moment. 'Please stop moving.' He saw her face turn; in that second David was sure she saw him, she closed her eyes as she pushed the barrel of the gun off her face and relaxed her body... in that instant David fired. Through his scope he watched as the bullet pierced the eye and exploded out the back of his head. Ten seconds later men began shooting out the door of the cottage. David shot one but two fell.

6:58 am EDT,

Carl watched Gianna's face, she looked up and closed her eyes. She saw something. David! Carl's mind flashed on the rifle in the apartment. Nick was moving forward, Carl went right. Two steps and the shot came from above his head. Yes! He watched Gianna slide down as her captor flew backwards. Carl was ready when they started coming out the door. He knew they had to cover Nick. He was going over the hood of the truck. All that would be in his mind was getting to Gianna.

6:58 am EDT,

Carmichael lay on the ground trying to breath as shallow as possible. The bastard thought he was dead. He had a Glock in his ankle holster. He knew he need six seconds to reach it and aim, cause he'd timed himself practicing the move. He watched for his opening. No way was *he* taking the Lady with him. Carmichael saw her bend her knees. She was gonna drop. The second he saw her let go he went for the gun. He was pretty sure three seconds had gone by when someone put a bullet through the asshole's eye from above. As the guy hit the ground Carmichael's Glock was trained on the door. He yelled to her, "Stay down ma'am I got your 6."

"I know you do babe."

6:58 am EDT,

Nick felt as if he was moving through water as he slid over the hood of Dark Lady. Carmichael dead... no... not dead... firing a Glock over Gianna's body. Nick stepped forward to lift Gianna, right in Carmichael's line of fire. Carmichael pulled up, the bullet smashed into the eave of the cottage. Nick picked Gianna up and took her down behind the truck. He looked at her bloody battered face. He wiped the blood off her eye. She opened her eyes. "Did the guy on the roof kill that fucker?"

Nick kissed her. "I thought I'd lost you." He held her as Carl, David and Carmichael killed the rest of the fuckers.

DJ and Sal came flying back into

town, when they heard the gunfire. They arrived as Carmichael finished off the last one. DJ froze when he saw the way Nick was holding Gianna, he thought she was dead. Nick said, "Help Carmichael." To Gianna he said, "Can you sit?"

"Yes. Nicholas help me stand please. Where's Carmichael?"

"I'm up ma'am, how's your head? Hope it's better than mine."

"NO. I think we're a sorry pair right now. Carmichael you did it again... you got more than me."

"I almost shot the Boss."

"*That* I wouldn't forgive you for." Carl handed Nick gauze and a cold pack from the first aid kit. "Did you see that shot? You're the best my boy but this guy is a close runner up. Where is he? Who is he?"

Nick snapped, "Gianna Stop Moving! Let me get this on your head."

"*Nicholas you're yelling*, I'm bleeding and you're yelling at me." David handed her a wet towel for her face. "Thank you. Are you my new sniper? That was a fucking incredible shot. Your timing was impeccable. Thank you for my life."

"I couldn't believe you saw me. When you closed your eyes I just took the shot the second the Glock cleared your forehead."

"Nick unzip me and get the vest off I can't breath. Please hurry."

Nick undid her zipper and said to everyone, *In the truck now!* Woman you didn't think to tell me you took two in the vest?"

Nick eased the vest over her head and handed it to DJ. "Holy Shit! How are you standing ma'am?"

"I'm not. Nick has me. Where's my gun? One of those bastards took Carmichael's 'baby'. Find it."

Nick looked at her shaking his head, "Carl drive. You get in the front and stop talking to her she has two broken ribs. DJ clean this up. I'll send help when we get back. David thank you. Come back to the farm so we can talk. I've got to get her to the infirmary now. *Woman, will you ever learn to stay in the truck when I tell you to?"*

"I wouldn't count on it. BUT I did stay in, until they shot Carmichael. And they're cracked not broken."

Nick gets in the back seat with her. "How would you know?"

"Cause I've had two cracked ribs
before. Nick let me put my head on your
lap, it hurts my ribs too much to sit.
Don't we have any drugs in this truck?
Morphine, Heroin, *Something*?"

"You can't have anything until Andy
checks your head."

"Honey I love you a lot but if you
don't give me something for the fucking
pain I will stab you." Gianna realizes
she's squeezing his hand so hard she's
left crescent indentations in the back of
his hand from her nails. "I'm so sorry
look what I did to your hand."

"It's okay Gia you're in shock just
try to breath. Look at me... Gia open
your eyes."

"The light makes my head hurt more."

"Gianna, let me look at your eyes...
Carl move this fucking truck. Gianna stay
awake your pulse are wide open, your
pules is racing and your skin is clammy."

"And they said you weren't romantic?
Is there still blood on my face?"

"No, just your hair. You're going to
have a nasty shiner."

"There you go again saying those
romantic things every woman wants to

hear. Is Carmichael alright? He's too quiet. Check on him."

"He's fine. I told him not to talk to you."

"*Well that was fucking rude.*"

"Will you be quiet and just breath please."

"Nick I need to talk... I'm going down the rabbit hole."

"You want to tell me what an asshole I am for leaving you out there and not checking the street first?... Gianna wake up."

"I'm here babe. The truck is swimming and I'm trying not to puke on you."

"Go ahead, I'm a Marine, I've been puked on before... Gia look at me... Gianna... if you don't wake up I'm going to go see that farm girl."

"*Fuck you will.* It'll be kind of hard to do if I shoot you."

"You are an evil woman."

"That's why you love me."

"I do love you, now stay awake."

"Owwww Mother Fucker! I just took too deep a breath. That'll fucking wake you up."

7:40 am EDT,
Dancing Goats Farm
Moon Mountain, North Carolina

Slowing as he nears the gates, Carl says, "Hold her Nick, the barn is open we're going through." Dark Lady leans right then left through the barn.

"Nick kiss me in case I die."

"Don't you dare die on me Woman! I'll kiss you when we get you on the gurney."

"Nick you know I hate hospitals, don't leave me. You're my anchor. Don't let go, I'm afraid I'll drift away on the wind."

Inside Andy says, "Nick, we'll take her, you wait here."

"*NO*, you'll work around me. I promised her I wouldn't leave her. Get to work."

12:58 pm EDT, October 10,
Damascus, Virginia

Rory sat in the big over-stuffed chair with Cindy on his lap. It was Beth's turn on the radio. Ann was stretched out on the loveseat. Their daily radio half hour had become the high point of their day. It had replaced TV, computer, phones and FM radio. Rory and Ann were working on building a solar setup so they could watch videos and use the computers. They were very careful with the little gas they had. Before the zombies they had gone out once and siphoned five gallons. Now that was on hold until the zombie threat passed.

Beth got the mountain compound on right away. "Hey Frank what's happening down there? Are you folks holding up alright?"

Hey Beth it's Pauline. The boys are gettin' wood up. It turned cold yesterday. Beth we're doin' fine. Tracy and Betty Lou said hi to y'all. We had zombies at the gate last night but they moved on. Oh, here's Frank. Y'all take care. Bye."

"Frank here. Have y'all had any more zombies?"

"Yes, Cindy put two down on her watch this morning. There's one or two, then a wave of them come. Guess they must still be selling the drugs here."

They talked about the news each group had gotten through the HAM network. Most of it was bad. The HAM network was getting larger every day. People were

getting organized in small groups,
pooling their resources and talents. The
bad Army had made itself known in
Virginia. They'd killed an elderly couple
and the group nearest them hunted the bad
Army down and shot all of them. People
were passing the warning along so others
were ready when the bad Army showed up.
In Virginia, they took to calling them
the BA. Some local groups were bullies
and raided other camps. Scavenging was
dangerous but necessary. The water on the
east coast seemed to stop rising but now
parts of the land were becoming salt
marshes as the land subsided. The
refugees from the flooded areas were
moving toward Oklahoma. It was still
unseasonably warm there. The Santa Ana
winds reached Phoenix now. Strong winds
off the Gulf of Mexico, which was now
three times it's former size, brought
inches of rain across the spongy
southeast. Icy winds had blown a snow
storm across the Rockies and the great
lakes. It was icy rain by the time it got
to Vermont.

Information from outside the US was
still hit or miss. Canada seemed to be
doing okay but were bracing for a cold
winter. Their native tribes said the old
ones had told them they knew this by the
behavior of the animals. North Carolina
was a mixed bag. Some refugees moved back
to the western half of South Carolina.
The North Carolina coast was miles
inland. If you could still go to the

beach, Raleigh would be a seaside town. They had trouble with the BA in several locations. But North Carolina people who had been farmers were doing better than most. The state was dealing with a crazy spate of zombies, which were now spreading to Virginia, Tennessee and South Carolina.

1:00 pm EDT October 10,
Dancing Goats Farm
Moon Mountain, North Carolina

Sadie was up and doing more than she should at this stage of her concussion. Lizzy hung out in Q kitchen so she wouldn't have to run when there was an issue. Her stitches were healing and they itched. Alexandra made her an ointment that worked very well. Everyone in the Q was subdued waiting to hear about Gianna. Reno and Lizzy spent a few hours getting to know Dave. He agreed to stay and have dinner. A real cooked meal sounded great to him. Lizzy called Simon and asked if he would make Dave a steak for Dinner. Simon said he'd cook him a whole cow for saving Gianna. Reno dealt with the people who stopped by and wanted to be part of Nick's plan. Some brought flowers for Gianna. Reno asked one of the women how they knew. She said word travels on the wind out here in the country.

Amber and Dawn kicked up production in the greenhouses. They had five girls

potting seeds all day. Gianna would want
to have lots of seedlings to give to the
people. Violet stopped by and told Amber
she was postponing the Octoberfest to the
28th. There was simply too much going on
at the present. Amber agreed. Bonny got a
message from Lizzy, to put the best brood
hens to sit. They were going to need more
chickens to pass out. She put the big fat
gold Brahma hen on a half a dozen Pekin
duck eggs too. Lizzy said to put the bull
in with four of the cows and make sure
the billy's were in with the does not in
milk. They were going to need more meat.
Bonny told Stephen it was good he'd
brought in a record year on the hay.
Stephen spent the day with the field
workers putting winter wheat down and
plowing a new field for peanuts. People
were going to need oil. They'd have to
put hoop houses over them and heat them
on freeze nights. Amber had talked to the
Water Wizard about growing wild rice. He
said he would work on expanding the marsh
areas around the stream and the ponds.
Amber had a new hoop house put up. She
was going to try a winter crop of
potatoes and sweet potatoes. One of the
teenage girls complained about the extra
work. Shouldn't the people they were
growing it for be doing the work. Amber
said, "You're right go pack your bags.
You're out, so I can make room for
someone who'll understand what a gift and
honor it is to live here." She made the
girl sit with her suitcase at the east
portal all day waiting for Sadie to have

time to put her out. When the parents complained and made excuses for the girl Amber said "You can go with her if you want." They said they wanted to talk to Gianna. That was really stupid. Amber whirled back around. "My Aunt is unconscious from being shot and beat with a rifle butt. I am her voice. If you don't like it, you can get the fuck out too." Then she walked away.
After they left Dawn said, "Are you really putting her out?"

"Fuck no. She can sit there all day and cry some sense into her empty head. Her parents have done a shit job of teaching her what it means to live here, so they can sweat it out all day too. AND they're going to have a lot of ass kissing to do for trying to play the Gianna card."

Dawn was laughing. "You are so much like her. Sadie runs things like her, but your mind works like Gianna's. Especially the dark side." The rest of the greenhouse staff put 100% in after that. Amber watched them and thought, 'That's a nice bonus. No wonder Auntie liked intimidation.' Tyler came by to say he'd hooked up solar panels for her new hoop house.

1:30 pm EDT,

The sisters had agreed to check in on Gianna together. On the way in Amber

223

saw the father sitting on his suitcase next to the girl at the portal. She was quite pleased. The others asked and she explained. They approved. Inside they found Andy, who said Gianna was still asleep. Yes, Nick was still there. Andy said Nick had always been a difficult patient but he'd never been rude until now. He wouldn't take anything to eat or drink. He just sat there next to the bed. He hadn't let go of Gianna's hand since they brought her in. She thought he might actually be resting. He had his head on the bed next to Gianna now. They said they would just look in and not disturb either off them.

They moved the curtain aside on the window. Nick's eyes were closed. Sadie said "Nick looks like shit. He's really screwed up about this."

Violet said, "Thanks sister obvious. None of us could see that but you."

Alexandra said, "Don't get bitchy you two. It won't help."

Amber said, "If y'all weren't talking, you'd see she's waking up. She just put her hand on Nicks head. Okay we're out of here. You wouldn't want someone watching you at this moment." Then she closed the curtain and hustled the others out. Violet started to protest. Amber said we'll stop by and see her at the house later. You know she's not going to stay here now that she's awake. They went back to their business.

Amber ran to the house and grabbed Gianna sweats and a T shirt. She knew they had cut her clothes off. She got back to the room and knocked on the door. Nick opened it. "I thought she might want these. Love you Auntie."

Nick laughed. "You think just like her. She was this minute threatening to leave here in a sheet." Amber closed the door. Outside she thought 'That's the second person to tell me that today.'

Andy protested Gianna leaving even though she knew it would do no good. Nick helped her dress and got her in the cart promising Andy he'd put her right to bed. Upstairs Nick realized one of the girls had housekeeping come in. The food trays were gone, the papers they'd left scattered about were nicely stacked and the bed had fresh linens. Getting in bed was as painful as getting cut was. Once settled Gianna said she was starving. Nick called Simon. "She's up and she's hungry."

Simon said "I heard she was up. I just put chops in to marinate."

Nick said, "Hold those for later make her a porterhouse please." Simon answered and hung up. Nick sat on the edge of the bed and told her "He's cooking now. You're having steak and grilled vegetables. No finger food, you need protein. I don't know how the hell word gets around here so fast. He already had lamb chops out for you. We just came across five minutes ago."

"I have to teach you how to listen to the wind. The wind is Her voice. How many times have you found me at night standing in the moonlight with the breeze lifting my hair? That's one of the ways Mother speaks to me. All you have to do is learn to listen." Nick listened to the words and thought 'I know her so well and some things she does are still a mystery.' "Can I have a vodka now? I've been poked, prodded, had my clothing cut off, my head still hurts, I want a drink."

"Yes, I'll get it when your food gets here. If I give it to you now you'll be drunk when the food comes and you won't eat. Don't bother with that pouting face, I'm not giving in."

"Nick I saw many thing while I was out. They're a bit fuzzy but more changes are coming. Come over here and I"ll tell you what I remember." Nick pulled his boots off and sat up next to her.

She talked and he listened until they heard Sadie.

"I'm coming up with sustenance for the wounded mother, so Nick please don't be naked."

"Sadie, she has a concussion and two cracked ribs. *No one is naked.*"

Sadie put the tray on the bed. "Yeah, just... checking Nick. Mom your face is a wreck but it will get better. The swelling is going down and the color is coming up."

"Thank you Sadie."

"Well someone has to tell you. He's not going to. He'll say, Oh I love you, you're beautiful. *No*, that's a lie. You're going to need make up to leave the house or you'll scare the children."

"Stop making me laugh you wicked child."

"Violet is bringing dinner. Alexandra will be by with some of her magic potions at some point. Amber will be by later, because Angelena just threw herself on the green and had a tantrum cause she couldn't see you *right now*. Her sassy ass is in time out. Don't know about Lizzy, she's very busy being me. So Nick put a pause on the honeymoon action and keep your pants on. Love you mom. By Nick." from halfway down the stairs. "Mom you want a Kamikaze?"

"Yes, Please."

Nick moved her tray on her lap and handed her a fork. "Eat Woman before that drink gets here. I've had a Sadie drink. She pours with a lead hand."

chapter 28
the shape of my heart

"One was lost
One was Gone
One was nearly Broken"

6:58 pm EDT, October 10,
Dancing Goats Farm
Moon Mountain, North Carolina

Alexandra sat on her Aunt's bed waiting for an answer. Gianna took a breath and began. "I'm not sure of the order of the events. You know I'm not good with time. I saw Forest on a road traveling in a older jeep. They were driving through a forest, maybe the Berkshire Mountains. Though I haven't seen them in decades, those mountains are hard to forget. It was cold. Nikki and the baby were wrapped in layers of blankets. The sun was setting behind Nikki through the passenger window, so traveling south? Maybe? I know he's a stubborn ass but I thought he would have set out for here as soon as the changes started to happen. When he didn't show the first week I forced myself to stop hoping. That seems to be a constant theme with that boy and me. I'm thinking he couldn't accept I was right and he was wrong. How do I leave my son out there and not go to help him? Is he even out there? Was it simply a mother's delusion? Fuck if I know. I know we have a war to fight and there's no room for fear. This makes me fearful."

"Have you told Sadie and Violet?"

"No. What do I say? I had a vision while I was unconscious from a concussion and oh yes, your brother, with his wife and child, may or may not be, traveling down the Appalachian Mountain range? Right, that's solid intel!"

"Did Sadie talk to him before she left Boston?"

"I don't know. Don't ask about him any more because it breaks my heart."

"Okay leave this to me. I'll get the sisters together and we'll see what we see. Any other delightful images you want to share?"

"Oh, Mother is not done. The winds of change will blow and there is war and fighting among the survivors."

"Aunt try not to get hit in the head again. We don't need any more nasty visions. Get some rest, love you." Alexandra passed Nick on her way out. "She's a little tired from all the visits. Night." She went off to find the girls.

Nick had gone off to talk to David while the Amazons spent time with Gianna. She was resting when he walked in the bedroom. Whatever Alexandra put on her face the swelling was gone and the bruising didn't look as bad as it had this morning. She opened her eyes. Nick asked, "Did Angelena wear you out with her bouncing?"

"Yes. I just want to curl up beside you and sleep for a week."

"That can be arranged. Let's leave the running of the world to the kids tonight. Did you talk to Alexandra about Forest?"

"Yes, and thankfully she took it upon herself to deal with it. If he remembers anything I taught him, he'll stick to the mountains and contact us when he finds a radio. Now, come over here and tell me, do we have a new sniper?"

"He's thinking about it. He's staying the night at the house. He's a Seal, so he has the skills we like. Lizzy made sure he was well fed. I left him drinking on the veranda with Reno. I told him if he wants to stay in town I'd send the HAM we got in Holly Springs back with him. Then we'll know what's happening

231

without having to get my wife shot and beat again."

"Oh that was very thoughtful of you Nick. I'm sorry, it was so stupid of me to get hit in the head. They rushed me and I looked down to make sure they weren't stepping on Carmichael. Not my smartest move. Did they find my gun?"

"Yes, and DJ cleaned it for you. It had blood on it. It's downstairs."

"Oooh... yawning is a very bad thing. Damn that hurt. The blood was probably from the guy I shot in the throat just before that pig hit me."

"Stop talking and go to sleep. I've got you." Nick watched her sleep. He's almost lost her again... he could not imagine life without her. He now understood how one could die from a broken heart.

7:20 pm EDT,

Ferret sat at her desk in the Shack, pondering how straightforward she should be with tonight's flog. Screw it they'll have to grow up sooner or later. If they're going to live, it better be sooner. They needed to get to work.

Tonight's Flog and yes as always...
Location Unknown

Now that we've covered the Why, this morning, lets talk about what's next. The winds of change are blowing folks. You'll need to change too, or not... and pay the price. As the hippies used to say, way back in the 70's, it's time to get back to the land. Treat the earth well and she will feed you. If you persist in poisoning the ground with chemicals you will fail. Treat the earth as you would be treated. Harmony is the key. Resist those who do not. The resisting may seem inharmonious. Remember the fields are burned to purge and revitalize the soil. Some will need to be purged. Do so knowing it's part of Mother's plan. (Oh, I can hear a few of you chaffing over 'way back' I get to say it cause I was born after *that* century.) The waters are not finished yet. More land will slide in to the sea. Choose your plot with care. Listen to the wind.

The Typist

8:00 pm EDT, October 10, Lynchburg, Virginia

Lynchburg was awash with zombies. The two idiot brothers, had stopped at a bar and grill, that was open and selling moonshine! They hadn't been to Lynchburg in several years but they remembered this was where all the locals hung. Sure as shit their Uncle was there. Everyone was either passed out or rip roaring drunk. This batch of hooch seemed to have a bigger kick than normal, but it was smooth as silk. Uncle Willy said "Aunt Bess has been prayin' y'all would find the way home. *Guess God was listening.* Sit boys and have a drink. Y'all just missed the fun we had with some Mexicans that tried to come in here."

The drunk on the next stool down said "They wasn't Mexicans they said they was from Salvador."

"Was that before or after we set his hair on fire?" Those not passed out started laughing and retelling each other how they had showed those Mexicans not to come into a place where white men were drinking. The brothers proceeded to get drunk. An hour later they were drunk enough to begin passing out 'samples' of their magic dust to anyone who wanted to try it. An hour later, *the passed out* were passed around... as a late night snack. The Spyder was again left without a driver in the parking lot.

2:00 am EDT, October 11,

In the wee hours of the morning the Spyder was found by twenty-two members of a BA group. The guy who found it managed to pocket a handful of pixie dust before the the leader claimed the bike for himself. After finding the massacre in the Bar and Grill they took what hooch they could carry and marched on to Appomattox. They arrived to find the

place empty. The leader said they'd sleep
in the courthouse. It was defensible.
Since they were out of food, they were
having a grand old time drinking. The guy
who snitched the dust from Ziggy's bag
began to pass it around. The next morning
Virginia lost the battle... again. Once
more the Spyder sat abandoned with its
deadly cargo. Ziggy would have been
pleased to know he'd started the
Brotherhood of the Traveling Dust.

6:30 pm EDT, October 11,
Dancing Goats Farm
Moon Mountain, North Carolina

David woke and for a moment forgot
the Apocalypse had happened. Then he
heard gunfire and it all came rushing
back. He swung his feet out of bed and
rubbed the sleep from his face. He hadn't
slept like that since the EMP. He walked
to the hall and found the bathroom.
Running water. What a pleasure.

Downstairs people were having
breakfast. They didn't seem bothered by
whatever was going on outside. Becky was
just leaving as she passed him she said,
"Morning, there are muffins, eggs and
corned beef hash on the stove. Help
yourself." She was out the door before he
could say thank you.

Reno asked, "How did you sleep?"

"Great. I had almost forgotten what

235

a real mattress felt like. Do you have tea here?"

"Yea, in that canister. There's a few kinds that we grow here."

"You grow you're own tea?"

"About 95% of what we eat, was grown here. Including that grass fed Angus you had for dinner. Everything is naturally raised. Nick and the Lady have lots of rules but if you follow them, life here is damn good. Now, that the ass fell out of the world, we have shit like yesterday to deal with, but we have this place to come back to. We owe you a lot for saving the Lady. Not sure what Nick would have done if she died."

"It was the least I could do. I should have watched where they went. I was beat and let my guard down."

"At least one of us didn't fuck up." Carmichael had just come in.

Reno shook his head. "You didn't fuck up you moron. You got shot in the head defending her."

David added, "And you still managed to cover her and not shoot Nick. I couldn't see you but I knew someone was shooting from the ground. When he stepped in front of you, I don't know how you pulled that shot up."

"Cause I would have wounded him and he would have killed me for it! You thinking about moving here?"

Reno thought about Carmichael's answer and said, "You're probably right about that!"

David said, "I want to give it more thought. It's been a while since I had to take orders from anyone. For now I think I'm going to stay in town. I would like to be able to come here once a week for a meal and a shower if Nick will go for it."

Charlie had come in. "He'll go for it. He already said he'd set you up with a HAM radio and supplies. A meal and a shower won't make any difference."

The men had breakfast and talked about what David needed to do to make his place safer. As they were clearing up, Nick and Gianna came through the door. Charlie said, "Ma'am what are you doing up? *Nick*?"

7:30 am EDT,

"Good Morning to you too Charlie, gentlemen. Reno, any coffee left?"

"Fresh pot coming right up."

Nick helped her sit. "Okay, that was

237

ugly. I may have to sit here for a while. Carmichael come here let me see your head." Carmichael bent down so Gianna could inspect his wound. "It could have been a lot worse. Next time you're watching my back, please watch your front as well. You're out of the nest for the next few days. You take one of the beds in the back bedroom until I clear you for the loft. I find out you're up there I will ground you for a month. Do you understand?"

"Yes ma'am."

"Reno see his stuff is brought to the room for him."

"Yes ma'am."

"David are we treating you well? Is there anything you need?"

"Very well ma'am. I was just talking to Reno and Charlie about a few things I could use to make the shop more secure."

Gianna looked over at Nick. Nick said "Tell us what you need." Reno served her coffee and the men discussed how they would fortify David's place. Once they had a list of supplies, Reno gave it to DJ and told him to take the pickup with the plow and load the stuff in. Gianna called Dawn for a box of fresh veggies. Becky came in and Gianna sent her to the pantry downstairs with another list of supplies.

Gianna asked David where his home was. He said it was one of the buildings that had burned. Then she asked who owned the cottage. He said the woman had been killed by the zombies. "Okay, Nick said your place is a bit Spartan. I think we should take items from the cottage and make your place more livable. Why don't you take that antique dry sink with the zinc top from the window of your store? Reno make a list. He needs a bed, a cupboard for his food, a table for the radio, oil lamp, laundry basket and small dresser, a two top and chair and any glass water jugs they come across. Secure the cottage. It may be useful at some point to have both sides of the street covered. Oh and a small fridge he can use as an ice box. Tell DJ to pick up a block of ice while he's back there. Nick how are you going to power the radio?"

Nick was smiling at the way she had assessed David's needs and rattled them off, without having seen the place. He loved how her mind worked. "One of the small solar generators with the panel on the roof."

"Perfect. Do you think we should send four of the regulars to get this knocked out?"

"I was going to, but with the list you just made I think we'll send six."

239

"Good idea. David have you found clothing since yours burned?"

"I've found some. I need to find warmer items like a coat and hat."

"As we organize the farms in the town, we'll check the empty places for the things you need. When you come here, bring your laundry, we'll have it cleaned to take back with you."

David looked from one to the other. "I don't know how to thank you both for all of this."

Nick's expression showed the seriousness of his statement, "David you're more than paid in full... You saved Gianna's life." Nick looked at Gianna and read her pain by the set of her jaw. He stood and put his hands on the back of her chair. "Say good by wife, you've been up too long."

On the way in the house Gianna said "One good thing about my ribs is you can't toss me over your shoulder like a sack of feed."

Nick said, "No... but I can keep you locked in the bedroom with me until they're healed... which should be three or four weeks."

10:30 am EDT October 11,

240

Smokey Mountains, Tennessee

Life was slow in the compound. The uncertainty of the future was beginning to weigh on the minds of some of the residents. Frank liked to have a plan for every situation. He didn't know what the condition of the country was so he was having trouble forming a plan. This made him uneasy.

Billy, the one most likely to implode, was handling the state of the country very well. He knew from the start this was a code red, so he felt pretty good about being right. Then, he'd rediscovered his wife and her new found talents. This made their confinement a bit like a second honeymoon. He slipped back into his country boy roots, filling his days with setting snares, tanning the hides and he built a small smoker to turn the meat into jerky.

Pauline occupied her time by inventing new recipes for cooking on the wood stove, to save on the propane use. She had started to write a book – The Prepper Wife. She filled the pages with all they had done and forgotten to do and the new ways they found to do everyday tasks. She listed the amounts they used of food and cleaning items. She devoted a whole page to the wonders of Baking Soda.

Betty Lou got better, every time Billy took her out to shoot. He made her a primitive bow and she got pretty good at that too. Her husband's pride and affection made Betty Lou feel she could master anything she put her mind to. She tried her hand at making rice flour. They all told her the noodles were amazing. She made a sourdough mother so Pauline didn't use so much of their yeast for the bread. Betty Lou felt the SHTF was turning out to be not so bad after all.

Dan had a bout of depression. He knew the food would only last them so long. He figured it would be years before things even started to get better. He tried to talk to Tracy about it but every time he did they got into an argument. She hadn't spoken to him in two days. He'd been spending more and more time with Harvey and Barbra. They were teaching him a great deal on living in harmony with the earth. Something the mountain compound members had not taken into consideration when they built it.

Tracy wasn't bothered at all by the state of the world. She knitted and read when it wasn't her day to cook or clean. She thought her husband was blowing this way out of proportion and she told him so most days. She only believed half of what came to them from the radio. She knew these 'zombies' were druggies. She'd seen many of them at the shelter were she had volunteered for years. They'd be fine once they ran out of drugs.

This happened to be her day for cleaning. She wiped down the bathroom with Pauline's baking soda spray. 'This does shine up nicely' she thought 'I'll have to remember to stock up on some when things get back to normal.' She wiped down the kitchen and swept the vinyl floor. The last job was dusting under her and Dan's bed. She found his book he'd been looking for. She went to call him and remembered he went to see Harvey about some planting thing. He was becoming a pain in her butt with this back to nature kick he was on. 'Where do dust bunnies come from? It's not like they had a pet in the house.' She took the dust mop to the balcony to shake it. On the way she thought up a new stitch for the afghan she was making.

Preoccupied with the pattern in her head, she let the mop slip out of her hand. It hit the wall where Pauline had shot the two intruders, and bounced outside the wall. "Damnation!" The men had gone deer hunting. Pauline and Betty Lou were in the back practicing with that silly bow. 'Like Betty Lou could kill anyone with that thing!' She went down the stairs to the garage. Tracy opened the gate and walked around to get the wayward dust mop. She retrieved it and was walking back when she thought of a way to work the new stitch into a sweater she'd started. She missed her head scarf slipping free of her back pocket where she had tucked it. The breeze caught it.

243

It wound up tangled in a shrub next to the gate. Back inside she bolted the gate then went into the garage. Still thinking about her knitting she pushed the button to close the door. It was dark inside after the bright Autumn sunlight. A pair of zombies came from around the front of the truck, blocking her path to the stairs. She held them off with the dust mop as she backed up to the bay door. She hit the button.

Betty Lou and Pauline heard her screams and ran for the garage. They rounded the corner of the building... Betty Lou put an arrow through the eye of one. Pauline took the other one down with her rifle. Tracy was dead before they had gotten half way to the garage. One zombie had yanked the dust mop from her hand as the second one ripped out her throat. Pauline circled the truck and found a child zombie. She killed it. Frank and Billy had returned empty handed. They were just outside the wall when they heard Tracy's screams but couldn't get in the bolted gate. They listened helplessly as Pauline and Betty Lou killed the zombies.

Dan was in the greenhouse with Harvey and Barb listening to jazz, something they'd introduced him to. They never heard Pauline's rifle. Dan and Billy dragged the zombies to the end of the drive while Pauline and Betty wrapped Tracy in a sheet. They couldn't let Dan

see her like this. They washed her face
after the the men put her in the back of
the pickup. The women got buckets of
water and washed the blood off the garage
floor while Frank and Billy dug a grave
in the back yard.

Dan wandered back two hours later.
He pushed the intercom button. He had
rigged it up to a car battery. "Hey open
up. What till you see all the food Harv
and Barb sent over. Think Tracy's scarf
blew over the wall. It's out here in a
bush in the drive." The four of them met
him at the gate. The girls took the box
of food in, while Frank and Billy told
Dan about his wife. In the kitchen the
women wept for death of their friend.
Between sobs Pauline asked, "Why in the
world did she go outside without a gun?"

1:00 pm EDT October 11,
Damascus, Virginia

Cindy tried to contact the mountain
compound first but they weren't on. She
tried other channels and spoke to the
person they had been in contact with in
Roanoke, Virginia. He said things had
gotten very bad there in the last twenty-
four hours. The zombie drug had made it's
way to Lynchburg. He figured 300 people
had died from zombie attacks. Two groups
of the BA had gone zombie and attacked
each other in Annapolis. In Tennessee she
talked to a woman named Sally Anne. She
said things were getting better since the

Army had left. Food was still in short supply but the killings, they had gone down since the Army was gone. Sally Anne said she and her family were in a cabin in the mountains. It belonged to her husband's father. Sally Anne said she had been in North Carolina for a while and it was kinda the same there. Then she had to sign off because her husband was back.

Rory asked Cindy to try Frank and them one more time before she signed off. A tearful Pauline answered. Rory and Cindy were horrified by the news of Tracy's death. Pauline said Dan was taking it pretty bad. They buried her in the back and Dan had just been sitting an drinking ever since. At the Inn the mood was somber for the rest of the day. Rory said the war had reached out and taken one of them. They needed to think about other weapons like baseball bats. They had a limited supply of ammunition. Ann said they should check their security measures again and add more to the barricade. They did, but their normal jokes and laughter were missing. The deaths of strangers was bad news. But the thought of someone they knew being eaten by zombies shook them to their core.

4:00 pm EDT, October 11,
Moon Mountain, North Carolina

In town DJ and the men had located the things on Gianna's list and carried them up to the storage room David had

246

been living in. They moved the rotting
bodies to the far end of the street where
they found the remains of the cow the
zombies had eaten. They used gas to set
the pile on fire. They had siphoned all
the gas from the cars they found in town.
They topped off the tank of the
camouflaged plow pickup and parked it in
the alley behind the Hardware store. They
wheeled a dumpster in front of it for
cover. The extra gas was stored inside
the back door of the store for David.
They boarded over the front door of the
Hardware store. David's roof gave him
access to the roof next door. That shop
also had a hatch with stairs leading down
to the print shop next door to the
Hardware store. They added cross bars to
both doors inside the Print shop and one
on the roof side of the hatch. The only
place David was vulnerable was the back
door leading to the truck. DJ said if it
was breached David should torch the
containers of gas at the bottom of the
stairs. The guys found four fire
extinguishers to keep at the top of the
stairs. David said he had camp stoves for
sale in the store and a case of twenty-
four bottles of fuel for them. While they
were getting those David took a pair of
butane torches off the shelf.

DJ laughed. "One of those will light
up the gas cans if it comes to it." David
said he'd rig up a hood and vent it out
the back window of the storeroom tonight.
The men helped him fill jugs with water

from a rain barrel for the bathroom in the store.

DJ had checked out the cottage as the men carried the stuff across the street. The dormer window in the attic was perfect for a sniper. And it had pull up stairs. They boarded up the ground floor windows and put cross bars on the back door. They screwed plywood to the front door but not to the frame. One of the men found a bull horn in the sheriffs station and put it in David's new apartment.

Gianna called DJ as they were leaving the Q. She told him the photographer's studio had fabric panels he used for a backdrop. She told DJ to get them to cover the windows in David's loft. Then he wouldn't have to crawl around when someone was on the street. Once the the solar panel was installed on the roof for the generator they were finished. Reno said, "Now, you're connected to the Q, 24-7."

The guys stood back and admired their work. David said, "This was so much easier with help. It was a bitch trying to scavenge and watch for zombies at the the same time. Thanks guys. And tell Nick and Gianna thank you again."

DJ said, "Don't mention it. I should tell you, Nick doesn't let any of us use her first name. We call her the Lady.

It's just part of the Feudal system out at the farm. I don't know how the hell you stood the isolation here. You snipers are an odd bunch. Carmichael can sit in that nest for days if he has to. You two will probably get along great, now that he knows you're not going to replace him as Gianna's guardian." That got agreement and laughs from the rest of the crew. It was common knowledge how devoted Carmichael was to Gianna.

David watched them leave from the roof. At the edge of town they killed three zombies coming down the road. Sal wiped the blood off the sword he'd found in the cottage. "Reno we should get more of these."

chapter 29
forever in my heart

"Evidently Love is Apocalypse proof"

1:20 am EDT, October 12,
Dancing Goats Farm
Moon Mountain, North Carolina

Nick woke to an empty bed. Now What?
After searching the house, he found
Gianna on the roof. She was standing in
the moonlight with a glass of wine,
listening to 'Forever'. "Gianna, why are
you up here alone, in the middle of the
night, listening to sad music?"

"My son." Nick didn't speak. He
waited. "I'm looking for a shooting star
to make a wish. Nick walked up behind her
and put his arms around her. "I want to
wish, he hears the words to this and
understands. no matter what, I will
always love him. He's my child who will
always be in my heart. I'm afraid I will
never see him again. I need him to know."

Nick pointed to the tail of a
shooting star as it streaked across the
sky below Mars. "Make your wish." In a
blink it was gone. "Will you come in

now?" She shook her head yes. At the ladder he said "How the hell did you get up here with your cracked ribs and a glass of wine?"

"Very carefully."

In a slightly irritated tone Nick said, "Give me the glass and hold my hand so you don't have to bend." When she was down Nick followed and closed the hatch. Back in the bedroom he intended to yell at her for going up there. When he saw the emotional distress in her eyes it stopped him. Nick got her back in bed and held her. He wanted to reassure her, but he couldn't. He wouldn't lie to her. Nick had no idea where Forest was or how to find him. He had promised Gianna he would find Sean and look how that was working out. He would have found him, if Mother hadn't turned the electricity off.

1:20 am EDT, October 12, Smokey Mountains, Tennessee

Betty Lou got up for a glass of water. On her way back to bed she saw a flicker of a light through the living room window. She looked out the window and saw Dan was sitting on the ground by Tracy's grave with a candle. She wanted to comfort him but thought better of it. He had taken himself off after they'd buried her. People deal with death differently. She went to bed and let the man grieve for his dead wife in peace.

251

**1:20 am EDT, October 12,
Culpeper, Virginia**

Another segment of the Bad Army had
found the Spyder and they were now
encamped in the home of a certain
influential congressman. Guess that would
be *formerly* influential congressman since
he was now dead. He would be turning in
his grave, if he hadn't roasted in the
jet fuel, at the sight of these men
grinding mud into his $20,000 Persian
carpet. The congressman's staff had been
hiding behind the estate's locked gates
until the BA rammed them with a pickup.
The leader said the staff were now the
slaves of the BA, which did not sit well
with two members of the staff who were
also members of Black Lives Matter. One
of them took it upon himself to dose the
stew the staff was serving the BA, with
two packets of drugs they'd found on the
floor, that had fallen out of one of the
BA's pockets. His plan, he explained to
the others was, to kill them once they
fell asleep.

The staff thought pixie dust was a
downer man, cause a bus boy told them so.
The plan quickly changed when the pixie
dust kicked in and BA started shooting up
the mansion. Some of the staff ran and
hid in the woods at the back of the
garden, the rest ran for the wine cellar.
Turned out that all of the staff made it

out except the guy who had done the dosing. After eating him, the zombie BA left the now bullet riddled mansion, to snack on most of the population of Culpeper. Yes, the Spyder once again sat patiently waiting for it's next driver. There were still 1500 of Spider Cat Man's half of the original cache of 5000 packets, of Ziggy's dust, he'd driven north from the little white clapboard church in Levelcross, North Carolina. This zombie thing could go on forever at this rate.

1:20 am EDT, October 12,
Dancing Goats Farm
Moon Mountain, North Carolina

Ferret was reaching out along the HAM radio network. She was asking people to pass a message that she was looking for a family member with his wife and child. She gave the best description she had and thought they might be coming through the Appalachia Mountains. If people even think they've seen them please pass the information along and to contact her. She gave the call letters JonJon had made up and her location as Mount Airy. Alexandra had taken her aside after the meeting between the sisters about Gianna's maybe vision, and told her to search wide. They needed to find him before Sadie got it in her head to go looking for him.

The farm had a farther broadcasting

range then most of the HAMS now in operation. They had a tower hidden among the tallest pines. Brian was a genius and he'd worked with the guys over in Studio City to create the farm's communication systems. There were two satellites that had survived the EMP. When they were in range the Catsear earpiece, they had created, worked as far away as Holly Springs and Moon Mountain. The Catsear was like a Bluetooth with superpowers. The name?... guys in Studio City all had cats.

Cats were big with lots of people on the farm. Not that there weren't dogs too. Collies and Westies were the herd dogs. There were a pair of Pyrenees Mountain dogs who lived with the horses. Irish Wolf Hounds lived on the hill in the forest with Jack-in-the-Green. No one knew how many. Alexandra had her Pitbull in the Hundred Acre Wood. The German Shepherds in the Barracks appeared more wolf in size and coat than dog. The alpha female, Luna, looked like a huge silver she wolf. Gianna had insisted they be trained as a pack. She said she wanted to preserve as much of their wolf memory as possible. Three male trainers told her it couldn't be done. She found a woman from the Rose Bud reservation who proved them wrong. The only drawback was Luna was pack leader and they responded better to women. Gianna didn't see this as a draw back. While selecting the regulars, she chose ten women to form the Amazon Unit who now worked with the Luna's pack.

When Ferretfirst saw the dogs she suspected there was more than a little timber wolf in the bloodlines, since North Carolina was one of the states with no laws against it. Ferret thought, 'Not that it would have stopped Gianna if there had been one.' Gianna thought of rules more like guidelines, to be modified as she needed.

The same tower used for the Catsear, was used for the farm's cell phones and radios. It had repeaters to boost the HAM radio signals. Finished with all the contacts for the day, Ferret called Antonio and asked if she could stop by with something she was working on. He said sure, it was quiet he'd enjoy the company. She headed over wondering how many cups of coffee he'd let her have? Freddy and Charlie were on the veranda when she came through the door. She went out to say hi and let them know she was in the Q since it was their domain for this shift. "Hey guys, just stopping by to go over something I'm working on for the sisters. I called downstairs and talked to Antonio. I forgot to ask him why Tiny wasn't on."

Both men said hi. Freddy answered her question. "Tiny had a date. Tiny doesn't get too many of those so Antonio, who gets plenty of them, said he'd do a double."

Charlie asked, "What are you working on or is it more secret Amazon stuff?"

Ferret wasn't sure how much to say, she went with, "Kinda. They have me looking for someone out there. I put out the info and I just want the guys to know if they hear someone looking for 'Missy' it's code for me." Both men looked at her. "*I know*. I had to pick something as far away from my name as I could. I don't know who's out there listening, who might still want to arrest me." With many questions left unanswered, she left them to wonder just who Ferret was. Antonio made two pots of coffee over the next four hours. They drank it as Ferret showed him why she was called *Ferret*.

4:30 am EDT, October 12, Statesville, North Carolina

Back on the the 9th of October, when the street-drug-trade partners tried to return to Statesville, they were met by a mob of twelve zombies coming up West Front Street. They took a right down Island Ford Road. They were so fucking freaked, that just before Third Creek Road they flipped the car. They ended up *in* Third Creek, roof side down. Jamal's brother went through the windshield. Kevin's brother snapped his neck. Glass went everywhere as did the bag of Ziggy's dust. The morons had a jar of gas with them. It smashed and the gas leaked on

256

the bag of packets. The car sank ass first weighed down by the heavy propane tanks in the trunk.

Not all the packets got doused with the gas, just a thousand or so. The plastic compromised and the other 700 floated away. They tumbled and bounced catching on rocks and sticks. Some got eaten by fish, who were later that day eaten by people. The packets floated under Buffalo Shoals Road. A few took a right down Back Creek. A dozen-ish made it as far as east of I-77. Several hundred were found by people... yes, many morons snorted or ate the dust. The greater part of the 1400 packets dissolved their contents into the slow moving waters of the creek. Water being in great demand since, the taps stopped working, some people in the area of Wellwood Drive were drawing water from the creek. They boiled it to be safe but they didn't filter it. They were enterprising folk, they bartered it to their neighbors for food. Boiling did nothing to Ziggy's chemical cocktail. The car was only 600' from where they took the water at 5:00 am that morning. They served the neighborhood Ziggy juice for breakfast.

By now the neighborhood was dead. A roving band of teens scavenging, took jugs of dusty water and 23 packets the dead owner of the house had gathered, when he was getting the Ziggy water on

the morning of the 10th. They found a few
dozen more in the other houses that
bordered the creek. Then they jumped on
I-40 south. The last of the Ziggy's
southbound drugs, were on their way to
what was left of Charlotte.

5:30 am EDT, October 12,
Dancing Goats Farm
Moon Mountain, North Carolina

Antonio said Ferret should hang
because Tiny was coming on in half an
hour. After she filled Tiny in he make
her one of his famous omelets. Antonio
reminded Ferret of her brother who had
died in a car crash when she was eleven.
Antonio thought she was a really smart
kid and he liked her strange sense of
humor. Becky found them laughing at the
antics of the beggars outside the gate.
When they were told to move on they
thought it a good idea to moon the guard.
Only when they bent over one of them
crapped. The crapper was more surprised
than the guards and ran away trying to
pull up his pants. The others followed
the crapper when the guard told them now
he have to shoot them. Becky said, "Let's
hope that's the only shit we have to deal
with today."

Antonio said "Hey I'm making omelets
do you want one?"

"Hell yes. Ferret, he makes the best
omelets. I'll be right back, need to

watch the changing of the manor house guards."

Becky passed Tiny at the top of the stairs. When he got to the bottom he said, "There's a rumor you're making omelets?" with a big grin.

Antonio said, "You got it Tiny. I'll go get started. Ferret, meet you upstairs after you talk to Tiny."

Reno and DJ had just walked in when Antonio got to the kitchen. Freddy was saying to Reno, "Let me fill you in on last night's *crap*." When he finished the story. Reno told him his guys would have to clean it up cause it happened on their shift.

6:00 am EDT,

Ferret came in while they were arguing about it. Antonio told her, "Just grab a chair. Don't pay any attention to them." When she sat down they all stopped and looked at her. Antonio said, "She's my tutor I'm paying her with breakfast."

Reno teased her about being too small to be a guard while he made coffee. Freddy beat feet to meet Dawn for breakfast, without having settled who was going to clean up the crap. Reno's phone rang, it was Tiny. David said a group of the rogue Army was in town ripping the boards off some of the buildings and shooting the place up.

"Shit, before I've even got a cup of coffee." Reno grabbed his radio. "DJ there's fourteen rogue Army in town. Get Pepé, the Humvee and one jeep. We'll take eight beside us. Charlie, you're still up." Reno went out on the veranda and called Nick. When Nick answered Reno told him what the situation was and what he planned to do then hung up.

Nick got out of bed and started to get dressed. Gianna said "Nick *Oh no you don't*. You said let the kids run the world... just last night."

"That was last night."

"And this is the morning. What the hell changed overnight?"

"Gianna, I have to do my job."

"I thought protecting your wife was your number 1 job" She tried a new approach. "If you die who'll take care of me?"

He stopped and looked at her. She was pouting. He looked away and kept getting dressed. Then because she was waiting for an answer, "I'll have Becky get one of the sisters up here."

That really pissed her off. "You promised me two weeks and we've had nothing but interruptions." She got out of bed and took her pants off the chair. "Fuck you Lorenzini. If you're going I'm going."

That got his full attention. Now *he* was yelling, "No-you're-not! Gianna get back in bed."

"*NO*. What are you going to do tie me up? Lock me in the house? Go! I'll take my own truck."

Nick stared at her. Short of locking her in the brig and taking the key, there really was no way he could stop her. "Gianna what the hell is wrong with you? Why are you behaving this way?" She ignored him and kept getting dressed. "Gianna I am not letting you out there in your condition." She slid into her boots. Took his leather off the chair and walked around him and out the door. He texted Reno and told him to go and keep his ear on so Nick could hear what was happening. Nick caught up with her in the kitchen as she was putting her gun in her holster. Nick reached for her...

Gianna pulled away. "Don't try to stop me or I will shoot you in the foot so you can't chase me."

Nick started laughing. "Evidently you've given this some thought, on your way down the stairs. What will people say after they find out you shot your new husband?"

"I'll tell them you were being your typical asshole self and you left me no choice. I'm sure *everyone* will understand. But if they don't, I really don't give a shit. Maybe I'll shoot them too." Nick was leaning against the counter with his arms crossed laughing as Becky came to the door with the breakfast tray. Gianna opened the door and said sweetly, "Just put it on the table Becky, Thank you dear." Nick was still laughing when Becky left. "I'm glad you find me so amusing." She took a scone and started to open the door.

Nick stepped up behind her and wrapped his arms around her, knowing she couldn't fend him off with her ribs still hurting. He was pretty sure he'd be wearing the scone in a matter of seconds. He was still laughing. "Please stop. Gianna talk to me. Tell me why you're behaving like this."

After twenty seconds of silence she said, "Well, since we're dressed we should at least go to the com room and listen to what's happening *without us*."

Nick kissed her neck. "It's our first married fight."

"*No! Not now. Stop it,* you're not getting any make-up sex. I'm mad at you. Now, are you coming?"

He smiled wickedly. "*That* would be up to you."

"NO. Nicholas, we can't stand here like this all day."

"Let's go back upstairs."

"No! Not now. That ship sailed when you said you'd 'send one of the girls to take care of me' so you could go off and try to get yourself shot... *again*! Now unhand me. You may stay or go, but I'm leaving. I want to know what is happening with our men."

Nick reached around her and opened the door. On the ride over he said "Gianna, I'm not going to retire because we're married."

"No? Well then I guess I'll have to fire you."

Laughing again... "You can't, we're married. According to North Carolina Law this place is now half mine."

"Evidently, *you've* given *this* some thought, on your ride over."

Nick pulled up to the Portal. "Woman, I learned years ago, I have to think in my sleep just to keep up with you." Nick got out and went around to help her up. He held on to her and kissed her.

With an almost smile hovering on her lips, she said, "*Still mad at you.*" and pushed him away.

Inside Charlie said, "They're chasing the bastards through town. As soon as they saw the Humvee they started to run."

The three of them stood around the kitchen table listening for five minutes... when the gunfire stopped. Reno said, "We'll be back after the bonfire Boss."

Gianna thanked Charlie. then left. She was walking back when Nick caught up with her. She couldn't drive the cart with the cracked ribs. He stopped and helped her in. When they got to the house she spoke. "*Somehow*... not really sure how... but somehow, Reno, the man you've trained and served with, and have known for fifteen years, managed to clean up the mess... *without you being there*. It's a *fucking mystery*."

She stubbornly pushed herself out of the cart, emitting several yelps from the pain. Upstairs Nick helped her get out of *their* jacket, then he pulled off her boots. Gianna stood, untied the lace on her sweats, and let them slide to the floor. She put her arms around his neck, smiled and said "*Now you can have make-up sex."* and kissed him.

6:30 am EDT, October 12, Damascus, Virginia

Rory stood on the front porch with his coffee, surveying their barrier. A mist hugged the forest floor across the road. A hawk glided above the tree tops. The scene was surreal. The ugly tangle of dying trees, brambles and vicious pikes against the beauty and elegance of nature. Rory mused, 'The problem is humans. If we can survive the zombies, raiders and winter, going forward I will do my damnedest to live in harmony with nature.' The thought of zombies brought Tracy's death to mind. What would he do if he lost Cindy? He should have married her years ago. He was crazy about her. Seemed like they'd been together forever. Out loud he said, "Hell why not? Now, I need to find a ring." He'd talk to Ann maybe she would have an idea.

As if she'd heard him thinking about her, Cindy stepped out on the porch. She wrapped her arms around him and watched the hawk. After a while she said. "It's so peaceful. I wish we could live in this moment forever."

Rory held her hand tighter. In his head her words echoed and he thought, 'That's all I want babe, is you beside me forever'. Any thoughts of her not wanting to marry him vanished. He talked to Ann right after breakfast. Ann loved the idea. She pointed out people married long before the marriage license was invented. They should take the truck out and see if they could find an abandoned jewelry store. She eased his conscience with, 'If the owners ever came back he could pay them then'. They'd tell Beth and Cindy they were going on a gas run. Then she went to work removing the screws from the garage door. Rory wanted to be back before lunch. Ann was so excited about their secret mission, she almost forgot to put the gas containers in the the truck.

Beth and Cindy sat on the porch with their rifles after they pushed the section of the barricade back in place. They were ready to move it, the second they saw the truck coming up the road, and armed in case they had to shoot anyone or *thing* that might be trying to harm their mates. As they waited they discussed the design for clubs they wanted to make. While weight was one way, to go a lot could be said for a strong but lighter staff studded with some of Ann's ten penny nails. They settled on several prototypes they would try out. Beth said there was a Hickory tree in the woods just beyond their back fence. They could cut a branch and drag it in. That would give them different diameters of wood to work with. A month ago either woman would have said the thought of this after breakfast chat, would have been absurd.

Ann and Rory saw no zombies on the way into town. The first two shops they stopped at had been looted badly. Rory found one ring that had been forgotten in the case. It wasn't what he wanted for Cindy. The third shop was on a side street and had been missed. The door wasn't even locked. They called out asking if anyone was there. After a minute Rory added "We're not here to hurt you, I just want to buy a wedding ring." When no answer came they cautiously moved through the store. In the back room they found a couple they assumed were the owners. They had been killed by zombies.

Ann pulled Rory out and closed the door. She found the case with the rings and put two trays on the counter. Rory then realized he didn't know what size to get for Cindy. Ann said she had it covered. Find a size seven. Rory picked a wide gold band for Cindy and a slimmer one for himself. Then Ann pulled out a tray with diamond engagement rings. She said "I'm getting a huge one for Beth cause I couldn't afford one when we married." They selected the rings they wanted. Ann went to put the tray back and hesitated... "Let's take all of it. The owners are dead. If family ever shows up we can give it to them. If not we keep it. We don't know what kind of social structure will evolve. We may be able to barter these in the future." Rory agreed.

In ten minutes they had the contents of the cases in a bag they found behind the counter.

Back in the truck they saw four zombies coming towards them. Rory backed out of the street and paused for Ann to shoot them. On the way home they saw a group of eight or nine a few hundred yards from the Inn. Rory looked at Ann. She said go for it. Rory hit the gas and ran four of them over. Ann reached over and started blowing the horn while he tried to keep the truck on the road as he crunched over the bodies. Beth and Cindy heard the horn and came running. Beth moved the barrier while Cindy covered the truck. One zombie had managed to get in the truck bed when the truck had slowed going over the bodies. As Rory pulled the truck inside the yard, the zombie reached in the driver's window and got a hold on Rory's shoulder. Cindy said, "Fuck you, he's mine." and blew a hole through it's head.

Ann jumped out and helped Beth put the other three down. They pushed the Civic back in front of the movable barrier section. Rory wiped the blood off Cindy's face and kissed her. "Thanks babe." While Ann and Rory were screwing the garage door down Ann said, "Good thing you decided to marry her. She might have shot you otherwise."

7:30 am EDT, October 12,

268

Moon Mountain, North Carolina

Reno stood at the south end of town watching the bodies of the rogue Army as they burned. David walked up and stared too. Reno said, "This is so screwed up. Never thought I'd be hunting down my own country's military personnel. How the hell do you make that choice? Killing the people you swore to protect?"

David said, "I don't know. I've been asking myself the same question since the last batch tried to kill the Lady."

Reno hit the edge of the fire that was trying to catch the roadside weeds on fire, with the extinguisher. He shook his head. "Charlie and I talked about how shitty it was to have to shoot the zombies we recognize. People we'd know from town. I thought that was bad but this feels some how worse."

David said "I can't understand how you hit a woman in the head with a rifle cause you want her truck. How the hell did they get in the Army in the first place? Didn't they screen for this shit?"

Reno said, "I don't think there were any apocalypse questions during the interview."

"Listen I salvaged two pairs of their pants before we put them on the pile. They're dirty but sound. Can you

269

take them back with you to be cleaned?
They're rather rank."

Reno lightened their mood by asking,
"The bodies or the pants?"

As David started to laugh Sal came
up. "Reno, DJ said to tell you, we're all
tightened up. Ready when you are. Oh, I
found two more swords."

Reno said, "Tell him I'm on my way."
The fire had just about burned itself
out. They started walking back. Reno had
seen the look on David's face at Sal's
find. "Sal found a sword and it worked so
well he wants more of us to have them for
killing zombies to save on ammo."

"The hand to hand would be more
dangerous but he's right about the ammo.
I had a better supply than most because I
sold it in the shop, but I'm counting
every bullet and shell. Unless Nick has a
bunker the size of NORAD filled with
ammo, you'll run out at some point too."

Reno was laughing cause Nick would love
one that size. "Not as big as that, but
we do make some of our ammo. Part of our
training when we were accepted to the
farm, was to master bullet and shell
making. We have four explosive experts."

Charlie told me, more were rejected
than accepted. How did they come up with
the number they have?"

"Nick said he figured how many he'd need to protect the property. Then added another twenty. Then Gianna did the numbers on what she'd need in stored and produced food to feed them each for five years. Then she told him to add another twenty on top of his extra twenty.

Nick said she told him 'what's a few more thousand pounds of food if it keeps you happy while you keep us safe.'

"Do you think they'll take on more like me?"

"She's made it clear no more civilians but skilled military will be considered. Maybe we'll pick up a few to station here in town in the cottage. That's most likely what she had in mind when she told us to secure it. She's always thinking ten steps ahead. Okay, we're out of here. Hope the rest of your day is quiet."

11:00 am EDT,

Mendez was feeling a little restless. He asked Charlie if he could go out on patrol? Charlie said Gabe could use a wing man on his run. He was delivering boxes of fliers to the borders they had set up. When they got to the first stop, Gabe got out and set a stack on the side of the road then got back in the jeep. Mendez asked, "What the hell is

271

that? How the hell does she think these are going to get to people?"

Gabe pulled a U turn. He was grinning when he answered. "You haven't been to the Gypsy Camp yet have you? Have you met the Airy-Fairys? There's shit that happens there on the farm you won't be able to wrap your FBI brain around. If the Lady says they'll get to where they need to go, they will." Gabe stopped the jeep "Turn around." Mendez turned to see a dust devil hovering over the pile of fliers. The pages were lifting and dancing around the cone. As he watched in disbelief, the dust devil moved on taking the fliers with it. Mendez turned to Gabe. Gabe said "Save it. I know you're going to say it was a fluke or a coincidence. You can tell me what you think after the same thing happens at the next two stops."

Gabe drove on. Mendez was dumbstruck when a new dust devil appeared at the next two stops. Gabe stole a glance as they drove back to the farm. At gates he said, "Mendez, there is so much you don't know about what goes on at the farm. When you're ready to learn, ask that little redhead you've been dating, to bring you to the circle one night. Before you ask... I'm engaged to her sister."

chapter 30
the Amazons

*"Intelligent
Bewitching
& Lethal"*

**1:30 pm EDT, October 12,
Dancing Goats Farm
Moon Mountain, North Carolina**

Lizzy was in the command room going over the report on the morning's events in Moon Mountain. Antonio had come back on in the com room at 1:00 pm, after catching five hours sleep. He liked working the day schedule. He had plans most nights and didn't want to have to schedule his dates to the daytime. Lizzy was halfway through the report when Antonio said, "Lizzy look at this." He'd had the headset on listening to the conversation at the gate. He switched it so Lizzy could hear.

"Lizzy said "Fuck... Let's not jump to conclusions Antonio.", as she dialed Gianna. "Mom, am I on speaker?"

"No honey, Nick's in the shower what's up?"

"There is a beautiful woman at the gate. She's demanding to see Nick. She has two children with her... they look about ten. She's arguing with Reno. OH dear ahmmmmm she just said Nick would want to see them. Their names are Rosie and Nicky Lorenzini. And mom she's wearing a wedding ring."

Gianna exhaled loudly. "I suppose shooting her is out of the question with the children there. Let her stay out there. Tell her Nick is out on the back property and you've sent someone to fetch him. I'll call you back he's just turned the shower off." Nick came in to the bedroom wearing a towel while drying his hair with a smaller one. Gianna lit a cigarette and waited while she considered the possible answers as to whom this woman was. She thought' If she's his wife I *will* have to shoot her and maybe him.' Then she said, "Nicholas, tell me about your past... past as in say eleven years ago..."

Her tone caused Nick to stop drying his hair. She had her Amazon face on. 'What had prompted this line of inquiry?' "Why?"

"Is there something you'd like to tell me that may have *slipped* your mind?"

Nick studied her face and demeanor. She was dangerously jealous about something. He was curious to see where this was going. "No Gianna. *Why?*"

"Because there is a woman at the gate demanding to speak to you. She has two children with her. She says their name is Lorenzini."

A wicked smile spread across Nick's face. He wondered how long before she started throwing things. He said "I love your jealousy. You very beautiful when you're jealous... and angry."

Gianna was smiling but her voice wasn't. "*Nicholas.*"

He walked across the room and took her face in his hands. "You know I love you, we're going to have to move my things out of the bedroom at the Q... and we'll need the room across the hall for Rosie and Nicky."

"Keep fucking with me Nickclas and I will hurt you."

Nick took his phone off the bed table, watching Gianna's expression as he spoke, "Reno, take the woman and the children at the gate to the living room. Have her wait for me there. Reno, tell her nothing." Whatever Reno's response was, Nick never heard it. Gianna snatched the phone and sent it flying through the bedroom door. Nick heard the phone shatter as it hit the banister.

Ann asked Rory when he was going to propose. He said, "I really just wanted to go in the house now and ask her."

Ann thought that was a fine idea. She'd stash the bag of jewelry in the attic and keep Beth busy upstairs. On the way back to the house Ann started laughing. She said, "Rory... we never did get any gas." They came in the kitchen door laughing. Beth said they must have been getting high on the gas fumes. That made them laugh even harder.

Ann pulled Beth into the hall and whispered "Come with me." Upstairs inside their bedroom Beth asked what was going on. Ann took her hand and slipped the three carat diamond on her finger. Beth got tears in her eyes, Ann kissed her. "Sorry you had to wait so long." They sat on the bed while told Beth what they had really been doing in town. Ann asked if she loved the ring cause if she didn't there were more to choose from. She showed Beth the bag from the jewelry store. Beth wanted the ring Ann had picked out, she didn't need to see the rest. Out in the hall, Ann pulled the stairs to the attic down.

Both women were in the attic when they heard Rory shouting, "She loves me! She said Yes!" Rory was twirling Cindy

around the kitchen when they got there.
Beth asked, "When should we have the
ceremony?"

Cindy said, "Today!"

Beth asked, "Do we have time for me
to make a cake?"

Rory said, "That would be really
sweet Beth. Cindy, you find what you want
to wear. I'll go pick you flowers."

Ann arranged the sitting room and
found what she thought was the perfect
music. She sparked up the generator and
plugged in the CD player. Beth put a cake
in the oven, got their best Champagne out
of the wine closet in the basement, and
made a tray of appetizers. When Ann was
pleased with her setup she returned to
the kitchen. Rory had returned. Rory had
come in with way too many flowers for one
bouquet. Ann sent Beth up to get dressed
and too help Cindy. Ann got matching
vases and put together a pair of
arrangements for the sitting room. Then
she sent Rory to change while she made
the bouquet.

Beth found Cindy sitting on the
floor in a pile of clothes. Cindy said,
"I packed for the apocalypse not for my
wedding day."

Beth picked up the pile and tossed
it on the bed in the next room. "Come

with me, I have what you need." In the back of her closet shelf Beth found the box she was hunting. She opened it and lifted out a strapless, beaded bodice, bell skirt wedding gown. "It's what I married Ann in. I think it will fit you." They fussed with the dress, Cindy's hair, then her makeup. When Beth was finished, Cindy looked like she'd stepped off a photo shoot.

Luckily, Ann was paying attention to the cake and pulled it out when it was done. Rory came in dressed in black jeans and a white shirt. Ann looked at him and said "There's a man's black jacket in the front hall closet. One of the guests left it." Rory put it on and Ann pinned a flower on the lapel. "You look damn handsome. I'm just going to dust the cake with powdered sugar then get dressed. Open that bottle and start drinking while I find out what my wife has done with your bride."

At 1:32 Ann returned and said, "Ready?" Grinning, Rory shook his head yes. Ann started the music. Beth came down the stairs and took her place next to Ann. As Cindy came into view. Rory held his breath when he saw her. Cindy took his hand as she handed her bouquet to Beth.

Rory said "I just want to live in this moment with you."

Cindy said, "This is our moment till the end of time." Rory put the ring on her hand and she his.

1:34 pm EDT, October 12,
Dancing Goats Farm
Moon Mountain, North Carolina

Gianna's hands came up... Nick caught her by the wrists... he pushed her back on the bed, taking care to keep those wicked nails away from his now naked person. He brought his face down to hers, "Gianna, if you don't stop kicking I will lay on you cracked ribs or not."

"She better be your sister or I will shoot her... and then you for tormenting me."

Nick put his face next to hers and said, "She's my younger sister Rose. She would never marry the guy that's why the twins have the Lorenzini name. Can I let your hands go now and hope you don't use those nails on my all too exposed flesh?"

"I wouldn't count on it."

Nick knew why she was still pissed. He'd teased her too long and he never told her he had a sister. "Babe we can't be fighting... we already made up. I really do love that you're so possessive of me but she's my sister. I don't even like her. Haven't spoken to her in eleven years. She lets the nanny bring the kids

279

to see me three times a year."

"But why did you never mention her? Or the children?"

"For the same reason you don't talk about Forest. It was on my list to tell you now that you're my wife... but we've been a little busy lately."

"You told me I knew all your secrets."

"Rose is not a secret, she a fucking curse on my life. A first class bitch."

"Nicholas you know I hate when men refer to women as dogs."

"Gianna, my sister *is* a bitch. I'm sure she's down there raising hell and making demands. Get dressed and you can see for yourself."

Nick opened the back door of the farmhouse. They could hear Rose, "You tell Nick I've been waiting long enough. He's to stop this childish game. My children need to be fed and a place to sleep. We've been traveling for over a day."

Nick shrugged at Gianna. "I told you." Nick saw the look on Gianna's face and said, "I think it's time for her to meet the Amazon Queen. I've been waiting for this for forty-eight years. She's all yours."

Gianna walked through the kitchen, the heels of her boots on the old wood floors, resonated ominously through the rooms. In the living room she put her hand on Reno's chest pushing him back as she stepped between him and the sister. "Thank you Reno, I'll deal with this intrusion." Gianna looked Rose in the eye. In what was referred to as her Connectcunt voice, she said, "If you're so concerned about your children's welfare, you should have taken better care of them. You come to my gate begging then I arrive to find you abusing my men? Children, would you like to go see your Uncle Nick? Lizzy take the children to see their Uncle."

"Yes ma'am."

Rose says, "I demand to see Nick."

Gianna raises an eyebrow. "You are in no position to demand *anything*. I can see Nicholas got all the breeding in the family. What is it you want from Nicholas?... Food? Shelter? Protection?Where do you suppose he's going to obtain these things you're demanding? Everything here... is mine. I don't take in beggars."

"I'm not a beggar! I'm his sister!"

"I know who you are and what you

281

are... you're a rude, penniless beggar. You're here at my door demanding food and shelter because you were either too *stupid* and/or *lazy* to provide these things for yourself and your children. I have zero tolerance for stupid people and I shoot the lazy ones."

Rose's face began to turn red with rage. Her fists were clenched. She said, "You bitch, get me Nick NOW!"

"NO. For the record, You're the bitch. I'm a Cunt and you'll watch how you speak to me or I'll have my men toss your sorry worthless ass out the gate. I know for a fact that Nicholas... dislikes you intensely. He's refused to speak to you for eleven years. Please explain to me why you think he would want to speak to you now?... Don't... say for the twin's sake, because then I *will* fucking shoot you. Reno hand me your sidearm. I just want it ready in the event this bitch turns out to be one of those despicable parasitical twats who survives off her children. Reno, please ask Nick if he will join us, I have a question for him."

Smirking because he knows Nick is standing in the kitchen listening, Reno answered, "Yes ma'am."

` Nick walked through the kitchen trying to wipe the grin off his face. Gianna was in rare form even for her. He stopped just short of Rose's line of vision. "Gianna, you had a question?" "I've met you sister and I find her lacking. No redeeming qualities at all. I suggest we shoot her, then you may keep the children. Opinion?"

Nick stepped into the room. "I don't believe you two have been formally introduced. Gianna, Rose Lorenzini, my sister. Rose, Gianna Lorenzini, my wife... Gianna, I believe the children like her." Rose sat there with her mouth open. Utter shock would be an understatement.

Gianna continued, "That is unfortunate. Reno take your gun back. Nick, I assume that means you don't want me to shoot her?"

"No, not yet... maybe later if she can't learn how to behave."

"Very well. Reno get housekeeping here. Have them box up the items in the bedroom and take them to the house. Make sure the linens are fresh on the beds for the children. Call Simon, have him send over food for short people. Is Becky here?"

From the kitchen. "Yes ma'am."

"Please see that Nick's sister is fed. Oh... Carmichael."

Becky says, "Ma'am I can bunk in the barracks until this is sorted out."

Gianna looks at Nick. "Perhaps the children would like to stay with their Uncle?" Nick narrowed his eyes at Gianna. His face said NO. A pair of ten year olds running around the manor was not conducive to continuing their Honeymoon activities.

Amber said, "They can stay with us. Angelena might enjoy the company."

"Thank you Amber. Nick?"

"I think we should let the children decide. Lizzy took them to the Hall to feed them and then to see the animals."

"Reno, hold off on the room Carmichael's in, but do everything else."

"Oh... Amber is there a spare set of bunk beds?"

"Yes."

"Problem solved. Amber please see they get put in the room Rosie will be staying in. That way if they want to stay here they'll be in the room with their mother." Gianna looked at Rose. "You, will stay here. You will mind your manners. When the room, is ready Becky will show you where it is. You have a bathroom in the room where you're

staying. You may sit on the veranda. Do
not leave the building. One rude word to
our people and you will be bunking with
Hansel and Gretel. Becky, eyes on her
when she's not in her room. Becky, show
her around the kitchen. If she leaves or
tries to go anywhere but her room and
this floor put her in restraints and call
me. Any questions?"

Rose sneers at Gianna. "Aren't
Hansel and Gretel those children from a
story book?"

"They were vandals and murderers who
ended up in a cell where they belonged."
Gianna looked to Nick. "Did I forget
anything?"

"Not a thing."

Outside Gianna asked Amber, "How
many of you were hiding in the kitchen?"

Amber said, "A bunch. Auntie you
were fucking great. I could have sold
tickets to that performance."

Nick asked, "Why did no one react
when she said she was my sister?"

Gianna said, "Oh, I texted Lizzy
cause I thought she might shoot her
before we got there. What do you want to
do with her?"

"I don't know. She is exactly the

type of person we would never let in here. I don't think she'd go and leave the twins. I don't think she will change. I do know she's scared of my wicked wife."

Gianna grinned. "This is a switch... for years I've been turning you loose on people, this time you turned me loose."

Nick was laughing as he helped Gianna into the cart. "You have no idea how much I enjoyed that. She should be okay for at least twenty-four hours. We'll decide after she screws up. I tried to find out what happened at the house in Asheville after the EMP but came up empty. I'm grateful the twins are here and safe. Do you want me to take you upstairs?"

"No, I'll be okay a bit longer. I want to go to the Hall and meet my new niece and nephew."

Nick and Gianna found the twins eating ice cream sundays. He introduced them to their new Aunt. Amber came in with Angelena. After hearing Nick was the twins' Uncle she said, "NO, he's *my* Uncle Nicky."

Gianna said, "Angelena, what have we talked about sharing? You have to share him, he's their Uncle too. In fact he was their uncle first. They're older than you."

Pouting Angelena put her hands on her hips and said "*Okay*... fine."

Nick asked if Rosie and Nicky wanted to stay and play or if they wanted to go back to their mother. They chose to stay and explore the farm. Nick knew Gianna had been too active and insisted he take her home. Before they left, Rosie asked who lived in the big house. Nick told her he and Gianna did. Rosie tilted her head and said, "So you're the boss here not mommy?" Nick told her yes. Rosie and Nicky said in unison, "Good!" As they were walking away, Rosie turned and said, "Uncle Nick, I like her, maybe a lot."

On the way back Nick said "Sorry it wasn't a better endorsement. They'll warm up as they get to know you."

Gianna said, "She's older?" Nick nodded yes. "I'd rather have her assessment of me. Shows she's thinking, holding back judgment until she has more data. Smart girl. I can't believe how much they look like you. *I could shoot her*. People would believe they're yours... just a thought." Gianna snatched the Excedrin off the counter as she went by.

She was getting into bed gingerly when Nick got there. He put a glass of water on the bed table and helped her. "Don't take those with wine. I brought

you this. You were up too long. No more
out of bed for you today." Nick got in
beside her. Gianna, are you ready to tell
me what this morning was about?"

Gianna thought about his question.
"Why did you try to break up the team? I
think I've proven myself out there. You
were going to run off to a new adventure
without me. The rifle butt in the head
was a bit dicey, but we *were* ambushed by
fourteen men. And I did manage to get
myself out of the way so David could take
him down. It's no reason to ground me."

"Gianna, it's *not* an adventure!"

She scoffed. "Save that bullshit for
someone who'll believe it. If it wasn't
an adventure, you wouldn't have done it
for twenty-six years. Isn't that why you
took my offer to build this place with
me? So you could continue to be a badass?
You think simply because I'm a woman I
don't get the rush from putting a bad guy
down?"

"Gianna, I don't want you hurt
again."

"Oh, and I should be fine with you
getting hurt? I don't trust anyone to
watch your back like I would. Nicholas,
every moment spent with you is a gift
neither of us thought we would ever have.
I want to be right here with you,
wherever here is, what ever shit storm

comes our way."

"Woman... what am I going to do with you?

"Keep me with you. Didn't you bother to contemplate the ramifications of your walking up my stairs?..."

Nick laughed, "No. As I recall, I was very drunk."

"Did you think I was going to fall into your arms and become the happy housewife, with dinner on the table at six?... What are you smiling about?" "Just thinking of you serving dinner at six in a cute apron."

"I can tell by the look in your eyes this fantasy has me wearing nothing *but* the apron. Stop it. You're not going to sex me out of finishing this conversation.

"If I surrender... will serve me dinner in just the apron?"

7:30 pm EDT,

Rose had tried to sleep after she had showered. She couldn't. The conversation with Gianna and the realization that Nick was married to *that* woman kept running around in her head. The investigator she'd hired to get information on Nick was a fuck up. His

289

report said Nick lived on a farm with a bunch of nasty bikers and some farmer women. The bikers didn't act like the drunks described in the report. The report also said the place was a rental. The title came back to a older woman who lived in a small town sixty miles away. That bitch didn't look like a farmer, not with those nails. It said nothing about Nick being married! How dare that bitch humiliate her like that in front of the help! That bastard Nick let her. He was enjoying it. She would make him pay.

This screwed up her plans. She had intended to find Nick so she and the children could live with him. He'd protect and provide for them, unless something better came along. She wasn't going to be held prisoner in this... this *farmhouse*. That servant girl, what was her name, Becky, was tolerable and not very smart. There had to be more to this place. Where was this hall? Her children were probably eating off paper plates with plastic forks, in some moose lodge with drunk Vets. The servants had moved items from this room to the house... That was it. She'd find the house the bitch had talked about and get Nick alone. She'd make him see she needed more for the children's sake. He'd never say no when the twins were involved.

Becky brought Rose a dinner tray to her room at 6:00 pm. Rose had to admit at least the food was quite edible. Rose

fell asleep after her meal. She woke an
hour later. She turned on the light. 'How
did this place have running water and
electricity?' She had to get out of here
and find Nick. She took the knife from
her dinner tray and tucked it in her
waistband. She picked up the tray and
carried it down to the kitchen. The
downstairs was very quiet. Rose walked
into the kitchen. She was startled to
find the servant girl there. Rose said "I
didn't want the smell of old food in the
room while I was trying to sleep." Then
she threw the tray at Becky. Becky
deflected the tray and grabbed Rose by
her hair and slammed her to the floor.
Rose pulled the knife out and tried to
slash Becky's leg. Becky caught her wrist
and twisted it until Rose released the
knife.

Reno came in as Becky flipped Rose
on her front and sat on her. Reno said,
"Is there going to be jello involved in
this?"

Becky laughed as she called Gianna.
"Ma'am, there's been a small altercation.
I may have been a bit rough. Yes ma'am.
I'm sitting on her in the kitchen. Yes,
on the floor. Reno just walked in." Becky
handed the phone to Reno. "The Lady would
like a word."

Reno took the phone and listened,
all he said was, "Yes ma'am, understood."
He handed the phone back to Becky and

left.

Gianna said, "Becky when Reno has the guard in the yard push her out the front door. I'll be there shortly." Then she hung up.

Two minutes later Reno stuck his head in the door and said, "All ready."

Becky pulled Rose up, marched her to the door and said, "Go." Rose found when she had gotten out of the house there were twenty-five armed vanguard circling the perimeter of the yard. She began screaming, swearing and slinging empty threats at the vanguard who ignored her. Rose call Gianna every filthy, nasty thing she could think of. The vanguard did not respond to her threats. Several did think they should shoot her for the things she was saying about the Lady.

Gianna called Theo. "Theo find the Amazons. Have them in the Q kitchen *Now*," and hung up. Gianna rolled over and looked at Nick leaning back on the pillows. Damn! "Sorry darling but we're going to have to pause this, your sister is causing a problem. Don't move, I'll be back shortly." Gianna hated leaving him but this had to be handled. She headed for the door.

Nick yelled "You're going out naked *again*!" Gianna snatched a silk nightgown off the bench at the end of the bed and slid into it on her way down the stairs.

Outside Alexandra slowed when she saw her Aunt coming out her front door. Gianna explained the situation on the way to the Q. Gianna walked through the farmhouse with the sisters falling in behind her as they arrived. On the veranda Gianna said, "To my left and right." Violet, Sadie and Lizzy went right. Alexandra, Amber and Dawn went left. Gianna stepped aside, to the women behind her, "A Circle ladies." The ten Amazons and their wolf/shepherds filed down the stairs and formed a wide circle around Rose who was standing in the center of the yard, still hurling insults and empty promises now exclusively at Gianna. As the last Amazon cleared the steps Nick came charging through the house onto the veranda wearing nothing but his jeans. Gianna put both hands on his chest and tried to back him up, he wouldn't budge. "I thought I asked you not to move. This is women's work darling, you have to go." She turned to Reno standing next to the door. "Reno you and the men may go now. We ladies have it under control." Reno ran down the steps and signaled to the men to return to the barn.

Nick said, "Your departure was rather abrupt... you left without kissing your husband." Nick pulled her to him and took what he came for... then he released Gianna and left to the sounds of the

Amazons cheering and whistling. Nick
didn't leave leave... he went down to the
com room to watch the show. Carmichael
was almost pushed out of the hay door as
other members of the guard squeezed in to
watch. Below, the barn had gone dark so
the others could spy from the shadows.

Gianna walked down the steps
signaling the sisters to follow.
Alexandra, never without her bow, shot an
arrow in the ground a few inches from
Rose's feet. Gianna said, "Rosie I hear
you've been a nasty twat tonight. My
Amazons and my daughters are here to help
me teach you what happens when you
disobey my orders." The sisters found
their places around the circle. "These
are my Amazons, you stupid stupid woman.
I'm sure in your arrogance you thought
Becky was a serving girl didn't you?...
Not only is she one of my Amazons, she is
also a lieutenant in my vanguard... the
elite of the elite who protect this
place. You thought you could overcome her
with a serving tray? Evidently Nicholas
got not only the breeding but the brains
too." Gianna walked slowly toward Rose.
She circled behind her... she took a
handful of Rose's hair... Gianna bent her
head backwards till Rose thought her neck
would snap. She didn't resist, the
Amazons were armed with fierce looking
knives. The one with the bow was glaring
at her. Gianna said in Rose's ear, "When
I'm in bed with my magnificent husband, I
become quite violent when called away

from him." Gianna released Rose shoving her to her knees. Standing over her, Gianna continued. "In the past week I've been shot in the thigh, smashed in the head with a rifle butt and took two 45 bullets in my vest that cracking two of my ribs. As one might imagine, Nicholas is most concerned, as you just saw, that I don't further injure myself this evening." Gianna stepped back four paces. "Luna come." The leader of the pack came to Gianna's side. "Luna hold." With Rose on her knees the huge dog was as tall as she was. Luna bared her teeth and growled inches from Rose's face. Gianna said, "If you move, she will rip your throat out." Gianna started to walk away.

Rose said, "You can't do this! Nick won't let you." Luna growled again.

Gianna laughed a very wicked laugh that echoed across the yard. Over her shoulder she said, "If I know my husband, he's watching the show from the com room. Evidently he has no desire to halt your punishment. " When she reached the edge of the circle Gianna said, "Divina, Luna is yours." Divina gave a high pitched whistle and Luna returned to her mistress' side. Gianna said, "Amber would you like to teach the unruly twat that it's rude to say nasty things about your Aunt?" Amber stepped into the circle and took the whip off her hip and began snapping it within inches of Rose as she circled her. Each time the whip connected with the ground Rose jerked away. Gianna said, "Violet it's yours. When you're done she's to sleep with H&G." Then she walked up the steps in search of her husband. Nick met her at the top of the stairs. Gianna took his hand as she walked by. "I believe we were in the middle of something extremely delightful..." On the walk to the manor house Gianna asked, "What took you so long?"

"We *were* in the middle of something delightful... I couldn't get my jeans zipped without injuring myself. That would have upset *both* of us."

In the barn the vanguard watched. They admired Amber's skill to be able to come so close to Rose's flesh and not connect. One of them wondered if the Amazons would kill Rose. Gabe said, "No. It's not about physical damage. This is physiological not physiological. She's useless as she is. They'll break her and rebuild her into a better human being. If she's an inherently bad human they won't be able to rebuild her. I don't know what they would do with her then. Don't know of the circle not working." The men watched as the circle of Amazons closed in on Rose. Gabe said, "They'll strip her now and take her to the clearing in the woods behind the Gypsy Camp." The Amazons closed ranks as they began to move forward toward the portal. They left Rose's clothing behind in tatters on the ground.

One of the men asked Gabe, "How the hell do you know this shit?"

"My fiance, Devon, is training to be one of the Amazons."

chapter 31
country boys can survive

"Moon Mountain Country Boys,
also have crazy mad skills"

11:30 pm EDT, October 12,
Moon Mountain, North Carolina

David heard the sounds of people in the street outside his loft. He lifted one of the window flaps he'd cut in the photographer's screen. Below there were four men, with a cart being drawn by a donkey. The cart was a perfect example of *country boy ingenuity*. The frame looked to be the wheels and axles from an ATV. They'd added bigger tires to give it height. The bed was a collection of salvaged planks. Two tin kerosene lamps hung off each side from modified shelf brackets. The bed held items the men had scavenged from around town. David recognized two of the men. The other two wore hats that cast their face in shadow. They were standing in front of the Hardware store talking. David went quietly down the stairs to better hear them.

Neil was talking. "I have no idea

where he would have gone. I mean after his house burned, this was the only place he had."

One of the ones David couldn't see said "We don't want to break in before we know if he's dead or alive."

The other one David recognized, Randy said, "If he's gone then I guess it'd be okay. Let's wait and check with a few people. Find out if anyone has seen him." The others agreed with him.

Then Neil said, "OK, but I still need to find parts for my hand pump. My family will need water in a day, two at the most. I've got to find a drive coupling. All I can find at the house are 1 1/4" and I need a 2". Let's keep looking. Maybe there's one we missed at the feed store."

The men started to walk away. David banged on the door and yelled, "That you Neil, Randy?"

"Holy Shit! That you David? Wow so glad you're alive."

David said, "Go around to the back of the building. There's a door past the dumpster. I'll meet you there." David ran up the stairs and called the Q. He told Tiny he was letting people in the store he knew. If Tiny didn't hear from him in a half hour, then David was in trouble.

David threw a tarp over the containers of gas, and opened the door. "Come on in go through to the store. Here, take this lantern." He handed Neil the rechargeable Lantern. Inside the store David said let's get that part you need.

Neil found it in two minutes. "David I can't really pay you. Are you even still taking cash?"

David said, "Don't worry about it. You need to have water for Lisa and the kids. Next time you come to town bring me a couple of jugs of water. If I'm not here put them outside the back door."

Randy said, "David, these are Sandy's brothers Casey and Walter. They're out at the farm with us since the lights went out. How are you doing here? Do you have food? We might be able to bring you something if you don't."

The men were all leaning on the counter in the store. David said, "I'm fine. It was a little rough till I connected with the folks out at the Q farm."

Neil said, "You mean the Bikers? Why would you even talk to them?"

David started laughing. "They're not really Bikers. Yes, they have a few bikes but they're all retired Vets."

Randy cut in, "I heard they've been helping out people in need and they're the ones who took out the Thackers."

Neil jumped on that statement. "That's bullshit. Don't believe the rumors Randy. Nobody has a tank."

David said, "Hold on all of you. Yes, they are helping organize the people still here. Yes, they did flatten the Thackers. They are helping to protect the town. They helped me with a band of rogue soldiers right outside my store. They came to bring me food and water and the Army bastards ambushed their sniper and the woman with the long silver hair, you've seen selling at the Farmers Market. Found out she's married to the tall intimidating one, Nick. Afterwards, they brought me to the farmhouse. They have solar! I had a hot shower and the best steak I've ever eaten. I'm their eyes in town now. They set me up with a HAM radio. I called them this morning when a second band of rogue Army came through wanting to burn the town. Reno was here in fifteen minutes. You should have seen those assholes run when they saw that Humvee rolling into town. They're really good people."

The four men looked at David with astonishment. Then Randy's youngest brother-in-law said, "Think I could get a ride in the Humvee?"

Before David could answer, Tiny's voice came through the radio up in the loft. "David are you okay? David come in."

"Shit I'll be right back." David ran upstairs. When he'd finished telling Tiny he was fine, he'd just got to talking, David turned to find they had followed him upstairs. He said, "Not as nice as my house was, but Nick sent seven guys to help me get this stuff up here and set it up."

Randy asked, "So how big is this farm? From the road it looks like eight to ten acres."

Neil said, "Lisa told me the tax records say the place is a thousand and twenty acres. You remember she use to work in the tax office here in town."

"Well I don't know about that. I only saw the front ten acres. I have no idea if there's more to it." The conversation was getting too personal in regard to the farm so David said, "Good to see you all and to know you're safe. Stop by when you're in town next time." The men took the hint and traipsed down the stairs.

Outside the door Rory took a hard look at the truck. "Hey David where did this come from? It looks like the one the Smith brothers had."

David said, "It was theirs, until they attacked the farm. Smith and a bunch of idiots tried to ram their gate with it. Reno said they killed all of the attackers. They tuned it up and painted it. Nick said to park it here so I have a getaway vehicle if I'm overrun. Mostly it's here, so I can ride out to the farm for a shower and a meal once a week."

The younger boy one piped up again. "I'd work for them for a hot shower once a week and a steak!"

"Sorry kid. To the best of my knowledge they only hire ex-military. You guys should stop by and talk to them during the day and speak with Reno or Charlie about how they are trying to make the town safe." David locked and bolted the door after them and went up on the roof to see if they made it safely out of town. He could hear them talking as they made their way around the building.

Neil, "That was real nice of him to give me the piece. Can you believe what he told us?"

Randy, "Well I can't see why he'd lie. We really have no facts on the people at the farm, just gossip."

Neil, "I don't think he's lying. I mean wow, who knew we had such cool people looking out for the town. After I

get the pump fixed we should go over
there tomorrow." Then they were too far
down the street to hear the rest. After
they were out of sight Tiny'd said to
call him when the guys had gone just to
be safe. David asked Tiny to pass along
the guys' names and that he'd told them
to stop by to hear about the plan. David
signed off feeling the stirring hope for
Moon Mountain's future.

6:30 am EDT, October 13,
Smokey Mountains, Tennessee

Betty Lou was on breakfast this
morning. She was making biscuits and
gravy. She thought the house was somehow
quieter without Tracy. Which was silly
since Tracy had never talked too much.
Maybe it's everyone else who was quieter.
Billy came in the kitchen and put his
arms around her. "Betty Lou, I don't know
what I'd do if I lost ya."

Frank came in as Billy was kissing
Betty Lou on the neck making her giggle.
"That's what we need, more laughter round
here. Good Morning you two lovebirds."
Everyone had noticed the change in Billy
over the last week. They were real
pleased in the new way Billy treated his
wife. Pauline came up behind Frank. Guess
the affection was infectious. Frank
pulled Pauline in his arms and said,
"Good Morning my sharp shooting honey,"
as he kissed and dipped her.

304

Dan came in, took one look at the love going on in the kitchen and said, "Thank God! This is a scene to start your day with. Nothin' like a little lovin' with your breakfast." He poured himself some coffee and smiled at them all. "Sorry I've been so distant. Y'all have been real wonderful friends. The best. Harv and Barb have really helped me understand their way of thinking about reincarnation. When you view death their way it's so much easier to accept. I just wanted to thank you. I'm sure Tracy is looking down and she thanks you too. Now Betty Lou, how about some of that good smellin' gravy on these southern biscuits?"

They all gave a sigh of relief knowing Dan was gonna be alright. Pauline was a bit concerned about the reincarnation talk but she felt Jesus would make an exception seein' as how Dan had just lost his wife in such a tragic way.

Over breakfast they planned their day. Frank wanted to make sure they were on the radio at 1:00 pm sharp. He wanted to know if Rory and Cindy were okay after they weren't on yesterday. Dan asked if Frank and Billy had anything they needed help with. They said not really, knowing Dan wanted to go to Shangri La. Dan told them about all the growing knowledge Harvey and Barbra were sharing with him. He explained they had given him a bed in

the greenhouse. Dan was growing food for
their household. They'd have fresh
vegetables through the winter. Come
Spring, he wanted to put beds in the back
yard. He'd been a decent gardener before.
He felt he could produce a lot more per
square foot with all they had taught him.
Everyone got real excited to know there
would be fresh food. Betty Lou said she
might like to come and help sometime if
Dan wouldn't mind. Dan said it would be
great.

Dan hadn't told them about his
project before since Tracy had been so
down on his ideas. He walked along the
path thinking again what great friends
they were. For the first time since
Tracy's death, he felt he was going to be
alright.

7:30 am EDT, October 13,
Dancing Goats Farm
Moon Mountain, North Carolina

Rose was still a spitting viper when
Violet went to bring her a breakfast of
grits, bread and water. When Violet put
the food on the shelf in the small
opening in the bars designed to pass
prisoners food, Rose tried to scratch
Violet. Violet grabbed her wrist and
twisted it. "Try that again and I break
your hand next time." Rose rubbed her
wrist which was already bruised from when
she tried to stab Becky the night before.

Rose looked in the bowl and said
"I'm not going to eat this shit. I want
my brother! Wait till he finds out what
you bitches have done to me. He'll kill
all of you!"

Violet crossed her arms and stared
at the foolish woman for a good long
minute. "You just don't get it. Nicholas
wants *nothing* to do with you... Did you
not see him on the veranda last night
kissing my mother? He knew what was going
to happen to you. The two of them
designed and built this place...
together. The man has lived with us for
ten years. He knows *everything* that
happens here. *Kill us?* Nick shoots people
who even *think* they want to hurt my
mother. He kills to protect her. Nick
said he didn't believe you could change
and you are precisely the type of person
we would never allow to live here. He's
washed his hands of you." Violet turned
and walked away. Rose threw the bowl of
grits at her. It smashed on the floor.
With out turning Vy said, "For the waste
of the food and the broken bowl you'll go
without lunch." She slammed the steel
door and locked it.

Violet met the sisters in the Hall
for breakfast. "Nothing has changed with
Rosie the Retched. Screaming Nick would
kill us all for what we had done to her."

Alexandra put her fork down. "She's
insane. I think I should simply put an

307

arrow in her heart right now. Sorry Vy, we're not going to be able to save this one."

"Not yet... let's give her a few days. Stranger things have happened around here."

Amber asked, "Vy did she ask about her kids this morning? She didn't last night. Becky did she ask before she tray-ed you?" Both women said no in unison. "Fucking cow. Not a word about her children, and screeching for Nick. Something's very *wrong* there. Anybody else pick up on that?"

Lizzy shook her head yes. Sadie said, "Yuck! I thought I was just being twisted when I got that."

Amber says, "Bet she hit on Nick and that's why he hasn't spoken to her in eleven years. That's why he turned her over to Auntie. You didn't see the wicked grin on his face when he said, 'Gianna Lorenzini, my wife' It was a serious fuck you."

Lizzy chimes in, "Yes, I saw that look. I wondered why it was so intense."

Amber said, "Holy Shit! That's what the kiss was about! They've been careful not to be affectionate in public. Nick shows up half naked and goes 'all Fabio' on her with that passionate kiss. Yes,

ladies, Rosie the Retch has a thing for
her brother! Nick wanted Rosie to know
just how much in love he is with his
wife." This brings hoots and other
boisterous outbursts, like 'go Nick!'
causing others eating to turn and stare.

Violet says, "We can use that. In
fact I did this morning."

Alexandra slammed her hand cn the
table. "Sorry there's no fixing that kind
of perversion. Just call me wher I can
put an arrow in her... I think Auntie got
it right off... Oh yea... that's why she
said 'When I'm in bed with my magnificent
husband'. I thought it was a bit odd to
say to his sister." This too brings hoots
and other boisterous outbursts, like 'go
mom!' causing others eating to turn and
stare again.

Violet gives them a death look and
they go back to minding their own
business.

Becky stood and said, "Well now that
we've gotten to the bottom of that slimy
mystery, I'm going to take Fabio and his
wife breakfast. And then maybe a shower.
I feel dirty just talking about this. See
you all later."

8:30 am EDT, October 13,
Moon Mountain, North Carolina

David was making himself breakfast

309

with eggs and ham from the farm. He was
whistling a country tune thinking how
different this was from the weeks of
hiding up here eating cold food out of a
can. Maybe a few people will move into
town when it's safe. He'd talk to Nick
and see what he thought about the idea.
He and Reno had a conversation, well, a
drunken conversation about country boys'
skills that were probably giving them an
upper hand now. David thought they could
use those skills to make the town more
livable. If the buildings were filled
with people and they put up a roadblock
that alone would make the place safer.
They could start up the farmers market
again. People needed to barter, why not
do it in town. They could barter skills
too. David warmed to the idea as he ate.
He was washing his dishes when there was
suddenly yelling in the street. Randy's
brother-in-law, Casey, the younger one,
was in the street waving him down. He had
nine people with him. They were in a hay
wagon being pulled by horses. David went
up to the roof to talk to him.

Casey said, "Hey David I have some
customers for you."

"Casey I'm not open for business. What
are you talking about? Wait there I'll
come around." David went down to see what
the hell was going on. He wasn't going to
give his stock away. When he got to the
front he said, "Folks, my store is
boarded up, not sure what he told you but

310

I'm not open." David took Casey by the arm and pulled him a few feet away so they could talk. "What the hell are you thinking? I have survived the EMP, looters, zombies and the rogue Army because I keep my head down and no one knew I was here. I do one guy a favor and now you show up and put me and my store in danger. What? I should walk all these people through my secret back door so they can all tell another nine people each? What the fuck were you thinking? I helped out an old customer and now you want me to give my stock to all these people? Say something damn it!"

Casey said, "They have stuff to pay you with."

"What if I don't need what they have? Still not telling me how they shop when the building is boarded up?"

"I don't know. I thought they need and you have. I didn't think about your safety I guess."

I guess you didn't. You'll be home at the farm and I'll be fighting off people who want to rob me and kill me. How old are you?"

"Fourteen."

David thought, 'Well that explains it. He's just a kid.' David thought from his height he was maybe nineteen. Shit.

David walked back to the wagon. "As you can see you can't just walk in and shop around. Are there things you came looking for? One lady wanted flour. David said, "Ma'am I don't have flour. I had a Hardware store. Tell you what, why don't you all get down and show me what you have and what you want." The lady who had flour wanted a camp stove, the woman who wanted flour had six quarts of preserved peaches and plums. David took the items from both women. He gave the flour to one and said he'd go in for the camp stove. One man wanted to trade homemade hard sausage for a shovel handle. David said okay. This went on for a good twenty minutes. Then David told Casey to come with him. In the store David collected all the items he'd bartered for and he and Casey carried them out to the people in the wagon.

When everyone was happy David said. "Sorry I was a bit ill with you when you all got here. Young Casey here didn't talk to me about it first. Today is Saturday. Let's say on Saturdays and Wednesdays people gather here in town and we'll have a Farmers Market here in the street. Tell your neighbors. The more people who come the better the chance of finding what you want. And if you know of anyone out there alone have them come and talk to me about moving into town in one of the empty places. Don't know if you've spoken to the people at the Q Farm. I have and I can tell you they are very good people. I'm working with them to help get us back on our feet. When we have more people living in town we can start to have the market on more days. If you know whether the people who own these buildings are alive or dead please let me know." David gathered facts on the buildings for another half an hour and they got back in the wagon. David gave Casey a jar of peaches because he felt bad for having yelled at him. When they left David went around, up and then down and opened the print shop and brought all his trade goods inside. He carried the food upstairs and put it in the cupboard Gianna had the men bring up. He needed to thank her for knowing what he would need before he did.

10:30 am EDT,

David called the farm and talked to Reno about his ideas and then how it spontaneously happened. He told him he was concerned about tonight but he'd deal with whatever happened. Reno said the ideas sounded great, he'd pass the info on to Nick and the Lady. Let him know if he was having trouble with intruders.

11:00 am EDT, October 13,
Dancing Goats Farm
Moon Mountain, North Carolina

Nick found Gianna on the roof sunbathing nude. He stood there looking down at her. She said, "What is it now?"

313

Nick said, "Is this something new, you going outside without your clothes, or I have I missed this behavior for the last ten years?"

"It's called skyclad darling, wearing nothing but the sky... To answer your question I believe you simply missed it. Though there may have been more frequent episodes of my public nakedness in the last week or so. You were rather all out there yourself last night. Those jeans and your *condition*... left nothing to the imagination."

Nick ignored her attempt to shift the topic to himself. "I can not imagine *me* missing *you* wandering around skyclad at *any* stage of our relationship. I think you're lying Gianna... to torture me. Come inside I want to talk to you."

"Why can't you talk to me here? Is the news so bad you think I'll throw myself off the roof?"

Nick is laughing. "No, I want to talk to you about something serious and I can't concentrate with you lying there naked." Gianna stood up and started walking toward the hatch. Nick picked up the towel and wrapped it around her. "*Gianna,* they can see you from all over the farm *and the Q.*"

She patted his cheek. "Only if

they're looking, Nick."

"Well, I don't share well either. Put this on."

In the bedroom she asked, "What type of *serious* clothing do you recommend?"

"Put something on to go to lunch. I'd like to eat in the Hall with the children." Nick sat at the table and watched her dress.

When Gianna was finished she studied his face. "This is about your sister and why you haven't spoken to her for ten years. I already know Nick." She came and sat across from him as she braided her hair. "Let me help you Nick, you sister has a very unhealthy attachment to you. She went too far with her desire and you cut ties with her. I'm guessing it wasn't the first time she tried it. When she was a teen maybe... and you brushed it off as a silly teenage phase?"

"Sometimes you scare me woman... just a little bit."

"Nicholas, it's not magic, or psychic, I just pay attention. The first time I heard her say your name at the door... all the hair on the back of my neck stood up. Then the second time when I was standing in front of her... the eyes... body language... the tone of her voice... all a dead giveaway. Then, there was your delight at her extreme discomfort and shock when you said '*my wife*'. If there was any doubt, it was dispelled by your passionate kiss in front of the vanguard and the Amazons... another message to her. Which is why I said what I said when I had her by the hair."

His most wicked grin slid across his lips. "I couldn't quite hear everything in the com room, what did you say?"

Gianna offers him her own wicked grin. Knowing he just wants to hear her call him her magnificent husband again she says, "Too bad you missed it, Amber tells me I was great. Let's go to lunch now, dear. She can't bother you any more, she's in a cell."

11:30 am EDT, October 13, Damascus, Virginia

Rory and Cindy celebrated their marriage, with Ann and Beth all afternoon then into the night. As they left for bed, Beth said they should sleep in and she'd bring them breakfast in bed when they woke. Rory moved their Big Ben alarm clock so he could see the time. He brushed Cindy's hair from her face then kissed her awake. "Hey sleepy head, it's almost noon. We've slept away our first morning of married life."

She snuggled closer. "Husband, if

you love me, you'll find me something for the pain in my head."

Rory picked up the walkie-talkie and called Beth. "Good morning or afternoon I guess. Could you bring Cindy something for her hangover please?"

"I have just the thing. I'll put the tray outside your door in ten." Beth had splurged and opened one of the quarts of orange juice they had canned. She made Mimosas for the newlyweds and a pair for herself and Ann to have with their lunch. She added a bottle of headache meds and brought the tray up. She placed the bed tray at the door, knocked, then returned to the kitchen.

Rory padded across the room to get the tray. Cindy watched him through half closed eyes, the sunlight made her headache hurt more. "I'm not sure why, but you're even sexier now that you're my husband. We may need to spend more time in our room so I can watch you wait on me *naked*."

Rory smiled and put the tray on the bed. He took two tabs out of the bottle and handed them to Cindy with her Mimosa. "Take these ma'am and I'll show you what *other services* we offer here at the Inn."

Ann came in from the yard. "One of the hens is sitting on the eggs and was a bit peckish when I took them. How are we

317

on eggs in here?"

"We're good. Why?"

Think I'll build a brood box for her and put her in the plant room. She can keep the eggs for the next two days. When things settle down, people are going to want chickens. It's just short of a month to hatch and five months till they start to lay. I don't think we can have too many when that time rolls around. There will be a percentage of roosters in each hatching also. What do you think?"

Beth smiled at her wife. "I think I married an amazingly smart woman. We're having an early lunch. The newlyweds are awake. I made Mimosas. If you think three days of eggs would be better we can have other things for breakfast."

Ann said, "This looks great. You would never know there was an apocalypse going on outside, they way we live in here. I'm so lucky to have you. And I think we're gonna make it with the help of those two..." Ann stopped, both women looked up...

Beth laughed, "Unless their bed comes through the ceiling in the sitting room.

12:00 pm EDT, October 13,
Dancing Goats Farm
Moon Mountain, North Carolina

318

Rosie and Nicky seemed to be settling in just fine. They'd had a sleep over with Angelena, who was behaving better at having to suddenly share Uncle Nicky. The twins were happy to see Nick at lunch. Rosie asked if she could sit next to Gianna and Angelena said that was fine, she'd sit next to Uncle Nicky. Gianna noticed they did not ask about their mother.

She'd gone with Amber to get the children plates. "Auntie, they were perfectly well behaved. They just asked to sleep in the same room. Guess it's a twin thing. They jumped at the idea of a sleep over. They haven't asked for her. This morning I told them Rose had to go on a trip. The boy just shrugged. Rosie asked if Uncle Nicky was still here? When I told her yes, she just smiled and ran off to play. They did talk about missing their nanny. I think Rose went off a lot and the nanny did most of the raising."

They brought the plates to the table. When Gianna put the plate in front of the boy, Nicky said, "I love macaroni and cheese. We could only have it when mother was gone." Amber raised an eyebrow at her Aunt. The look on Nick's face said he was thinking ugly thoughts about his sister.

They went back to get plates for themselves and Nick. Amber said "I wanted

319

to broach another subject away from Nick. It has to do with Rose."

Gianna continued selecting food for her husband. "I already know. Got it before we even went through the door yesterday."

"Good, cause I was elected to tell you. We all put it together at breakfast when we compared impressions and then I pointed out Nick going '*all Fabio*' on the veranda, that cinched it for us."

Gianna was laughing so hard she had to put the plates down. "*'Going All Fabio'*? That's priceless. I can see that's going to be a new phrase around here."

"Alexandra said you'd figured it out cause of what you said during the neck stretching. Are you going to talk to Nick about it?"

"Already did. He sat me down and I could tell by the look on his face what was coming. I spared him the embarrassment, by telling him I knew. He's fine now."

"*Yes!* I love confirmation! Wait till I tell the girls we were right."

Lunch was a pleasant affair. Gianna pondered a more permanent situation for the children. Violet had texted her about the scene when she'd brought Rose her breakfast. This was going to be a long process. Nick didn't want them in the manor house during the honeymoon. Gianna wasn't sure how she felt about it. Rosie interrupted her thoughts by asking if she might get to see the manor house some time. Gianna told her yes, when things calmed down. Then Rosie told her she thought Gianna was brilliant for having created the farm. The world was bad out there. The trip here had been pretty scary. She said she used to worry about her Uncle. Now she knew he'd been safe and happy in this great place. Nicky had been listening to their conversation. He said walking through the portal was kind of like going through the gates of the Emerald City. Everybody was so busy and happy, and it *was* pretty green in here. Then he looked at Gianna and said, 'Thanks.' Gianna excused herself from the table and called Theo. "Darling what cottages do we have vacant near Amber?"

"We don't. You want a place for the twins don't you? Let me talk to some people. I may be able to move them out to one closer to the farm area. Hector works with Stephen and Tia works with Bonny. They may like being closer. I'll call you back." He was gone before Gianna could tell him how much she loved how he was always in her head.

Nick said he wanted to check in with Reno if she was up to it. Gianna told him she was. When they got there, Gianna told Becky she thought they could do away with the men stationed around the manor house. Nick cut in and said *No*, not yet. Becky smiled and went off to work with Carl and Mendez. Reno sat down and brought them up to speed on what was happening in Moon Mountain.

1:00 pm EDT October 13,
Smokey Mountains, Tennessee

Frank was on the radio as promised at one sharp. Ann was on today she said "Hey Frank, how is everyone doing? Is Dan better?"

"We're all doin' better. The people at Shangri La have been a big help to him. We were worried when y'all weren't on yesterday. Somethin' come up?"

Ann thought she'd build up to it. Beth was smiling waiting to hear their reaction to the news. "Rory and I went to town yesterday morning to hunt for gas. We did a little scavenging too." Beth rolled her eyes at Ann's explanation for the bag of jewelry now in the attic. Ann continued. "We ran into three zombies there. Put them down with no problem. Coming back we had a mob of them between us and the Inn. Rory ran right over the top of several of them. Beth and Cindy had the barricade open so we blew right in. One had gotten in the truck bed and was about to take a bite out of Rory when

322

Cindy blew it's head off declaring 'He's mine.'" She gave Frank a chance to answer.

"Damn I'm glad y'all got through it okay. Knew there had to be a reason why y'all weren't on."

    "Oh, that happened in the morning. We were busy getting the bride and groom ready after that..." She waited to see what Frank would say.

    The next thing Beth and Ann heard was Pauline squealing with delight. "Y'all telling me that boy finally married her? Tell me what she wore. Bet she looked lovely. Did y'all have a weddin' cake and flowers? Was there music? Betty Lou come here Rory and Cindy got married!" Frank got out of the way and pointed out to his very excited wife, she'd have to stop mashin' the button down if she wanted to heard Ann's answers.

Beth and Ann were laughing their asses off listening to Pauline. When she stopped mashin' the button, Ann and Beth answered all her questions. Rory had told them he and Cindy wouldn't be down for radio time but to go ahead and break the news if they wanted. They didn't get to talk to anyone else because Pauline used up their half hour with questions. Both women thought it was worth it. They hadn't laughed so much in ages.

Nick listened to what Reno had to say about David. He had his thinking face on so Gianna said, "Road trip time I believe."

Nick smiled at her reading his mind. "Yes, I think you're right as usual. Reno we'll take the Dark Lady, you follow with two guard and two regulars." Nick saw the question on her face and added, "Tell Carmichael he's riding with us. Check with David and see if he needs anything from here."

After he'd hung up with Gianna, Theo called housekeeping and had them go through the cottage near the farm. Then he called Hector who said they'd love to move. Asking was merely a formality. They would go wherever Theo suggested. As it turned out they really did want the new place so that was nice. Theo told him to get Tia and go to their home and pack their things. They could take whatever furniture they wanted. Let housekeeping know what they would be bringing to the new place so they could move out items that weren't needed there. Then he called housekeeping back and told them to send help to get them moved and to fit the cottage near Amber out for the twins. He was in the middle of talking to the woman

324

he thought would make the perfect nanny
when he got a text from Alexandra. The
woman was ecstatic at being asked. She
went to find the twins so they would have
time to get to know her e they moved in
tonight.

1:30 pm EDT, October 13,
Moon Mountain, North Carolina

Then Theo texted Gianna with the
information in Alexandra's text. Gianna
said Do nothing until she spoke with
Nick, which would be a while since they
were on their way to town. She'd talk to
him when they got back. They had just
arrived at David's when Gianna finished
texting Theo.

Gianna went to get out of the truck
when Nick put his hand on her arm to stop
her. Nick got out and told the men to
sweep the street and the buildings. David
made his way down while Gianna waited in
the truck for the men to give the OK. She
did it because she knew Nick felt he was
to blame for last time they came to town
and she didn't feel well enough to get
shot again yet. She waited after Reno
gave the all clear for Nick to tell her
she could get out. It was good to let him
think he was the boss of her once in
awhile. He smiled knowing she was
pretending to be the obedient wife.

Nick and Gianna walked up and down
the streets with David as he told them

about the ownership of each place. Gianna said they should clear out the feed store to use for the Farmers Market. Then it could go on even if it rained and they should let the people set up tables they could come back to each time. They needed to find a wood stove for there so it would be heated when the weather changed. Nick said he wanted the road at the south end of town blocked for now. Reno told them he found a forklift he thought he could fix to move the concrete barriers from the parking lot. While they were talking, Casey returned with an elderly couple who wanted to move into town. Gianna offered them a tiny shop four doors down from David's Hardware store. They asked if they could move in now. The back of the wagon held things like their bed they brought from their house. Gianna said yes and had Casey and one of the men moved their things inside. She told Reno to secure the building for them. David and Nick watched Gianna managing everything and smiled. David told Nick what he knew about Casey when he asked.

4:30 pm EDT,

When the wagon was empty Nick called Casey over. "I hear you're very enterprising. I also hear you're willing to help David. I'll pay you with a hot shower and a steak once a week."

Casey grinning said, "Yes sir! I'd do it anyway but those two things would surely be nice."

Laughing Nick said, "Okay you are David's assistant. You can come out to the farm when he does. Just so you know we don't eat steak every night. However David can have one whenever he wants for saving my wife's life. But we'll see that you get one the first time you come. From now on you run your ideas by David first. No more surprises like this morning."

"Yes sir I mean no sir."

Gianna came up to where they were talking. "Casey would you look around for a broom for Miss Massie?" She looked at David and asked, "Sheriff or Mayor? Then because he looked confused she said, Pick one. No one is going to argue with your choice. Nick will see to that."

There she was in his head again. Nick liked David for Sheriff but he waited to see what David said. David looked to Nick. Nick said, "Sheriff, no question. Let's see who else wanders in over the next few days. See if we don't find you a deputy. If not I'll post one of the regulars out here in the cottage for back up until one comes along. Tomorrow have Casey clean out the Sheriff's station and paint it."

David said, "Thanks Mayor. If anyone is the new Mayor it's you. You're dumping sheriff on me."

Nick opened his mouth to protest. Gianna spoke first. "You want to boss this all around, you have to be Mayor. Down the road you can appoint a new one. Now, they need you. You stared this Nicholas."

Nick looked at her like he wanted to slap her. Then said, "Fine Mrs. Mayor."

"If that was meant to irritate me it didn't. You know I love bossing people around." She grinned at him because it was irritating him. "Come on Mr. Mayor, it's time to take Mrs. Mayor home."

Nick realized she was in pain. He'd forgotten about her ribs because she was acting as if she wasn't hurt. Nick rounded everyone up and they left for home. Gianna put the seat back and closed her eyes. Nick saw her pain and drove faster. Gianna was actually more tired than in pain. She was thinking how to deal with Theo's text.

Chapter 32
The BOYS ARE BACK In TOWN

*"The day Nick almost shot
the Deputies, but not the Sheriff"*

**4:30 pm EDT, October 13,
Moon Mountain, North Carolina**

David watched them leave town. They were a pair of dynamic people but Reno was right, they did play rough. He saw how the Lady baited Nick. David imagined it got worse than that. Casey had been eavesdropping on the conversation after he'd found the broom. He walked up and said, "Hey Sheriff, does that make me a deputy?"

David laughed. "No, you know what Nick said, you're my assistant."

"Don't you mean, Mr. Mayor?"

"If you like your head where it is, you better not call him that. Nick or Mr. Lorenzini will do from you. And no more cartloads of people before I've even washed up the breakfast dishes. If you don't follow my instructions, I'll lock you in a cell. Tomorrow we're going to reclaim the Sheriff's office. Do you know how to use a paint brush and roller?"

"Yes I do. Can I call you Sheriff?"

"If you have to. Lets take a look at what has to be done in there before you leave."

"OK. Can I ask a question?" David shook his head. "When are we going out to the farm?

"Maybe after the Market on Wednesday." The office was dim in the late afternoon sun. David looked at the crazy shit the drug dealer had left on the walls. They'd need stain killer over the marker. He didn't want that shit bleeding through the paint. He looked at the desk. He'd need to sand that down. He made a note to ask Reno to bring a cordless sander from the farm when he came to put the barrier in place tomorrow. He'd needed a file cabinet for the files that had been tossed on the floor. The Deputy Sergeant's office was a half glass-walled room at the back. David thought, 'It wasn't too messy guess the asshole didn't use this room.' The bathroom would need a lot of bleach and jugs for flushing. David wondered how long before the sewer system became an issue with folks moving back in town. He'd need to get some outhouses dug for solid waste. Where would they get wood shavings? Did these issues not belong

under the Mayor's job description? Yea,
he'd remind *Nick* about these toilet
issues. David closed the door after them
and made another mental note to change
the lock in the morning.

He sent Casey on his way and stopped
to talk to his new neighbors. Massie and
Ray Booth were in their 80's. David was
glad they'd moved to town. They'd be
perfect pray for outlaws to rob and kill.
He said they should come and supper with
him tonight. They would work on getting a
wood cook stove in here for them. Ray
said they had one at their place. David
told him they would get it brought here
for them. Nick's people had a trailer
they could put it on. He'd see about
getting that done tomorrow or the next
day. David told them they could bring
anything they wanted to their new place.
At some point they would see about
putting a few more walls in here for
them. He'd brought them two jugs of water
from the rain barrel for flushing the
toilet. He said he'd give them a bottle
of drinking water when they came to eat.
He told them how to find the back door
and went to his place to put some food
on. The lady had brought him mac and
cheese and fresh tomatoes. She'd given
him some ham when they set the place up.
He'd add some to the meal. She also
brought him a new block of ice. As David
was cutting the tomatoes he said, "Look
at me entertaining!"

331

Casey went flying into his sister's house excited to tell her what he'd been up to all day. He ran into his older brother Walter and almost knocked him down. Walter whacked him in the head and said. "Watch where you're going. I've been working all day while you ran around annoying people."

Sandy asked, "Where have you been all day?"

Casey was glad she asked in front of Walter. "In town. I brought people to trade with David. After he finished the deals he said we're going to have a Farmers Market again. Every Saturday and Wednesday. I met the people from the Q Farm." Randy came in and took a seat to listen to Casey's animated tale. "I gave the Booths a ride to town. David said people could move to town to be safer. I got to help Mrs. Lorenzini get the Booths set up in their new place. She said we're going to clean up the feed store for the Market. Her husband Nick is still a little scary but he made me David's assistant. Guess what my pay is, just try and guess." They all looking at him with no clue. "I get to go to the farm and have a hot shower and a steak! Every week!"

Walter said, "You're a liar."

"Ask David or Nick if you don't believe me. Ha, you can't cause you don't know Nick. Nick made David the new Sheriff. Mrs. Lorenzini said Nick had to be the new Mayor for now, while he gets the town set up and running again. He wasn't crazy about being Mayor but she said he had to. AND I got to sit in the Humvee! Reno said he'd take me for a ride too. He's coming back tomorrow to block the southern road so assholes can't try to burn the town again."

Sandy said, "Casey don't swear in front of the little ones."

"Sorry, I'm just so excited. Tomorrow I'm helping David clean up the station and paint it cause the crazy drug dealer wrote weird stuff on the walls. It was his drugs that made the people act like zombies."

Randy said, "You've had a hell of a day. Good for you. Who is this Reno?"

"He's Nick's second. He's the boss when Nick isn't around. Oh no wait." Casey flew out the door. He was back in a minute. He gave his sister a package. "Mrs. Lorenzini brought two of these for David but she said he'd be fine with just one. I had a few bites cause it smelled so good but just out of the corner."

Randy and Walter crowded around to see what Casey had brought them. All Sandy could say was, "Oh my God they have cheese!"

Casey said, "She said they make their own cheese. This is two year old cheddar." Randy was smiling at his wife, he knew how much she loved and missed cheese.

Sandy looked at her little brother grinning. "You did real good my boy. It was very generous of you to bring it back to share with the family. I'm very proud of you Casey. Should I heat it up?" Everyone said no. They all took a seat. Randy put the baby in the highchair. Six year old Randy Jr. sat next to his dad. Sandy carefully spooned out the creamy golden goodness of mac and cheese for her family.

5:00 pm EDT, October 13,
Dancing Goats Farm
Moon Mountain, North Carolina

When they got home, Gianna said they should have an early supper with the children and their new nanny before they moved them into their new cottage. Nick asked her what nanny and what cottage and when did she arrange this? She said she put it in motion while they were having lunch. She texted Layah, while Nick was questioning her, Gianna texted Layah should find out what they wanted to eat and call the order in to Simon, let's eat at 5:30. Slightly annoyed, Nick said, "Stop texting and talk to me. Who is this woman you've put in charge of my niece and nephew?"

Gianna said, "Just yours? Did you not tell them I was their new Auntie?" Nick realized he was being a bit obnoxious and sat on the bed next to her. Gianna was resting her ribs. "Her name is Layah. You know her she's one of the Airy-Fairies. Blonde, late 40's, never had any children. I believe she couldn't. I think her husband left her when they found out. Level headed and a lovely woman. The cottage is the one next to Amber. I thought you'd want them near where you could watch them from the window. And Amber can keep a close eye on them."

Nick took her face in his hands. "Every day you do something that makes me fall more in love with you. Let's go see the cottage before we meet the kids to eat."

As soon as they walked in, Gianna saw her girls had been there, by the framed photos on the wall. Some of the children alone and others with members of the Tribe. Six great shots of Nicky and Rosie with Nickolas. Even one from lunch today of Gianna and Rosie talking. Gianna pointed them out to Nick. Tough guy almost got teary eyed. The walls of the cottage, were a soft cream. The girls had filled the house with brightly colored accessories, conducive to creating a happy environment for children. Their closets and drawers had clothing, some new and others shared.

Most people traded clothing there on the farm. They had the 'Shift Shop'. They brought stuff they didn't want and took if they wanted. A storeroom in the back was stocked with new clothing Gianna had purchased in the event that they could no longer buy clothes, such as the one they now found themselves in. There was also a seamstress studio stocked with blots of fabric and drawers filled with trims and notions.

The children's bathroom had toothbrushes and robes. It was a three bedroom cottage. The nanny's things were already in her room. The girls had turned the third bedroom into a playroom with books and games. Gianna checked the cupboards in the kitchen. She found them nicely stocked. She turned to Nick to see what his reaction was. He pulled her to him. "More and More every day. They're just like you. I see you in everything they did here for the twins." Nick just held her. Gianna sensed there was more he needed to tell her.

The twins were so excited to have a meal with just Nick, Gianna and their nanny but mostly Nick. Nick remembered

Layah as soon as he saw her. Hamburgers were what the twins had ordered, another one of Rose's forbidden foods. Rosie regaled Nick with their adventures around the farm and shopping for new clothes. Nicky asked if he could have his own horse. Nick said maybe a pony for his birthday. Rosie said if he's getting a pony she wanted her own goat. Gianna asked when their birthday was. Rosie told her November 16th. Gianna said the baby goats wouldn't be born until December and January, but she could pick another one if she didn't want to wait. Rosie said she'd wait for a new baby.

6:00 pm EDT,
Moon Mountain, North Carolina

After the family had eaten their pie, Nick told them he had another surprise. He walked across the green, both children holding his hand. They went wild when Nick told them this was their new cottage. Nicky yelled, "It's right next door to Angelena!" They ran through the house wildly. Nick went to tell them to calm down but Gianna stopped him. When they found Layah's room they ran down and said, "We get to keep her too?" Nick told them they didn't own Layah, but yes she would live with them. When Nick said it was time for him and Gianna to leave they hugged and kissed and thanked him.

Rosie came to Gianna and took her hand. There were tears in her eyes.

337

Gianna squatted down and wrapped the child in her arms. Rosie whispered "You're the Auntie I always wanted." Gianna kissed her and they left. From the doorway Nicky asked, "Can you see us from the big house?"

Nick turned and said, "Yes, I'll be watching you two, so you best mind Layah." Nick was silent on their walk to the Q. He held Gianna's hand so tightly she found he'd left red marks when he finally let her go. While Nick was talking to Reno and Charlie, Gianna's mind was elsewhere. She still had to talk to Nick about the text, now that the children were settled and he was pleased with the arrangements she'd made. She was very disturbed that the children never asked about their mother. She needed to get to the bottom of that. What really worried her was the darkness lurking behind his joy in the children. She'd give him the space to open up when they got home.

Gianna was jolted back to the room when Tiny yelled up the stairs, David was in trouble. Gianna waited in the kitchen. There was no point in going down with Tiny, Charlie, Freddy, Reno and Nick in the small room. Reno came racing up the stairs and out the door. Gianna wondered where her gun was. No, she wasn't going back to the house for it, she was not giving Nick a chance to leave her behind.

338

Gianna went out on the veranda to watch the preparations. Reno pulled Dark Lady out. Well that made it clear Nick was going. Freddy and Charlie ran past so fast they nearly knocked her off the steps.

Nick came up behind her and took her by the arm. "I see no point in asking you to stay so please find a vest." He hustled her down the steps to the barn. She found Carmichael and told him to get her a vest and a Glock. Nick found them standing by the side of the truck. Gianna was getting her vest on. Nick said, "Get in you two." Outside the gate Nick told Reno to take the lead in the Humvee. Gianna knew he did that because she was in the truck, otherwise he'd be leading. This pleased her because the assault vehicle would take first fire not Nick or her pretty truck. She needed to remember to ask Nick when did her personal vehicle become his go-to assault truck? She waited for him to finish the plan going on in his head. He'd tell her before they got to town what they were walking into. Three miles out he spoke. "David was in his place with the Booths, when a group of men in Army uniforms rolled into town. About twenty. They didn't act as badly as the others but they wanted food and water. Said they won't leave until they get some."

Gianna asked "Did we bring some?"

"No."

Gianna looked at him with her are you out of your mind look. "Carmichael give me your Catsear." She put it on. "Freddy get forty MREs, three cases of water, a case of beer and an armload of whatever Simon has of leftovers to feed twenty. Throw in a few loaves of bread. Get them here NOW." She gave the earpiece back to Carmichael. Nick was starting to tighten his grip on the steering wheel. Evidently he thought she was wrong. "I find feeding hungry men tends to make them much more agreeable. *As previously discussed,* not here for a ride along."

6:40 pm EDT,
Moon Mountain, North Carolina

Reno slowed as they entered town. He stopped the Humvee thirty feet from the line of men and their transport truck parked in the center of the street below David's window. Nick stopped the truck behind the Humvee as tight in as he could get. The other trucks flanked the Humvee. Nick got out, gave Gianna his stay here look and walked to the front of the Humvee. He addressed the group. "This town is closed. Back your truck out of here."

Gianna heard but couldn't see anything because Nick had parked her out of harms way. "My men need food and water. We ran out yesterday. Just give us

340

some and we'll leave. We're not looking for a fight."

"A fight is what you'll get if you don't leave. Now."

Gianna had had it and she was out of the truck. "Jesus H Christ this is fucking ridiculous." She marched toward the front of the Humvee with Carmichael on her heels. When she reached the front she said, "Hold your fire." And stepped out in front of the Humvee. She handed her gun to Carmichael "Stay." She took four more steps forward. She pulled her hair pin out and let the wind catch her hair. "Gentlemen, I'm an unarmed woman. What seems to be the problem?"

"Ma'am, we just want supplies."

Nick was at her side really really pissed. "Gianna..." he said menacingly.

"Nicholas, they're just hungry boys. Am I correct gentlemen?" Twenty men said Yes ma'am. "Okay, here's what's going to happen... we're all going to put our guns down. *Reno.*"

"Yes ma'am"

"If one of our men fires I'm going to shoot you and then the asshole who fired."

Understood ma'am"

She took another step toward the line of dirty raggedy men. "Boys, I need you to lower you weapons. It's going to be hard to eat while holding a rifle. I have one of my trucks on its way. It should be here shortly. They had to gather the food. I give you my word, as a mother, I will feed you." She waited... as soon as they began to shoulder their rifles she said. "DJ get me every container of water in these vehicles. Now. Carmichael there's water under the seat in my truck."

"Ma'am I can't leave you."

"MARINE do as you are told. Nick is standing right next to me!" Nick nodded to Carmichael over Gianna's head. Gianna heard Pepé racing towards them. "Move one of these trucks back so the food truck can pull up." Carmichael was at her side with the water. "Follow me." She took two bottles out of the box and walked toward the men. They began to crowd her. "Gentlemen please, that angry man, is my husband. Don't make him nervous. Let's form a double line." The men fell in line. DJ appeared on her other side and started passing out water. Pepé pulled up and Nick had the men pass down the cases of water. When all the soldiers had water Gianna asked, "Nick would you please bring the food truck forward." Gianna turned to walk to the truck and the men moved to follower her. She turned and pointed at them, "STAY." At the back of the truck she pulled the basket with the bread out. Nick was watching. "Nicholas don't just stand there, cut chunks of bread." When he was finished she took the basket of bread and went back to the men. "I need you to sit in two lines on either side of the street so we can pass out the food. How many are you?" Several said twenty. "Okay start with the bread and water. Eat slowly or you just puke it back up, understood?" Twenty yes ma'ams answered her.

Back at the truck Nick was cutting apples in half. When she was close enough he said, "You are the most fucking exasperating woman in the world... but you were right."

"I love you too and food we can grow, bullets we can't."

Sal stepped up. "Ma'am, there was no time so I just grabbed real bowls and spoons and forks."

"You did great Sal, thank you. You saved a lot of bloodshed getting here so fast." Simon had sent a pan of mac and cheese and a pan of roasted potatoes, peppers and sausage. The men who had come to kill, now served the food. David and the Booths came down and helped serve and collect the dishes. Gianna walked the line passing out one beer per soldier. She was greeted with hoots and thank yous. Mrs. Booth called her over to look at one boy's hand. It was a badly infected cut. Gianna yelled. "Reno bring me a medical kit." They got him up and off to the side. She doused the hand with water and peroxide when the kit arrived. She pulled up his sleeve, the swelling was past his wrist with red lines starting up his forearm.

She gave him something for the pain and called Nick. She showed him the hand. Nick yelled for Sal. "Get the food out of Pepé then get this man to the infirmary before he loses the hand. Call Charlie and have him call Andy." To the boy he said, "I'm sending you with two of my men. You need to see our doctor or you're going to lose the hand or die. Blood poisoning is going up your arm. You will have to leave your weapon here." The boy looked at Gianna, she shook her head yes. He handed his rifle to Nick and followed him to the truck. As he walked away Gianna asked his name. He told her, Geno Carbone.

7:45 pm EDT,

When the last scrap of food had been eaten, the dishes, beer and water bottles collected, David told Nick they would fit in the feed store for the night. Nick got their attention. "Men, we have fed you and are offering you a place to sleep. There are no beds but you'll be out of the weather. Do not fuck up."

Gianna stepped up. "What my Marine husband, Captain Lorenzini, is trying to say is, we've had to deal with other bands of Army men. They shot me twice and hit me in the head with a gun then said they wanted to rape me. They are all dead. Their bodies are that pile of burn rubble at the edge of town. More attacked our farm, they're dead too. A third group came in and tried to burn the town. Their bodies are also in the burnt rubble. I think you can understand why my husband was ready to shoot you. I believe, you are simply lost and hungry and not like them. I trust you will be honorable and not betray my trust. Do I have your word?"

They stood and said yes ma'am. The leader saluted Nick. "Sir we are in your debt for you kindness. We are at your service." Nick said, "At ease soldier. You'll follow David. He's the Sheriff here and a SEAL."

From the line one of them said, "Thank God we found the real military."

Gianna laughed. "You have no idea. They don't get any realer than my men." Reno stepped up. Gianna said, "Reno, sorry I had to say I was going to shoot you honey. You know I trust you with my life."

Reno laughed, "Yes ma'am, I knew

what you were doing. It was Nick I was
worried about you having to shoot."

8:00 pm EDT,
Dancing Goats Farm
Moon Mountain, North Carolina

They rode home in silence. As soon
as Nick stopped the truck, Gianna was out
and handed her vest to Carmichael.
"Ma'am."

"We're fine. You did fine. In fact
it made them more frightened of Nick so
it worked for me. Good night, get
yourself some sleep." She stopped in to
see how Geno was doing. Alexandra was
there. She said they could fix him.
Gianna thought she wanted to stand under
a hot shower for an hour or maybe two
should do it. Nick found her fifteen
minutes later, she was laying on the bed
still in her towel. "I just need to lay
flat for a few minutes. I bent over too
much." Then because she could feel he was
still fuming. "I think you did a very
nice job on those apples dear. They were
all the same size, very impressive."

Nick got on the bed with her. "You
do lie awake and dream of ways to drive
me insane. Gianna, I asked you not to
take stupid risks."

"And standing there facing twenty
men, who were so hungry, they were
willing to face us wasn't stupid? What if

346

they shot you in the head? Or some place else equally important?"

Nick pushed her hand away. "Now who's trying to sex their way out of a situation? Keep your hands on your own side of the bed. And what's with the hair?

Gianna rolled over to face him. "They're soldiers. Facing a big scary *you,* and all your stuff. They see me hand my gun off, I let the hair down... now they're looking at their mother or grandmother. They don't want to shoot their mother. I tell them to be good boys and mommy will feed you. It's not that complicated Nick. The biggest danger was you not getting what I was doing. Reno got it he said he did, but he'd been worried *you'd* be the one I had to shoot. You can't think of me as your wife out there... Now who's hands are on the wrong side of the bed? Stay over, there we're talking. Those boys are lost. If they had a home to go to, they'd have gone by now. They chose not to join the rogue units. That says a lot about who they are. After tonight they'd follow you into hell."

"As long as I had a loaf of bread."

Gianna's laughing at the image of Nick leading his soldiers with a loaf of bread tucked under his arm. She manages to get out, "Well, whatever works for you babe. I think we may have men now to

347

station in the cottage."

"How can you tell me not to think of you as my wife? You are my wife and I don't want you shot again!"

Still laughing, "Well you just told me I couldn't use sex so I had to think of something to say. Hey, watch the hands bub. We're still talking here."

"Do we have other things to talk about? Because I think we've worn this topic out."

Gianna sat up and wrapped the sheet around her. "Yes, we do. Nickolas, something is bothering you. I saw it in you eyes tonight with the children. What is it?" Nick looks at her, he knows he can't ever hide his secrets from her when she starts like this. "Nick, we've been here before, when something dark and painful rose up from your past. Just spit it out babe. You know I've got you. What else did your bitch of a sister do to you?"

Nick sighed and ran his hands over his face. "She destroyed my family. When I left the Marines I went home to my parents' house. I was home two days when she climbed into my bed naked, while I was sleeping. When she woke me I threw her out of the room. She said she'd make me pay. If she couldn't have me no one would. I took my things and left my parents' house within the hour. The next day I called my mother to tell her why I'd left. All hell had broken loose. Rose told my parents I'd raped her. I tried to explain but my father wouldn't listen. Rose was his darling baby girl who could do no wrong.

Our relationship had been strained for years. He never forgave me for joining the Marines and not taking over the restaurant. My mother kept saying why would Rose lie? I left my number with my mother and then traveled around the country. Mom called me two months later and told me Rose was pregnant. Rose said the baby was mine. I told my mother it wasn't mine and hung up on her. Eight months after the bitch said I raped her, she gave birth to twins. When mom saw the babies she knew they weren't early babies. I asked her to tell my father to do a paternity test. She had tried but he said Rose wouldn't lie to him. He wouldn't insult her by asking her to do it. Mom had it done on the sly. She could be crafty, that one. She tried to show it to my father and he said I'd had it fixed by one of my friends in the government.

Over the next two years I'd make trips to Asheville and mom would meet me for lunch or dinner. It was the only way I could see her. I had just left the first of those dinners the night I found you. Despite Rose's behavior, Mom loved the twins and would bring them with her

349

when she came to meet me. Rose was screwing her way through every rich guy in the country so she didn't know. Four years into building this place with you, my parents were killed in a car accident. The nanny knew about the secret visits but didn't know how to find me until she found a box with my number in it in my mother's dresser two weeks after they died. I told mom about you and the farm. At our last meeting she said I should marry you. I had our rings made just before they died. You probably don't remember I went through a really dark few months."

"Nicholas I remember. I was so afraid you were going to leave here."

"Rose found out about the visits because Rosie was asking to see me after my parents died. Rose made the nanny tell her everything. She did but she hid the box and mailed it to me later. It had photos we'd taken when I'd visit. Letters and things. Then Rose's lawyer called me about the estate. My fathers Will left everything to Rose but in North Carolina half was my mother's. Her Will left her half to me. Told you she was crafty. I told the lawyer I wouldn't contest my father's Will if I could see the twins. It cost me two million dollars to see them three times a year for a day each visit. It was worth every penny. Rose fired the nanny which she did a lot over the last six years. But I still got to have them and that's what mattered to me. Rosie is the spitting image of my mother. She acts like her too."

"Nicholas, I wish you had told me. I would have skinned that bitch right out there in front of the vanguard. But... this makes what I have to tell you a lot easier. Nick, Rose is dead. We didn't kill her. She threw the bowl of food Vy brought her this morning. Vy told her no lunch for wasting the food. Alexandra found her hours later, when we were on our way to town the first time. Rose had gotten a piece of the broken bowl and slit her wrist."

"That's why you made the cottage for the twins?"

"No, I put that in play during lunch. Rose may have been dead but I didn't know it at the time. I was very concerned that they haven't asked for her once. I was worried they might be in shock from whatever they've been through. I just wanted them to have a stable place where they could feel safe. Then, Theo got the call and texted me. You have no idea how many of our people were involved to make the cottage happen tonight. There was a couple living in there this morning. Nick say something."

"Where is she?"

"I told them to move nothing until I

spoke with you. Shit just kept coming up all day. I didn't want to tell you before we ate with them this evening. I wanted you to have the joy and not be thinking about the bitch dead."

"Tell them to burn her on the zombie pile. Fuck, now we have to tell the kids."

"Nick, I wouldn't. Let them settle in and be safe. If they ask about her we'll say she's away and there are no phones. When we think they are ready we can tell them she died in an accident. Then they won't have an abandonment problem as if she just left them, which she did but they don't need to know that. She's done enough damage to your family. Let's just give the children the best life we can. Nicholas you put as much into this place as I have. Your family should benefit from what we created. Remember when you said, 'I think the children like her?' I'm not sure they do. You know what Rosie said to me when I hugged her? 'You're the Auntie I always wanted.' Not, *where is my mother.*"

chapter 33
A LITTLE HELP FROM MY FRIENDS

"In which we learn
Nick is ambidextrous."

8:00 am EDT, October 14,
Moon Mountain, North Carolina

David was installing the new lock in
the Sheriff's station when Casey came
rolling into town. Once again the wagon
had people in it. "I'm going to kill this
kid." David waited until Casey had run up
before he started yelling. "What the hell
did I tell you yesterday?"

"Wait, wait I can explain... I
didn't bring them they were walking to
town already. I just gave them a ride. I
mean they were gonna get here sooner or
later. Just thought you could deal with
them before we got started."

David admitted it did make sense.
"Okay that was smart. Get in here and
start putting those files in the cabinet
in the back office."

"Yes sir."

"And Casey don't read them!"
David went to deal with the people in the
wagon. There was a man, woman and a
child. They looked pale and underfed. "Hi
I'm David how can I help you folks?"

The man jumped down and put out his
hand. "I'm Todd. Todd Jennings. Folks
call me TJ. This is my wife Donna and our
daughter Emma. We're not from Moon
Mountain. We've been staying with family
here. We had to leave Winston-Salem when
the zombies started breaking into houses.
One of the neighbors came by yesterday
and told us you're trying to put the town
back together. They've been kind but
there's no room for all of us there. I'm
an electrician and not bad with a hammer.
We were hoping we could get one of the
free houses."

David caught the sound of trucks
coming. He said, "I think we can work
something out. I need skilled laborers.
Know anything about solar?"

"Yea I've installed a few systems."

"Let's get the girls out of the
wagon. We need to get it down the side
street, trucks are coming into town."
Todd got his wife and daughter down and
David led the horse around the corner
down the side street where Reno and
Carmichael had been so piggish about the
zombies. Back on Main Street David yelled
for Casey. When he stuck his head out the

door David said, "Get a bucket of water
from the rain barrel for the horse." Reno
stopped the truck about where the wagon
had been. David smiled, "Morning Reno."

Reno Got out of the truck. "Hey
David. I brought one of the forklifts
from the farm. I'll get around to the one
at the feed store. Nick wanted the
barriers in place ASAP." Reno looked at
Todd and his family. "New people?"

David introduced them to Reno. David
said they wanted a place and Todd was an
electrician. Was the Lady up? He wanted
to ask where he should put them. Reno
said yes, give her a call. As he turned
to leave he suggested Todd have a look at
the forklift. Maybe he could get it
going. David saw the looks on their
faces. He told them he had a HAM radio.
He left them sit on the bench across from
his place and went to call Gianna. She
and Nick were in the cottage with the
twins. Tiny called her and she left Nick
there and went to deal with David. He
told her what he knew about Todd and
Donna. Gianna said put them in the card
shop next to the cottage. There was a two
bedroom apartment upstairs. Todd could
use the shop area as a workroom for all
the projects David would be giving him to
do. He told her they had nothing and they
looked rather starved. She asked him to
feed them something. She be in town after
awhile. She'd replace his food they ate.

David went out and told them the
good news. He showed them their new home.
He told them to stack anything they
didn't want down here near the door. Make
a list of what they would like. He'd be
back. He threw three ham sandwiches
together and carried them over. They were
busy at work and making progress already.
He gave them the food and a water bottle.
Told them the Lady would be here after
awhile with more food. Then he checked on
Casey. The boy was doing a great job.
Then he went to the feed store.

9:00 am EDT,

Many of them were sleeping. They had
been walking for two weeks. Some were
having one of the two MRE"s Reno had
given each of them last night. David told
them the Lady was bringing more food and
water. When they were up to it, would
they start to clean the place up. David
told them they would be using the space
for a Farmers Market in a few days, if
they could get it organized. He said to
waste nothing. Then he went to find Reno.

Reno had just gotten the first
barrier in place. David told him The
Booths needed the cook stove and stuff
from their place. Reno asked if any of
the Army boys were up. If they were he'd
send one of his guys to drive the truck
and trailer, if he could get four or five
of the guys to move the stuff. David said
he'd have them by the truck in five. When

356

David got back to the feed store, the place was a rush of activity. Everyone was up and working. David found the leader and told him what he wanted. David took the five men over to the truck, then went to get Mr. Booth. When Mrs. Booth found out they were going she insisted she go too. They got to the truck as Sal was loading the men in the bed. The one that called the front seat got booted to the back so the elderly couple could ride inside.

David looked at the board over the door to his shop and thought, 'I can't keep running around like this.' He took it down. After he'd freed the front entrance he got two more deadbolt sets for Todd and the Booths. He looked at his stock and thought, 'Can't keep doing this either. We need a locksmith to re-key the locks in town.' David had an idea and went back to the feed store. On the way he said out loud to no one, "It's fucking exhausting being the Sheriff." Inside David was amazed. The place had been a holy mess from looters. It was 90% squared away in just under an hour. David found the leader, he'd found out the last time was he was there, he was named Blake, and asked him to make a list of all the men and their skills in or out of the Army. David told him they were doing a fine job, then come and find him when the list was done. He checked on Casey. David walked in and said, "Holy shit, this is really coming along."

Casey was beaming at the praise. "I even filed them alphabetically. You were running so I went to the store and found a can of stain kill. Think it might need two coats."

David smiled at the kid and said, "Think we might have to go to the farm tonight." Casey let out a hot damn and started painting faster. On the way to the Jennings David mused at how the world had changed. People were now willing to bust their ass for a meal and a shower. The place no longer looked like a ransacked card shop. The floor was swept, a work table set up, the items they didn't want or need were neatly stacked or in boxes. Donna had found a line in the back yard on which the bedding was airing. Todd had asked Casey where the rain barrel was and got a bucket of water for her to clean with. Emma had removed the 'totally boy' stuff from her room and stacked it by the door.

David gave Todd the lock set as Blake came to the the door. "Sir the feed store is as completed as well as it can be without more direction from you as to what you want done with the salvaged items. Where would you like us next? And here is the list. The last five names are the men who went to help. They may have more to add to their skills." David scanned the list and found what he hoped would be there. "Have Juan report to me.

I have a whole town that needs re-keying. Blake how did you get them to work so fast?"

"I told them they needed to make that lady want to feed us again."

David started laughing, "Well done Blake. Find Reno and ask him if he needs a few hands. Bring the rest here they can start on the print shop." Blake went off and David turned to Todd. As he went to speak he remembered the guy liked to be called TJ. "TJ I'll take that lock set back. Blake has a locksmith among his men. I'll have him make a set of keys for your front and back doors when he gets here. I have a key cutter in my shop but that's as far as my knowledge goes.

11:30 am EDT,

They were about seven minutes from town when Gianna said "Nick I've been thinking."

Nick smiled and said, "When aren't you thinking?"

Gianna said "Well... when we're, Oh, hi Carmichael gee I forgot we weren't alone... never mind. Any-way, I was thinking about our new soldiers."

"Gianna, you know I don't like when you think about other men."

359

"Nicholas please wipe that smile off your face and listen. I thought you should pick the six to eight best. The ones we or rather you could train to be our unit in town. Separate from David and whoever he selects for deputies. I would install them in that cottage. Any thoughts?"

Nick is smiling again. "I have lots of *thoughts*... on the subject of a team assigned to town, I think it's an excellent idea. We can take two at a time to the farm for training. I like the leader. Since you've been so busy thinking about other men, any ideas on other candidates?

"No, not my area at the moment."

"What do we do with the rest?"

"Haven't got that far yet. We should work that Geno boy in as a regular now that he's seen the farm."

"Already have Charlie on it."

"I know you're the Mayor but I'm calling a meeting when we get there."

"As long as I don't have to speak it's fine. Why don't we make *you* the Mayor?"

"Because we're dealing with southern males. They respond better to you."

David was in the street working with the Army boys when they pulled up. He had a bench table set up in front of his store. When Nick and Gianna got out David said, "Thought you might like a table to work from."

Gianna said, "Thanks that's perfect." Amber was walking up with a tray of seedlings. "Just line them up on the table honey. Lee, bring the cage here and the bucket of compost." Gianna turned back to David, who was now talking about the potential of the Army boys with Nick. They were going over the list Blake had made. They had to stop and get out of the street because Sal was back with the Booth's things. This gave Gianna a chance to cut in. "David I want everyone here as soon as you can round them up please." Nick was grinning and about to cut in. Gianna squinted her eyes at his and trying not to smile said, "Don't you dare say it. If you do I promise you'll be very sad tonight."

She walked away but heard Nick tell him she should be Mayor. She marched back and said quietly, "Nicholas clearly you've forgotten the manor house has three bedrooms. One us may be sleeping in a different one than they woke up in." Nick held on to her as she tried to leave. He whispered in her ear, "I have no intention of sleeping anywhere but with my wife." Then he kissed her neck.

361

She looked up at him, "Nicholas what has gotten in to you today? You are a heart beat from out of control. Behave yourself." She went back to emptying the trucks shaking her head. Amber and Gianna had the table set up and went to see what they had done in the feed store. Blake was waiting for her reaction. "This is wonderful. Thank you all for working so hard. I can see my trust was not misplaced. On their way to the Jennings Gianna stopped by the Booths' to see how the items from their home fit. She told Mrs. Booth it was very homey and warm. Gianna was very pleased at the transformation of the card shop. She introduced herself to the Jennings. "This is lovely. Are you pleased with the location?"

Donna said, "Yes, thank you it's so much more than we expected. Emma is delighted with her new room. She's been sleeping on the floor at our family's since we got here."

12:00 pm EDT,

David had everyone in town gathered by the time Gianna had finished at the Jennings. Gianna said, "You've all done so much today you really should be very proud of yourselves. I wanted to tell you about our farm. I do not have a magic food making machine. We have animals and greenhouses. Nick and I created it to care for our people. We only produce so much. I feed the approximately 150 people who live there. When we have extra we will share. When Nick realized how desperate people outside our gates were he pushed me to ramp up our production. We have hens sitting on duck and chicken eggs, all the dairy goats have had a date in the past week as have the cows. My niece Amber has had people working extra hours to get seedling growing. All this takes time. Eggs take almost a month, to hatch, then four to six months to lay, cows carry for nine months, goats five, seedlings grow at their own pace.

You will have to find ways to make it through the winter. Work together. Y'all need a smoke house to preserve the food you catch. Donna, I selected that location for you because it has the courtyard garden area. I brought you two hens to give you fresh eggs. I'm hoping you will share them with the Booths who don't have a garden space. TJ you'll have to make the a coop. Amber brought seedlings of winter veggies. She even brought you compost for the beds. I'm sure there are the makings of several hoop houses to be found. I was thinking you could put one on the south side of the feed store. Work it as a community garden. We can get you started, you will have to do the work. My people have put in hundreds of extra hours the last ten days or so to help those outside our farm. I can't expect them to continue to do this much longer. We will help when we can but you can't look to me to keep you fed. My 150 mouths must come first. I believe as more people come to live in town it will get easier. David's reopening of the Farmers Market is a perfect way for you all to work together. If you step over to the table we brought some things for you today. Amber passed out the supplies and Gianna went to see what Nick and David were up to.

1:00 pm EDT,

She found them in the freshly painted Sheriff's station, sitting with their feet up on the desks. Gianna sent Casey off to claim a veggie box for his family and get a sandwich. "Well, what have you two been up to? Did you select your deputies?"

"Yes, ma'am I did. I have four in mind. We were just talking about where I should bunk them."

"I was thinking you might want to turn the print shop into a place for them. Your escape hatch would still be viable and if you needed them on the roof, they're right there. Nick, how many did you select?"

"Eight for the cottage."

That's thirteen with Geno. Now what do we do with the other seven? Should we put them in one place together? Do they have skills we want?"

David showed her the list and said, "I think that would work for now. I like the loft above the feed store. It would also give me eyes on this end of the street. Teach them how to run the farmers market. They could have their own hoop house there's room for two."

"That sounds great. They could take the plow truck and check the houses of the dead for supplies and furniture."

Nick smiled at her. "That was a very nice speech Gianna but there's a problem... these people have no way to feed themselves."

"You're telling me this why?"

"Because we have food."

Nicholas, if this is going where I think it is... you'll be back in the farmhouse never mind the other bedroom."

"Gianna, we already discussed that and neither is an option. That subject is closed. Now back to the food."

"David, is there something in that desk I can stab my husband with? Rusty scissors... anything like that?" David sat watching them, thinking yea they play rough.

"NO? Okay then it's time for me to go home."

She turned to go and Nick caught her by the wrist. "You can't look at their starving faces and say no."

"You're right. I can go home behind my walls, that we built because I knew this day would come, and not see them. I warned them for decades and they called me crazy and did nothing. Now you're asking me to reward them for their stupidity? By taking food from the people who've worked with us for ten years. In the last two weeks you've added five more mouths to the feed bill and there's Geno and the eight in the cottage. Where does it end Nick? I've given hundreds of pounds of food already. When does it end... when we're all eating one bowl of rice and beans a day? That's not what our people signed up for or worked for."

"Gianna you know you're going to give in so stop."

"Nick, are you high? What you're asking me to give, can't be bought and replaced. It can only be grown and that takes months of time and labor."

"None of which these people have. Give me a few bags of rice. Nick pulled her down on his lap.

"Rice, are you crazy? Do you see a fucking rice paddy around here anywhere? Nicholas-have-you-lost-your-mother-fucking-mind? You don't know that we've already cut back on the food we serve by 10%. They can have the surplus produce. Do you even know what we grow? NO. Because you've never worked the fields, greenhouses, orchard, or gardens. Stop smiling at me. And let me go. You know, a hundred years from now, they're going to look back and see ours was the shortest marriage in the history of the apocalypse!"

"Gianna, that's just silly. First I told you I will never let you go. Second, I'm the Mayor and I made a new law, No divorce in Moon Mountain."

"You *have* lost you mind. And for that new law of yours, you can stay here. I'm leaving."

"Only if I let you go, which I never will. Another topic we've already discussed and settled."

"Like the food? No. Another topic discussed and settled. Oh Nick, we waited all those years and now Alzheimers has set in. Now I'm stuck with you, come on my poor addled husband, lets go home." Nick released his hold because he was laughing so hard. Gianna was up and out the door. She turned to look at him laughing at her, the bullet hit her in the back and she went down.

Nick was out of the chair and to the doorway in three seconds. Gianna was on her side coughing grabbing her ankle. The shooter saw Nick in the doorway and bounced one off the stone lintel. As Nick pulled back he saw why she was grabbing her ankle as she slid a Glock out of the holster. She released the safety and rolled on her back. She shot the bastard three times as the army boys poured out of the feed store. Nick dove for Gianna. He rolled her, covering her with his body. Ten seconds later Reno and their men came charging down the street. But they were all dead. The boys shot the five attackers and then shot them again, and again. Blake had to yell cease fire to get them to stop. Nick rolled off Gianna and saw a 22 slug in her vest. He loosened the straps and rolled her gently to him. She put her hand on his chest and started yelling, "Nickolas, why the hell did you do that? You don't have a vest on!"

Nick laughed at her. "You have *got* to stop doing this to me woman!"

"This was a deal breaker. I am never setting foot on this street again." Gianna suddenly realized all the men were standing around her. "All of you Stop staring at me like I'm dying. Nick get me off the ground." On her feet she sees Reno laughing. "What the hell are you laughing at?"

"Ma'am Nick's right. You have to stop getting shot."

"Sage advise, asshole. Reno I want every one of the men who came out of that building shooting, in the truck and on their way to the farm in two minutes. Thank you gentleman. Go with Reno."

Amber pulled up in Dark Lady. "Nick get my Aunt in this truck." She jumped out and ran around to open the door. She got in the back.

1:30 pm EDT,
Dancing Goats Farm
Moon Mountain, North Carolina

On the way home Carmichael said, "Ma'am I am so sorry I wasn't there. I was helping Amber load the truck."

"Carmichael you were where you should have been. I wanted you to protect her. Didn't I tell you to stay with her? Don't worry about it. We're never coming to this fucking town again. Nick you still haven't answered my question."

Nick took her hand. "Gianna it's my job to protect my wife, with my body if I have to."

"Where did you get this *crap* advice from?" Carmichael and Amber were trying not to laugh.

"I read it on the internet." The two in the back lost it.

"Nicholas, I believe I've shown you I have *much better* uses for your body, than using it as a human shield." The laughing escalated

"Gianna, I can do both, I'm ambidextrous. I believe I demonstrated that to you last night." Laughing harder.

"I believe you did *indeed*." Carmichael fell off the seat.

Nick pulled up to the veranda. Carmichael and Amber fell out the back doors laughing. Charlie was on the steps. "What the hell happened?"

Amber managed, "Auntie got shot again." Then doubled over in laughter.

Nick was helping Gianna up the steps. Charlie asks, "What the hell are they laughing about?"

Nick smiling says, "I have no idea."

Carmichael manages to get out, "The Boss is ambidextrous." Neither can stop laughing.

Charlie growls, "You two get to the infirmary! There's something wrong with

both of you," and slams the door. Gianna
yells for Charlie just outside the back
door. "Yes ma'am."

"Nick stop. Charlie I have my new
soldiers coming in. Get them a place in
the barracks. When they're clean, feed
them anything they want. I'll see them in
the morning. Okay Nick need very hot
shower please."

3:00 pm EDT,

After the hot shower Nick was
massaging one of Alexandra's magic salves
into the impact point on Gianna's back.
Her chin was resting on the edge of the
bed. So she can sip her Purple Kamikaze
through a straw. The salve and the drink
are starting to take effect. "Nick, thank
you I'm feeling so much better, thank you
honey. Why didn't you have a vest on?"

"I got sloppy because I woke up
feeling invincible."

"You *were*, rather not your stern
self today."

"Gianna, I feel like a ton of shit
that's been on my back for eleven years
is gone. You've been my best friend
almost since the day I found you. Last
night you helped me let go of that shit.
I shouldn't have hidden it from you for
ten years but now it's gone. Seeing Nicky
and Rosie happier than I've ever known

371

them to be, you don't know what a that means to me, or maybe you do, that's why you made it happen. I woke up and the anger that's always in the back of my head was gone."

"This new found freedom made you forget your vest, behave more than a little sensual in public, which is completely out of character for you, and then go 'all Fabio' on me again?"

"What the hell is 'all Fabio'?"

"OH, I didn't tell you about that. Well Nicholas, you're getting a reputation around our village. 'The Romance Hero', to the infirmary was the first time...

Wait, you need some background data. The Amazons gave her the name of Rosie the Retch. They were all having breakfast the next morning and started comparing their impressions of what she was all about. Nick, they got it. Amber is the one who strung the bits together. She figured you wanted the retch to know you were in love with your wife, which is why you showed up on the veranda and as she put it, 'half naked and went 'all Fabio' on me. That was the second time.

The third time was today, when you dove in between bullets to cover me, with no regard for your own life. That was an 'all Fabio' thing too. Then the ride home... yea I promise you after the way those two were laughing, with a little help from your friends babe, by tomorrow everyone will know, Nick is ambidextrous in bed." Gianna stole a glace over her shoulder. "Nick you look confused."

"Yea... Who he fuck is Fabio

cḣɑpⱦeꝛ 34
SⱦAⱯIꝴG ALIVE

"If I can stay alive long enough..."

9:00 pm EDT, October 14,
Dancing Goats Farm
Moon Mountain, North Carolina

Gianna woke with a start. She looked for her phone to call Andy. She answered on the third ring. "Andy, sorry to bother you at this hour. We need to get everyone on the kelp tabs ASAP. I know some take them already. And some eat the seaweed we grow in the shrimp tanks. I'll have plant samples cut in the morning. Let me know what you find. Thanks." She texted Dawn about collecting the samples. Nick wasn't in the room. She assumed he'd gone to check on their new soldiers. She didn't know how many of them had come to her rescue, but if they were willing to run into a gunfight with no cover, she was willing to train and feed them. She thought about getting up but she still hurt too much. "The guys are right, I really do have to stop getting shot."

"Are you talking to yourself again?"

"Yes, Nicholas, I am. You'll be pleased to hear I'm agreeing with you about not getting shot again. We're not going to leave the farm ever again. Then, we'll all be safe. Please don't start arguing with me over this. The rest of the world is not our problem. This new 'Messiah' roll of yours is not attractive, and very irritating!"

Nick had been standing by the door watching her animated declarations. He was smirking as he tossed 'their' leather on the chair and sat on the edge of the bed to remove his boots. When he was done he laid back on the bed and put his hand around one of her ankles. "You woke up rather feisty. You must be in pain." Gianna ignored his remark and continued braiding her hair. "Your new soldiers are doing fine, by the way. They went a little crazy when they found out they could have steak and apple pie à la mode. You're right, they're just kids. Blake is the eldest at twenty-five. Reno brought in eight. David is down in the Q with Casey. The kid worked so hard David brought him in a few days early. David said they'd cleaned up after we left, then started on the loft apartment in the feed store. The ones I had picked for the squad in town, set the cottage to rights. Two of the ones Reno brought in are two from my list, Blake and Roger. Since you've piggishly taken the extras as your solders, David only has one left to put in the feed store. He wants to know if you would give at least one of them back?"

Gianna was lying back on a stack of pillows filing her nails. Nick wondered if she was filing them down or to a point. "I'm glad they enjoyed their dinner. I'll review them tomorrow and decide then. You could always give him one or two you picked for the cottage."

"I could but I won't. Who's going to train your new soldiers?"

"Nick, don't be an ass. That's your job. Since we won't be leaving here anymore, you'll have plenty of time to see it's done correctly."

Nick rolled over and moved up alongside her. "Gianna I'm very pleased you won't be going out there again, but don't think for a minute you're grounding me."

Gianna stopped filing and pointed the file at him. "Nick, you do realize this is a metal file don't you?"

Nick laughed at her. "Gianna, I don't think you're in any condition for a little hand to hand with me right now. You know you'd never win even if you weren't injured."

"If you persist in this foolish notion, I could wait and stab you after

376

you fall asleep."

Nick was laughing at her again. "You could but I don't think you will. Before you decided to get shot again, we were having a conversation. You realize, if you hadn't run out on it, you wouldn't have gotten shot. We have to provide food for the men in the cottage if they're part of our security force. We also need to see that David and his deputies are fed so they can protect the town. Are you really going to let the old people and the little girl starve to death watching the men eat?"

Gianna threw the file in the bed table drawer and slammed it closed. "I'm putting it in there, because I'm truly feeling like I want you hurt you with it right now! Why do you persist in making this my responsibility? When we started this place you said you agreed with me, that we couldn't save everyone. Were you bullshitting me? Was it your plan all along to raid our supplies when things went south? What is wrong with you?

Back in August, when the news said the barrier islands were losing 6' a year, they should have begun to stockpile food. Or when the storms and the oceans began to consume the southeast they could have done something. The fucking lights went out two weeks ago! They've done little to nothing for themselves in that time. We killed the zombies for them.

377

Flattened the Thackers and wiped out how many bands of the rogue Army? By babying them we're starting the same cycle all over again. Why can't you see that?"

"Gianna you run a feudal village here, how is that any different?"

"Because our people knew to prepare. They understood they needed to work together. If one of them is hurt or sick, two more step up offering to do their job. I don't have to tell them. They just do it. For the last few years my job has been to keep track of what is going on outside so they could continue the life they've built here.

Your men protect them and they feed your men. The men have learned how to grow food and care for animals. The Tribe members have learned how to defend themselves. We don't make them do these things, they choose to. Nicholas, we're not the only place like this. There are thousands of us around the world. That doesn't count the preppers. We have friends in the Smokey Mountains who started their place back in the 70's. Not only are they doing fine, the preppers down the road from them are starting to work with them to become more like us."

"Gia how is that different than what I'm asking you to do here?"

"Because they're preppers. They have

food, ammo and a secure place to live. They're not looking to Barb and Harvey to keep them alive. They want to learn how to stay alive after their food runs out."

Nick threw his hands up. "Arguing with you is like arguing with Google... you have a fucking answer for everything! Gianna, I will not stand by and watch children starve!"

"What are you going to do... Go on a hunger strike?" This image caused her to start laughing. "They won't die living on the extra produce and milk we give them. Vegetarians have proved this. You need to stop this foolish request for me to give up staples I don't know how to replace yet. They should get off their asses and put in winter wheat and get fields ready for oats in the spring. There are still some bags of seed in the feed store. You should tell David to secure them from mice, so he can pass them out when the fields are ready to plant." Gianna leaned back and crossed her arms. She was watching Nick's face as he continued to try to think of an argument that would get her to give up the food in the storerooms.

After five minutes all he'd come up with was, "It's not enough Gianna!"

She was laughing at him. "Well I guess we're back to: the shortest marriage in the history of the apocalypse!"

"Gianna! If you say that again I'll..." He knew he'd never hurt her, at the moment he couldn't come up with something to threaten her with. "I will think of a way to punish you for saying for that!" She was laughing at him. Pissed and frustrated he said, "You are the fucking most exasperating woman to ever have drawn a breath!"

"You're just saying that because you know I'm right."

"NO, I'm saying it because *you're exasperating.*"

She thought this was a good time to use one of his lines on him. "Nicholas, You're very sexy when you're angry." It wasn't. He threw the pillow at her and stormed out.

An hour later Nick returned. Gianna was half asleep when he got into bed. Still in a combative mood she said. "Poor Nicholas, whatever shall you do with your exasperating wife?" He pulled her to him and showed her.

**11:00 pm EDT, October 15,
Moon Mountain, North Carolina**

David deposited a clean and well fed Casey at his sister's drive and headed back to town. In spite of the town being

380

attacked again and Gianna getting shot
again, it had been a very productive day.
They had gotten the bodies burned and
drove the attackers truck through the
brush and brought it into town on one of
the dead end side streets. He now had his
own vehicle for the Sheriff's office.
Nick told him to put the pickup with the
plow in front of the cottage for the team
he would keep there. The printing shop
was cleaned out in the back. The four
deputies already made sleeping areas for
themselves. Gianna had told him to move
the printing machines to the back room at
the feed store.

Nick's team in the cottage squared
it away but still needed single beds.
They'd put doors on the living room to
make another sleeping room. They shared
some bedding and towels with the new
deputies and the soldier in the loft.

Gary was eager to taking over the
feed store and Farmers Market
responsibilities. He worked on the loft
and started sealing the seeds in rat
proof containers. He'd worked a few
summers in a feed & grain back in Georgia
before joining the Army. When he ran out
of containers he hunted around town for
more and parts for hoop houses and
gardening tools. David said he'd supply
the tools and take payment in veggies
when the crop came in. Gary told him
there was usable lumber in the block that
had burned, he was going to salvage some

for the raised beds in the hoop houses. He asked David if the Lady had any cats out on the farm. He wanted one or two to keep the Farmers Market free of mice. And did David think they would give him anymore compost and maybe soil? David told him he'd pass along the requests. It wasn't until Gary asked for the cats that David realized the zombies must have eaten all the ones that used to live in town.

The Jennings and Booths had been upset by the attack. David pointed out the barriers Reno had put up that morning had kept them from riding into town and doing more damage. Now with men posted at that end of town, they'd be even safer. Things were getting better. As a few more people moved into town they would get even stronger.

David rolled into town and found all was quiet. He saw the second story window of the cottage open and the end of a rifle extended beyond the sill. There was the glow of a candle in the deputies barracks. He drove to the south end of main street and saw Gary was seated in the loft door facing south. David parked the truck in front of the cottage and tossed the keys up to the guard in the window. As he fell asleep his last thought was, it had been a damn good day for the town of Moon Mountain.

Nick met Layah and the twins on their way to breakfast. He was keeping his promise to have at least one meal a day with them. Inside he told Layah she should go and eat with her friends, he'd see the children were fed. Nicky had a plate stacked with too much food. Gianna told Nick to let him do this. He'd stop once he felt safe. But she'd told Nicky he did have to take what he didn't finish to the proper pens to feed the animals his leftovers. Rosie had lots of questions which she began asking as soon as they sat down. "Uncle Nick why don't we have to go to school here? The children all seem very smart how do they learn?"

Nick thought,'Mom hope you're watching, she's turning out just like you.' "We have school in the winter months. After breakfast they gather here in the Hall in front of the fireplace and they work on one subject a day. They study all the normal subjects. Gianna feels the arts are very important. There are classes in painting, sketching, sculpting and more. There are music classes where you can sing or learn to play an instrument. You'll learn about poetry, the performing arts like, dancing and acting. You can perform in the productions they put on if you want. In

the spring the classes move outside.
You'll learn how we grow the food you're
eating right now, how to care for the
animals."

"What about gym class?"

"We don't have one. You can join one
of the dance troops, or take yoga or Tai
chi."

"This is the best place to live. I
wish we could always live here."

"You do and will always live here from
now on." Nick braced himself for
questions about their mother. 'Damn why
wasn't Gianna here?'

Rosie surprised him with, "I've met
the Airy-Fairies. They're Layah's
friends. I love hanging out with them.
Did you know they have real fairies
here?"

Nick was laughing at her excitement
and out of relief. "Yes, I believe we do.
I've never seen them though. Gianna says
I'm looking with the wrong eyes."

"You must be, cause they taught
Nicky and me how to, and we saw them. He
got excited and tried to catch one. Layah
told 'him they're not bugs, we never
catch them.' Also they have the most
beautiful names here. Layah says you can
change your name whenever you feel the

old one didn't fit you any more." She put her fork down and put her hand on Nick's. She looked up at him with a most serious expression. "Uncle Nick, I'm changing my name. I hate Rosie. It's her name. Layah said I should think about it a few days and see what name comes to me. I'll let you know when I pick a new one."

Nick was taken back by the realization that Gianna was right, she did not miss or even like her mother. "Make sure you let me know so I can find you. I don't want to be calling you the wrong name. Nicky are you changing your name too?"

"Hell no, I have your name!"

Nick looked at Rosie. "Why didn't you ask Layah about school?"

"I was afraid if I asked, then the fun would be over and she'd remember we had to go to school."

7:30 am EDT,

After they'd eaten they went to feed Nicky's three extra pancakes to the ducks. When he was done he told Nick, "I think I should take less food next time. Well, maybe just one extra pancake, I do like feeding the ducks."

Nick said, "I believe Amber or Dawn will give you greens to feed them if you

385

ask."

They found Layah on the green doing yoga among the grazing sheep with the rest of the class. She jumped up when she saw Nick. The twins ran off to find a place next to Layah's friend Aja and her boys. Nicks said, "Layah you're doing an excellent job with them thank, you. Let me know as soon as Rosie picks a name. I want to support her in this. Anything I should know about?"

Layah said, "I'm so happy you understand how deeply she feels about this. I know she was your sister but I have to tell you the children don't like her. Seems she never spent time with them and fired a nanny every time they got close to them. I was waiting to tell you this after breakfast, when I tucked Nicky in last night, he said I hope she never comes back. From her bed Rosie said me too. Gianna told me what happened so I wouldn't encourage the children to believe she was coming back. She wanted to hear anything like what I just told you so please let her know."

Nick said he would and went to find his brilliant wife. He'd been busy with another part of building the farm when she had designed the schooling system. Then hadn't given it much thought when she explained it to him. As he was explaining it to his niece he got what an amazing plan it was.

He found Gianna in Alice's Restaurant with Simon. Nick smiled when he saw they were weighing out two pound bags of flour, dried beans and dried fruits. Dark Lady was parked outside the door, filled with boxes of store bought canned goods. He could hear Amber adding today's fresh produce, milk and eggs to the boxes. Nick came up behind Gianna and put his arms around her waist. He whispered in her ear, "I love you." Simon told Nick to stop trying to shag his help and to carry the bags out to the truck.

8:30 am EDT,

Nick pulled the Dark Lady through the barn to find the plow pickup and David's new-to-him Chevy pickup waiting in the Q.

He looked at Gianna. She shrugged, "I didn't see any reason for us to go there when they were perfectly capable of coming here."

When he saw Gianna, David said, "Glad to see you're up and around. Hope you're not too sore."

Nick said, "She is but she's too stubborn to stay in bed. But if she hadn't gotten up, you wouldn't be picking up this food. She also interviewed the men who came to her rescue and these two want to go back with you to the feed store to help Gary run it."

Gianna stepped closer to David and said in a low voice. "I think the three of them are gay and feel safer together. Keep a close eye on them. If anyone gives them the slightest bit of shit bring the bastard to me. I will have Amber take her whip to them. Make it clear to any person who wants to live in the town, I will not tolerate bigotry, racism, or prejudice of any type. The punishment will be swift and violent. Make it clear to the people you are bringing the food to before you give it to them. If they don't agree wholeheartedly. They don't get the food. Only kind loving humans get to live in the town."

David looked at her and smiled. "Trust me, no one will give them a problem, we look after our own."

10:00 am EDT, October 15, Moon Mountain, North Carolina

David called everyone to the table outside his shop. He relayed Gianna's message and waited for reactions. They said they had no problem with blacks, Jews, or gays, as long as they were nice people. David said they might want to add Pagans to their list since most of the people at the farm were Pagan. Mrs. Booth said, "I had no idea Pagans were so nice. I never met a Pagan before."

388

David handed out the food with the warning, "You have to ration this food. They didn't have it to give. Nick had to do a lot of talking to get the Lady to take it from her peoples' supplies."

"We'll have to thank her next time she's here." Said Donna Jennings.

David shook his head. "Don't think that will be any time soon. She's mad that people keep shooting her on this street. Nick said she's going to stay safe behind her walls for a while. Gary, she sent these for you." David lifted an animal carrier out of the cab of the truck. "She's expecting so you'll have kittens in about a month. Her name is Tara." A beautiful green eyed cat looked at Gary and meowed. "She also sent you two hens and a rooster to protect them. You can take the truck to the farm when you're ready for the compost and soil."

Brent, one of the soldiers who had returned from the farm, said, "I'll take care of the chickens. I use to raise them."

Everyone took their supplies back to their homes. Gary had found an 8'x8' room under the feed store made of block. He didn't know what they had used it for but he was going to use it as a root cellar. He told Brent and Scotty to put the food down there. He'd put some shelving in there this morning. Brent made a fenced

area for the chickens inside the store
and went out to find stuff to build them
an outside run?

11:00 am EDT,

David stopped back to tell them that
two of the guys in the cottage were going
scavenging. Did one of them want to go
along. Scotty said he'd go. David let
them take both trucks because they needed
beds. Casey went with them too. He knew
which houses belonged to the people who
had died.

David was just going up to his place
when Troy, one of his new deputies,
caught up with him. There was a group of
people coming up the road to the barrier.
David yelled for six of Nick's squad who
were in the cottage to follow him. David
got to the barrier as the first of the
group did. He scanned the crowd for signs
of trouble. He didn't see too many
weapons, just tired dirty people. He
said, "What do you folks want? This town
is closed."

A woman in her late 50's stepped
forward. She said, "I'm Dolly Parks, I
understand why you have your road closed
and don't want strangers in your town. If
we had a place I'd do the same. We don't
want to make any trouble. Could you think
about letting us pass through? A few in
the group have family in Mount Airy.
Doubling back will add two days to our

walk. We're so close. We have our own food, we could give you some."

David asked, "Do you speak for the group?"

From the back of the group someone shouts, "We ain't got no niggers or fags just Christian white folks."

Dolly yells, "Shut the hell up! Don't pay any attention to him. He attached himself to the group yesterday. If I had any bullets left I'd have shot him ten miles back. Yes, I speak for our group."

Brent standing next to David says, "I'll be happy to shoot him for you."

David laughs, "Not yet. Why don't you help Dolly over the barrier so we can talk in my office. Dolly, I'm David Nelson. I'm the Sheriff here." In the station David offers her a seat and a glass of water.

She's grateful for both. "Haven't had a chair since we left Winston-Salem four days ago. The zombies were so bad we had to fight our way out. I got bitten by one." She rolls up her sleeve. The bite is swollen and red. "Don't worry, I haven't shown and signs of turning yet."

David smiled, "Dolly, you're not going to turn. It's a drug that causes them to go zombie. But you need to get that cleaned. I'll see if we have some medication for you." David yelled for Kevin. He sent him next door to the clinic and tells him to look for the supplies Casey put in one of the cabinets this morning.

Kevin came back with alcohol and an antibiotic ointment. "I can clean this sir. Ma'am, if you'll let me."

Outside there's some type of ruckus going on. David says, "Take care of the lady."

The same asshole who was yelling, is now trying to climb over the barrier. David walks up and puts a bullet in his head. "Gary, drag him to the burn pile." Then he went back inside. Dolly looked up questioningly. "I shot him for you. I don't want assholes walking through the countryside with that kind of attitude."

Dolly starts laughing. "I like you. If you were a little older I'd like you even more."

David chuckles, "I'm gay."

Dolly says, "Damn, just my luck. In the middle of the frigging apocalypse, I run across a handsome, not afraid to do what needs to be done man, and he's gay. Do you have an older brother?" Kevin is laughing so hard he's having trouble wrapping her arm.

David says, "No I don't. How many of
you are there? And how many have family
in Mount Airy?"

Brent stuck his head in the door.
"Gary's got him on the pile shall we
torch it? You know out at the farm they
call that 'taking the garbage out'."

David is still smiling from Dolly's
comments. "I should have turned him over
to Amber's whip but he was too annoying
to take out there. Go ahead and burn the
trash."

Dolly says "Who's this Amber?"

"She's the niece of the woman who
owns a farm outside of town. She told me
this morning if anyone behaved like him I
should turn them over to her, so her
niece could take their skin off with her
whip."

Dolly leans forward on the desk.
"I'd like to meet this woman. Sounds like
we're two peas in a pod. There's twenty-
two of us well twenty-one now that you
shot that asshole. Eleven have family in
Mount Airy. Why?"

"Well I have no idea about the other
nine until I meet them but you'd be
welcomed in the town if you wanted to
stay. We have a young couple with a

daughter who are refuges from Winston-Salem for the same reason as you." Kevin had finished with Dolly's arm. "Kevin, put the supplies back, burn the items you used to clean it and help the people over the wall. Send Gary in to me. Dolly we are just getting back on our feet here. The people out at the farm have been a serious help in making this happen."

"Did you want me sir?"

"Gary do you think we could let these people rest in the feed store?"

"Yes sir. As long as they don't touch Brent's chickens, he's gotten kind of possessive of them already."

David stood. "Come on Dolly, let's get your people off their feet and some clean water to drink. We can talk more when they're settled." Out at the barricade David watches the people as they climb over. "Dolly which ones don't have a place to go?"

"Those three clueless college girls. We helped them escape from a second floor dorm. That tall drink of water is a fireman. I think he bats for your team. The two middle age sisters. I thought they'd be a pain in the ass but surprise surprise they grew up in Maine. They can start a fire with one match. And they taught us how to filter stream water through crushed charcoal and sand. Last the retired golf course couple. Think he said he was an engineer. She's a waste of air."

David was chuckling through her whole description of the people. "Dolly I hope you stay I could use the entertainment."

In the feed store they found three of the men from Nick's squad fussing over the college girls. Brent is warning people not to go near his chickens. Gary is telling them where they can relieve themselves cause he doesn't want human crap near the spot he's putting the hoop house. Dolly asks, "What are you going to do with this place?"

"Upstairs is a loft Brent, Gary and Scotty are turning into an apartment, so I have eyes at this end of town. They are left over Army. Down here we'll be holding our Farmers' Market. Come on I'll show you the rest of the town. The Booths and Jennings are standing halfway down the street. David introduces them to Dolly and tells them what's going on at the feed store. They head down to meet the people. David tells her how they ended up with the Army boys, and how Nick and Gianna have helped the town.

12:00 pm EDT,

As they're walking back through town Dolly asks, "So handsome, how does a body

395

get one of these free houses?"

"The Sheriff has to approve of you and then I call Gianna and ask her where I should put each person as they come along." Behind them the trucks are pulling back into town, loaded over the tops of the cabs.

Casey yells "Wait till you see all the good shit we got!" as the truck goes by.

Dolly asks, "Why does this Gianna get to tell people where they can live?"

David shakes his head. "Dolly I'm going to let you ask her yourself."

"Why... is she a bitch?"

"No, but she's tough as nails. Yesterday she took a 22 slug in the back of her vest right where we're standing. She got her Glock out of her ankle holster rolled over and plugged him three times, before Nick could get out the door to cover her. The real reason she's in charge is she has talent for building a community. She built a small sustainable village on her farm. Don't let her hear you call a woman a bitch. She says women are not dogs. She prefers cunt.

"Oh boy, I like her already. When is she coming to town?."

"Not for a while, that was the
second time she got shot here in two
weeks. Let's find out who in your party
wants to stay."

1:00 pm EDT, October 15,
Dancing Goat Farm
Moon Mountain, North Carolina

All ten of them wanted to stay.
David called the farm and asked Reno if
he could talk to Gianna about where to
house new residents. Reno said he'd find
her and have her call back. Stay there.
Reno found them walking the twins home
from lunch. Rosie wanted to go with her
Auntie to the Q. Nick started to say no
but Gianna said fine. Rosie got to check
out the com room with Antonio while
Gianna told David where to house the
people. David asked when she'd be back
town. "When assholes stop shooting me
there. So it's on you David. Make the
street safe and I'll come back."

Back on the farm they found the 'two
Nicks' as Rosie called them, on the green
playing with the sheep. Gianna asked if
the children would like to see the manor
house. She was answered by squeals of
delight. They explored the downstairs and
ran up. Rosie asked "Who lives here?"

"Just Uncle Nick and I."

"Why just the two of you in this big
house?"

"He likes to be alone. You know that. Don't ask silly questions you know the answers to."

What's in here?"

"That's our room and stay out of it. You wouldn't like me going in and touching your stuff would you? I think not Missy."

In the living room Gianna said, "I think we should sit, it's time for a talk." Nick looked at her warningly. "Sit Nicholas, don't get your knickers in a twist." This started both kids giggling cause no one talked to Uncle Nick like that. Gianna sat with one leg over the arm of the chair so Rosie did the same. "I think you know she not coming back, that's why you asked Nick those questions at breakfast. Am I right Missy?" Rosie tried to hide her smile behind her hand and shook her head yes. "You have your answer. What else do you want to know.

Nicky said "What will happen to us?"

"Well, I thought we made that clear when we gave you that lovely cottage to live in. We want you to stay here with us. It makes Nick very happy when he looks out the window and sees you two laughing and playing. Do you like it here?"

"Yes, but what if she comes back and takes us away?"

"That will never happen because we won't let her in the gates. She can jump up and down and scream but she'll never get in."

"But what if she has a gun?"

"Well... I have lots of big guns, and did you know I have a tank? Maybe Uncle Nick will show it to you this week. Her name is Audrey." Nicky looked up at Nick who shook his head yes. The boy smiled ear to ear.

"You know Uncle Nick and I built this place. Well, that makes you rather like the prince and princess here, like Angelena. But you must always be kind and don't hold it over other peoples heads okay? Now what is your new name?"

"I met Alexandra today. I want to be an Amazon like her, so I would like to be Athena."

"Perfect. One of my favorite Goddesses. She is the patroness of Wisdom, Poetry, the Arts, Strategy and *Warfare*. A name befitting an Amazon." Gianna stood. "Come on little Amazon, let's find some ice cream to celebrate."

1:30 pm EDT, October 15,
Moon Mountain, North Carolina

David explained to the town's newest
members what the town rules were. They
were happy to agree to them. David gave
William and Harriet Bradley, the retired
golf course couple, the small house on
Elm behind Donna and TJ. Elm was the side
street on the corner of the Jennings
place.

He offered the one across from it to
the Booths. Gianna thought it might be
quieter for them. Massie was worried the
young men might be ill with her if they
had to move her cook stove again. Blake
said it wasn't a problem. He liked the
new location for them. He could keep a
closer eye on the place on Elm Street
from the back of the cottage. Safer
sounded good to Ray. The Booths packed up
and moved for the second time in a week.

Gianna put the college girls, Mandy,
Livvy and Cora next door to the squad.
The boys would end up hanging around
wherever the girls lived. Might as well
put them where David could keep a lid on
things. The upstairs of the shop would do
nicely for three. Have them clean it and
bring any inventory that's downstairs to
Dolly at the dress shop across the
street.

She put Dolly next to David's
Hardware Store. The Dress shop had a
second floor apartment that should be
plenty of room for her. Have her

inventory the clothing and clean up a shop. She should set up a Shift Shop for the town like the one we have at the farm.

David found out the sisters, Della and Franny Olenick used to have a bakery. Gianna put them in the bakery restaurant. Have them clean it and figure out what they needed to get it open again. There's a two bedroom apartment on the second floor for them.

The tall drink of water was indeed a Firefighter. They both agreed he should take over the tiny Volunteer Fire House on the corner of Elm and Main.

Gianna asked if he'd made any headway with organizing the warehouse behind the Sheriff's station. He said they'd made a start. He'd moved the supplies people didn't want from their new places to racks there. Casey was asking if he could have a bed in town. David had the deputies add a bunk for him in the new deputy house, the former print shop. They were going to get the equipment moved tomorrow. Gianna suggested they make a door in the wall and slide the equipment to the real estate office next door. Find out what kind of engineer William was. See if he can come up with a way to run them.

David told Gianna about the bite on Dolly's arm and and asked if they could get a few basic medical supplies. She said, "Between you and Saint Nick, you're going to nickel and dime me till my cupboards are bare!" Then she said she'd have Alexandra and Andy put some together for the town. Gianna told him to find someone with medical training. He told her Livvy was studying to be a nurse, at least it was a start. David had replaced the bottom half of the clinic's door with plywood and Casey had done a good job of cleaning it. The floor had been cleaned with bleach to remove the drug dealer's blood and anything not packaged was burned.

When everyone was in their new place. David took a break on the bench on the sidewalk outside the squad's cottage. The town was really starting to take shape. He'd had the squad remove the wood from the front of the store. He could see through the shop windows, Dolly was already busy arranging the Shift Shop. She'd loved the idea when David had told her. She'd asked how Gianna knew she'd spent years in retail sales. David said, "She just knows shit."

1:30 pm EDT, October 15, Damascus, Virginia

The newlyweds had spent the better part of twenty-four hours in their room. Once they emerged Rory and Ann started making daily runs to town. They found the Inn that had been attacked by the '*more*

402

was the way to go', zombie boys. Ann filled boxes as Rory carried them to the truck. The dead owners had put back a truckload of food. Rory found their cat hiding under the veranda. Ann found a closet, with as she put it, 'A shit load' of cat food and the carrier. They found twenty gallons of gas in the garage and building supplies that made Ann's eyes twinkle. Rory suggested they come back for them. The cat was freaked and he didn't like leaving the food unattended while they searched. Reluctantly Ann agreed.

Beth went nuts when she saw the cat. Theirs had died back in the spring. Cindy looked at the huge amount of food and told Rory it was the best wedding present ever! With these boxes they went from, we'll manage to get by, to we're in very good shape. Rory and Ann went back for a second load. After the tools and building supplies were loaded they found a store room in the basement with cases of canned food. Once the twenty-one cases were loaded, they siphoned the four vehicles, collecting another fifteen gallons of gas. Ann got in the truck and said, "Where the hell did you find this?"

"In the back of the owner's closet. This is the boost we needed as far as ammunition and fire power goes." There were at least five hundred rounds, two rifles and a hand gun." As they left Ann said a silent thank you to the dead owners.

4:00 pm EDT,

Rory was checking to see if the
movable barrier was properly in place
when he saw a group of people walking up
the road towards the Inn. He yelled for
the women. Cindy reached him first with
his rifle in hand. Beth and Ann were
right behind her. The people were filthy
with road dust, the tragedy they'd lived
through, written on their faces. The
three women used the Civic for cover.
Rory walked to the barrier when one of
the group called out to him.

The man's face was bruised, one hand
was swollen. "Could you please spare us
some water? We haven't found any in a
day." Beth went to get a jug. "The
zombies over ran Danville. The Bad Army
was worse. They caught us as we were
leaving town. That's how I got this." He
pointed to his face and hand. We're just
trying to find a place to sleep tonight."
Beth returned with the water and began to
fill their bottles.

Rory stepped back behind the car.
"Ann what do you think about sending them
to the Inn by the creek? We got most
everything out already."

"Well... they might cut into the
rest of our foraging if they stay. It's
hard to say no. Just look at them."

Cindy said, "We took in so much food today we'll be fine if we don't get anymore. How many are there? Fifteen? I'm going to get them one case of the kidney beans you brought back in the last load." Beth went with her to get more water.

Rory went back to the barricade and told the man about the Inn and how to get there. "It's a big place. You'll have room for your whole group. You'll have to remove the three bodies the zombies killed and board up the window they came through. How are you set for food?"

"We ate the last of that this morning."

"My wife went to get you a case of beans. You'll have to find your own after this."

Cindy handed the case to a young man who'd been listening to what Rory had to say. Rory said, "I believe that place has a well but you'll have to find a way to draw the water by hand. I wouldn't drink the creek water until you make sure there are no bodies floating in it upstream. We'll stop by tomorrow and see how you've settled in." The man named Phil, thanked them for their kindness and turned his people around. He wanted to get them to the Inn before dusk. In the kitchen Cindy said to the others, "Guess we have it pretty fucking good here. The cities seem to be a very dangerous place to be."

4:00 pm EDT, October 15,
Smokey Mountains, Tennessee

Frank and Dan were having the same
conversation while watching the camera
monitors. The zombies had moved over the
state line into Tennessee. They had
killed at least a dozen in the last two
days. The walls were holding well.

The beggars were hardest to deal
with. It helped to know Harvey put a box
of extra produce out on the road every
day. Now that Dan was working almost full
time with them production had jumped. It
didn't really cost them anything but
labor to grow the extra food. They'd been
saving their own seeds for years. They
had fantastic compost piles to keep
replenishing the soil so just labor and
water from the rain barrels.

Harvey and Barbra generally got the
World News, as they called, it from
Ferret. They passed the information on to
Dan. So far they hadn't had to deal with
the rogue army but they were seeing the
refugees fleeing the cities. That's why
Harvey started leaving the food. No way
in hell would they open their gates.

5:45 pm EDT, October 15,
Dancing Goat Farm
Moon Mountain, North Carolina

Antonio heard the message and yelled upstairs for Reno. "There's a nearly a company of rogue Army marching east. They will be here in approximately thirty minutes. We didn't get word sooner because someone had to run through the woods to the Baker farm. The people are fleeing into the woods."

"Sound general alarm in the farm too. Get Nick here now." Reno ran up the stairs. On his way to the barn he thought, 'The Lady is going to be ripping mad when she finds out Nick is out there. Nick's going to lose his mind if they attack and he's not here.' He couldn't think about them now he had orders to give.

Gianna came out of the farmhouse behind Charlie. She looked around the yard, then went into the barn. She'd seen Reno going up the tower. Halfway into the barn she had her answer... the Humvee was gone. She ran for the com room. Antonio heard her pounding down the stairs and cringed. *Antonio where is he?*"

She had her really scary voice on. "Ma'am I don't know. I can't raise him. The satellite must be out of range. He went to town fifty-five minutes ago."

"I'll deal with *you* later. Get me Theo." She put a headset on. "Theo talk to me."

"The Tribe is armed and have reported to the Sergeant. The Amazons are on their way. The children are in the Hall. No I don't know where he is at this moment."

"We'll have a discussion later on how long you've known he was off the property. Send me another ten regulars." She hung up and turned her attention back to Antonio. He was pretty sure at this moment he was more afraid of her than Nick. "Antonio have you raised David yet? Get me Violet." She began to pace listening to Reno and Charlie get the men in place. She cut in. "Get Carmichael in the cupola. Violet get up on my roof. They're coming from the west." David's voice came through the HAM. "David please tell me my asshole husband is there."

"No, he left maybe twenty minutes ago."

"If he doesn't die in this, I'm going to kill him when I get my hands on him. Antonio will tell you what he's walking into. If we can't hold them here, they'll be coming your way." She threw the headset on the desk and grabbed a Catsear. There was still no sign of movement from either direction.

Charlie saw her coming and wasn't sure which was the greater threat. She took the stairs two at a time. Reno saw his life flash before his eyes. When she'd reached the top Charlie said, "I was asleep ma'am."

Reno took the full force of her rage. "When the fuck will you stupid men learn? When I say *I know* it means I fucking know! You're standing in the middle of the fucking apocalypse *aren't you*? You live here *why*... because I told you *I knew* this would happen. When that obstinate husband of mine ignores my warning, the least you morons can do is tell me he's left the property and placed himself in grave danger! Nick left the town twenty minutes or so ago... Yes, they should come face to face in about ten minutes, with asshole Nick, on the wrong side of the gate! By the end of this day you'll all learn that I am far more dangerous than Nick. Heads up boys... *This is not going to go well for Nick.* Which is why I told him to stay inside the fucking gates!" In their ears they hear Violet say she sees movement through the trees. Gianna says, "Carmichael can you see Nick coming from town?"

Twenty seconds later, "Shit, yes ma'am. What the hell is he doing out there?"

"If he lives we can ask him later." She looks at Reno. "Carmichael, *my strange child,* knows Nick shouldn't be out there... but *you* didn't think to tell me. Give me those fucking binoculars.

Have them ready to open the gate if he gets here in time." She's watching Nick and she can't stop him. "Give me the flare gun."

She fires it as Carmichael starts firing and says. "Ma'am they have scouts running through the woods."

"Nicholas-are-you-out-of-your-fucking-mind?" Nick saw the flare and is driving faster toward the gates. Gianna turns, the Amazons are standing on the new walkways on the inside of the gates. Lizzy is there too with a rifle rather than a bow.

The two Army jeeps saw Nick as he saw them. Nick skidded the Humvee sideways in front of the gate to keep them from ramming it. Gianna screams, "Open that fucking gate." Charlie signals them not to open it. It's too late... forty plus men swarm up out of the woods and overrun the Humvee. The vanguard and the Amazons are inflicting heavy damage but four of them have Nick. They drag him out of the driver's seat. One Army guy jumps in the drivers seat. Gianna says "Lizzy take out the tires on the Humvee." In seconds Liz has the two facing her down, an Amazon farther down on the wall puts an arrow in the other back tire. Gianna takes out the last one, through the thigh, of one of the men holding Nick. Lizzy goes to work on the tires of their jeeps next. The leader backs the

second jeep out around the corner when he
sees what's happening.

Lizzy manages to hit the front
grill. "You won't get far now fuck face."

They have a rope around Nick's
throat and are using him as a shield as
they retreat. Gianna raises her gun and
aims for the bastard's head. Carmichael
says, "NO, ma'am not even I can make that
shot."

Nick is watching his Gianna's face.
He sees her lower the gun. He watches her
change from wife to Amazon. He can't see
her eyes from here but he knows they've
gone black. As they are dragging him down
the road he thinks, 'If I can stay alive
long enough...' Then they hit him in the
head... everything goes black.

6:10 pm EDT,

Gianna stood watching, waiting...
they had Nick tied to a lamppost in the
front yard of Thompson's farmhouse.
Nick's face had been battered and is
starting to swell. His mouth is bleeding.
He keeps spitting blood. An asshole in an
Army uniform, is shouting in his face.
He's taunting Nick with a Bowie knife
against his throat. He runs the tip under
Nick's jaw, leaving a fine line of red in
it's wake. Gianna waits... drops of blood
are falling on Nick's chest. He's been
stripped to the waist. His ribs are

bruising already.

A group of thirty-five men are gathered on and around the jeep Lizzy hit. There is a puddle of anti-freeze on the ground under the radiator. They're watching the torture of Nick and are cheering their leader on.

Reno's in her ear. "We're in place. Alternating Vanguard Amazon from your twenty around both sides of the farmyard. Looks like there were more than we were told. We left thirty-four on the ground at the Q. I'm looking at close to sixty five here. No idea how many are in the house. Ma'am, are you sure you want to leave the back open? They'll escape out the back of the house into the woods."

Gianna hisses through her teeth, "*Indeed they will.*"

Gianna takes a breath, then notched an arrow and raised her bow. Alexandra standing on her right can see her Aunt's hands were trembling with rage... and fear. "Auntie, please let me have the honor."

"Yes, the cracked ribs aren't helping my aim. You're the better archer. I wish you could stop him but not kill him. I would so love to skin that mother fucker alive."

With a wicked smile Alexandra

412

answered her, "Oooooh that I can do Auntie."

Gianna looked to her eldest on her left and nodded, Violet raised her hand to the Amazons... a war cry zaghareet exploded into the air, so feral and primal... their enemies' blood ran cold.

Alexandra raised her bow... the Amazons followed... Alexandra's flamed tipped arrow flew... followed by twenty others... the metal beneath Gianna and Alexandra's feet vibrated and shook... when Audrey spoke.

www.ingramcontent.com/pod-product-compliance
Lightning Source LLC
Chambersburg PA
CBHW050900250626
47155CB00001B/36